THE
BLACK KISS
OF DEATH

A NOVEL BY

KEON SMITH

DEDICATION

This book is dedicated to my two daughters, Zahiyah and Zariya. There's no crown on this earth that you don't deserve. And, even though the sun sets and night falls, you two will forever shine in my eyes.

To all the people who are gone, but not forgotten: Brian, Mookie, Don, Tay, Putt, Aunt Stacy, Lonnie, Toya, Shaq, and my grand-pops, Richard Smith. And, to all the females who continue to struggle in a man's world, but still manage to keep their heads held high and succeed. This one's for y'all.

ACKNOWLEDGMENTS

Life is so precious in a world where death knocks on your front door, night and day. Therefore, I want to thank God first and foremost for giving me the awareness, will-power, and strength to wake up and face another day in the life of reality.

Next, I want to thank my AK (Shakita Banana) for staying by my side on those long, lonely nights when I was looking for a cure for a hustler with a death wish. You kept me safe in a concrete jungle when wolves were on the prowl searching for victims.

Shout out to Shabree Nicole White for giving birth to my two crown princesses, Zahiya and Zariya, and being strong enough to take care of them by herself while I sat behind hell's gates waiting for an opening. Bree, you're the best!

SPECIAL THANKS

Special thanks to Alexis Elena and Dominique Price. Another special thanks to the women who once, or still, have my best interest in life, starting with my grandmom, Mary Smith, to my mom and the CEO of Between Men and Wolves, Bernadette Prater, Tasha Washington, Katifah Bundy, Makeyda Jones, and Shabree White. If I failed to mention anyone else, it was because I couldn't remember your last name. No hard feelings, though.

To my two little brothers, Marcus and Michael Prater, my Aunt Donna, and my cousin, Corinna.

Last, but not least, a special thanks goes out to Shaunta Jones, Deveryn Epps, and the rest of my family at Skyler Publishing Group. Thanks for your dedication, commitment, and belief in me. This book is the beginning of the hunt, so, for all you lost sheep out there, BEWARE OF THE WOLF!

"Every gangster has a story.
    And, every story has a beginning.
    This is our story."

— KENNY MONTEGA

PROLOGUE

"Wake up, Sleeping Beauty," a voice said just before Diamond felt cold water splash up against her face and body.

As she painfully gasped for breath, her eyes opened to see that her arms were over her head and her wrists were duct-taped to the pipes hanging from the basement ceiling. She was also without her shoes and shirt. The only thing she had on was a pair of blue denim Alexander McQueen jeans and a black LaPerla bra.

As she looked over her shoulders, she saw Bain dangling upside-down, quiet, but alive. Before she could speak to him, the muscular African-American dressed in all black back smacked her to reality.

"That was for this," he said, pointing to his broken nose and swollen black eyes.

Diamond looked at the rest of the men standing behind him and smirked with sarcasm. Some had bruised faces, others had bruised egos. Before she could say something that would surely get her killed, the door upstairs opened, and a darker man who looked like he ran with the Ape Gang appeared.

Defiantly, she stared the man with beady eyes down. He frowned and asked in a raspy voice, "What is your name?"

Diamond never flinched, nor did she respond. The man looked at his enforcer and gave him the signal while stepping back.

"With pleasure," the man with the broken nose said, stepping up.

He struck her in the stomach with an uppercut, then in the side with a hook, ensuring that she had no air to breathe.

"Now, I will ask you again. What is your name?" the beady-eyed man said, louder than before.

When Diamond was finally able to inhale, she curled up her lip with disgust and spit dead in his eye. This time the beady-eyed man needed no help from his men. He returned Diamond's remark with a hard slap to her face. Before she could cooperate, he punched her in the stomach. Embarrassed, he wiped what he could of the spit from his face and grabbed her by her long hair, pulling her head back.

"You think you're big shit, bitch, huh? You think you can use those pretty lips of yours to get your way out of this? I'm here to let you know it's over."

"If I ever get out of here, I'm gonna kill you so quick your heart will still be trying to function with that tiny brain of yours." Diamond threatened.

The man laughed as he looked at his soldiers, who were amused, as well. "When the boss gets here, the only one doing the killing will be me. Since I hear you like to kiss, you can kiss your pretty ass goodbye in a few minutes."

As he released her hair, he struck her in the jaw again with his closed fist. His cell phone rang in his pocket. The man pulled it out and answered it. After speaking briefly, he closed the cell phone and looked at one of his men. "Go let the boss in," he ordered.

Diamond could no longer hear the man talking. Her mind was somewhere else. She was dazed by the punch, but she still held her ground. She knew she was going to die, but there was no way that she would give anyone the satisfaction of seeing her beg for her life. She had remembered hearing a story about a man who once tried to kill her father. When he was captured and placed into the same sort of scenario as she was, he, too, held his ground to the very end. The next generation hadn't changed one bit. In fact, it was worse. Diamond's mind was in a daze, thinking about her life from the moment she was born, in search of where it all went wrong.

CHAPTER 1

27 YEARS AGO
SALIDEEN CARTER

*O*ut in the wide fields of Cuba, a large Boeing 737 cargo jet touched down on the dirt strip and came to a complete stop near the tall grassland. As the back hatch began to open, a black limousine approached, followed by an entourage of armored SUVs and pickup trucks. These vehicles housed a small fleet of henchman, armed with fully automatic assault rifles. With them, was the Cuban drug lord, Diego Elcano. Together they approached the plane.

It was a bright, warm and windy day in Cuba; one of the best days Diego had seen in years. Out of the mouth of the jet stood a half-black, half-Saudi man who sported a thick, dark beard and curly hair. He wore white linen with cream, crocodile skin cowboy boots. Diego smiled as he extended his arms. "Salideen," he greeted.

The short Cuban gave the young man a hug and a pat on the back. "So, what did you bring me today?" Diego asked as Salideen's men began pulling the crates and cases out of the plane.

"Come, take a walk with me, Mr. Elcano. There's something I would like to show you," Salideen said, throwing his arms around the short Cuban's shoulder and leading him over to the new supply. It was obvious from the man's behavior that he and the Cuban had a good rapport with each other. No one normally would dare get that close to the boss.

Salideen opened the crate to expose the mini AKs inside. "These are AK-74s. They shoot at rapid fire, just like their cousin, the 47, but these are lightweight. It's like holding an Uzi, but with more fire-power. See," Salideen said, taking one out of the crate and placing it in his hands.

Elcano was impressed by the lightweight machine gun. "Do you have ammunition?" he asked.

Salideen pulled out a fully loaded clip and handed it to Elcano. He stepped back and watched as the Cuban took out the empty clip and replaced it with the loaded one. He pulled back the lever and slid a bullet in the chamber. He looked at one of his men. Once the others saw who he was focusing on, they moved out of his way, leaving the lone man out in the open. Elcano aimed quickly and fired the powerful weapon, almost cutting the henchman in two.

"Beautiful," he said, inspecting the smoking torch.

"I knew you would like it," Salideen replied. "Now, over here is something much meaner."

Salideen opened another crate to expose a giant machine gun that almost looked like an anti-aircraft gun. "This is the .50 caliber Gatling gun. It has a revolving eight-barrel gas compressor."

Elcano's eyes really looked hungry for blood now. "Do you have ammunition?" he asked.

All his henchmen nervously looked at each other then at their dead colleague on the ground.

"I'm afraid I didn't bring any .50 caliber bullets with me, but I promise you I'll send them, just as soon as I get to where I'm going," Salideen assured him.

A big wave of relief came over the men after hearing that. Once the men were done conducting business, Elcano had the money loaded onto his plane. "So, tell me, my friend," Elcano said, walking with Salideen, "how is everything going?"

"Pretty good, I guess. Right now, I'm on a big paper chase."

Elcano chuckled. "Just like your father. If only you would settle down and marry my daughter. Think of the power we can obtain."

"I know. But like I said before, Pearl is a beautiful young woman, and she deserves the best. I'm not that guy. I've still got a lot of growing up to do. And, faithfulness is something that is not on my list."

Elcano nodded. "That's why I respect you so much, my young friend."

"What about Castor? His family has been in control over in Colombia for a long time. Now, he has inherited his family's business. He would make a great ally," Salideen suggested.

"Yeah, but for some reason, I don't trust Colombians. Nonetheless, I believe this is the only choice I have."

Just then, Salideen's satellite phone rang. "Excuse me, Mr. Elcano, I have to take this," Salideen said.

"By all means, I'll just have my men load these things up on the truck."

Sal answered the phone. "Hello?"

"When are you going to bring your butt home?" a sweet voice said on the other end.

"I didn't know that I had a home in Philadelphia," he replied.

"Don't get smart."

"Brenda, why do you have to be so demanding?"

"Because I miss you," she whined.

Salideen smiled. "Well, if you miss me so much, why don't you get on a flight to Vegas so we can spend some time together?"

"Vegas? Why can't we spend some time here?" Brenda questioned.

"Because I'd rather have you in a hotel than -- "

"Than the ghetto. You know what?" Brenda interrupted with an attitude.

"Come on, baby, don't be so defensive. Look, come to Vegas. Please."

"No," Brenda snapped.

"I'll buy you a new fur coat," he bribed her.

There was silence over the phone for a few seconds before Brenda huffed, "When do you want me to leave?"

Salideen gave her the time and place, and then ended the call.

Once Elcano and his men grabbed all the merchandise, Salideen twirled his index finger in the air signaling for the pilot to start the engine.

"Let's wrap it up!" he shouted to his men.

Within seconds, the engine of the plane came to life. Five minutes later, Salideen and his men were preparing for take off on a trip to Vegas.

CHAPTER 2

CHARLES WHITE

On the docks of Los Angeles, Charles White and his crew waited for the Russian Mafia to show with the two kilos of cocaine that they planned to purchase. It was a quiet night; a cloud of fog had blanked most of the area. Charles, who was only 19 at the time, checked his watch once more. In his hand was a briefcase. Ordinarily, $34,000 wasn't much for a man with such a big appetite, but all the robberies, high-jacking, and extortion schemes that nearly got them all killed in the past had made him appreciate that kind of money.

When two cars pulled up, six Russians got out, along with their boss. He kept his distance because his wife was in the car. In fact, the fog was so thick, he was almost invisible.

"Do you have the money?" the Russian asked with one hand stuck inside his black, full-length, wool coat.

He was an up-and-coming lieutenant who went by the name of Zelinski. His demeanor was the same as Charle's, perhaps even worse. As much as Zelinski didn't care for blacks, he knew he had a job to do.

rles replied, holding up the briefcase.

ans. To him, they were dangerous and

because no one else would. Everyone

ng were cut-throats looking for a come-

The Russians, however, were the only

h him.

he Russian commanded.

od friend, Sam, then at the Russians.
Taking a deep breath, he approached the limousine where the men were. When he got there, one henchman checked him to see if he was armed. Finding nothing, they allowed him to proceed.

Zelinski," Charles said, extending his hand.

The Russian mob boss didn't return the gesture. "How much is in the briefcase?" Zelinski asked.

Charles didn't let this discourage him. Instead, he smiled before placing the briefcase on the hood of the limousine and spinning the code to the lock. Once the briefcase clicked open, Charles raised the case to expose a chrome .45 Smith and Wesson. Zelinski's eyes bulged when he saw the gun and no money. As Charles grabbed the gun inside, one of his men opened up on the Russians with an assault rifle and chopped them down like lumber.

Zelinski turned and tried to flee, but Charles put a chokehold on him from behind and placed the gun to his temple. "Where do you think you're going fatso?" Charles said.

"What do you want?" Zelinski asked.

"For one, you can get the fuck in the limo," Charles commanded as his crew approached with guns in hand. "Check the vehicle. Find the work so we can get out of here."

His crew did just that. As Charles opened the door, the woman inside screamed, so he dipped into the back seat and smacked her with his gun. "Shut up, bitch, before I leave you stinking out here."

"Do as he says," Zelinski instructed.

Charles sat in the back seat with his gun on both of them.

"You're a dead man. You do know that, don't you?" Zelinski said calmly.

"I'm the one holding the gun here," Charles replied.

Just then, a female opened the door. "There's no money in the trunk, and the driver doesn't know where it is, either. Should we kill him?"

"No, Bonnie. Tell him to take us back to the mansion."

"What?" Zelinski said.

"That's right. We're taking you to your crib. We know you got something in the safe. You didn't bring coke, so I'm guessing you guys were gonna rob me. Ain't that how it goes?" Charles explained.

Part of his suspension was true, only Zelinski didn't get the green light from the higher up to rob Charles. He got the green light to kill him. Charles had been doing dirt to folks for a long time. His thirst for money was everlasting and his care for consequence was at a minimum. The Russians figured that they would kill two birds with one stone by murdering Charles and making a little money while they did it. Now that their plan backfired, their future was at risk.

"I have no idea what you're talking about," Zelinski fussed.

"Oh, I think you know exactly what I'm talking about," Charles replied.

Zelinski cursed himself for underestimating Charles. He thought it would be fast. But now, he was paying for it dearly.

The limousine pulled off, with Charles' crew following in the other vehicles, posing as Russians. They entered the gates of the mansion and pulled up to the front, where two men were waiting. As soon as they opened the door, Charles dropped them both with two bullets to the head.

"Let's go," he said, before pulling Zelinski out of the car.

The mansion looked a lot like the place where Tony Montana killed his right-hand man in *Scarface* when he found out that he was screwing his sister.

"Honey, what's going on?" Zelinski's wife asked as she approached with a confused look on her face."

"It's a robbery," Bonnie said, snatching her up and putting a gun to her head.

"Oh-my-god! Unhand me!"

Bonnie pushed Zelinski's wife forward with the gun still to the back of her head. Charles and his crew followed them inside the house where two guards were posted. Without hesitation two shots were fired, killing them dead. Zelinski's wife cried hysterically. It was the first time she saw death, and it wasn't pretty.

"Take me to the safe," Charles demanded, pointing his gun at the Russian lieutenant's head.

"I'm not taking you anywhere."

Charles pulled back the hammer of his pistol. "Wait, please don't kill me," Zelinski's wife pleaded, stepping forward. "It's in the back."

Charles nodded at Zelinski and smiled devilishly. He gave his crew the signal to escort them down the gallery while he followed. When they got into the cigar room, Zelinski's wife showed him the safe hidden behind the bar counter.

"Open it," Charles said with hungry eyes.

"I don't know the combination," she said.

Charles nodded to Zelinski. "You open it," he said, pointing his gun back at Zelinski.

"Fuck you. I'd rather die than give you shit."

"Ah, so you welcome death and don't fear it. That's really stupid, especially for the people you love."

Boom!

In a flash, Charles shot Zelinski's wife in the abdomen. The loud noise caused the Russian mob lieutenant to jump. When he saw his wife collapse to the floor, he rushed to her side. Charles aimed at her head to end her suffering.

"Goodnight, my love," he said.

"No!" Zelinski shouted. "I'll tell you."

After getting the code, Charles opened the safe. Inside were stacks and stacks of hundred-dollar bills. They stuffed them into the empty briefcase, along with a small plastic bag. Also inside the safe was a small, black sack with a reddish-orange diamond inside. *Jackpot*, Charles thought as he came from behind the counter and aimed his pistol at Zelinski.

"Your service is very much appreciated. Now you can die."

Before he could shoot, a hail of bullets came through the window, splintering the liquor bottles on the shelf.

Charles and his crew got low and fired back at the shooters trying to swoop in through the window. "Chuck, we gotta go!" Sam said, as he fired his two Colt .45s at the Russians.

Charles glanced at Zelinski and regretted having to flee without killing him. Bullets whizzed by his head. He shot it out with the Russians, all the way to the limousine. Charles turned around as three Russians took cover behind the pillars out in front of the entrance with their fully automatic weapons.

"Chuck, get in the car !" Two-Gun Sam shouted as Bonnie started the engine.

Charles fired two more times but missed before jumping in. Two-Gun Sam followed. They peeled off while firing at the Russians running out of the mansion.

As the car sped away, inside the mansion, Zelinski held his wife in his arms as she gasped for breath. Just then, his son and daughter walked in and watched their mother die in their father's arms. The moment Zelinski lost his wife, he lost all sanity. Charles White had made a very dangerous enemy.

That night, Charles and his crew counted up $530,000 and divided it amongst each other.

"I know that Russian had more money than this," Charles said, sounding a bit disappointed.

"Are you kidding me? This is more than enough to start our business. Besides, we had to get outta there," Bonnie stated.

"Always remember something, Bonnie. When you settle for thousands, there's always a chance you'll meet the bottom again. You achieve millions, and now you can walk on your own two feet. But if you think in billions, then you can run things. And that's what my plan is. To run this whole city," Charles proclaimed.

"So what's your plan?" Sam asked.

"Well, first, I gotta go to Vegas and wash half of the money,"

Charles explained. "The other half we'll use to find a connect. As far as the diamond, I'll sell it to the highest bidder. You guys just sit tight and wait until I return."

With that said, Charles rounded up half of the money and headed out the door.

CHAPTER 3

CHARLES WHITE

*W*hen Charles got to Vegas, he stayed at the MGM hotel. He won chips up and down the Vegas strip before cashing in a few hours later. When he hit the lobby, he noticed a pretty, brown-skinned female with a nice figure and short hair. Intrigued, Charles went up to introduce himself.

"Excuse me," he said, causing her to turn. "Have we met?"

"Not unless you're from Philadelphia," a stocky, light-skinned guy said out of nowhere before putting his arms around his woman.

"Oh, I apologize. You two are together?" Charles clenched his teeth.

"It's okay, my friend. No need to apologize," the man said.

How the fuck did he get a black girl so fine? He must have some money, Charles thought.

"Hey, can I offer to buy you two a drink?" Charles offered, thinking quick on his feet.

The man looked at his wife, who smiled, then looked back at Charles and said, "Sure, why not? By the way, the name is Salideen, but you can call me Sal. And this here is my wife, Brenda."

Charles shook Sal's hand, then the lovely Brenda's, who looked to be no older than 17. After a few shots of Hennessy, Charles and Sal learned a lot about one another. From there, they began to meet up every night and have drinks together. As they sat at the bar, they engaged in small talk until Brenda grew restless.

"I'm gonna try the slot machines," she said, getting up from her stool.

She stood and glanced at Charles before strutting away. Both Charles and Sal watched as she walked the floor like she owned the place. "I can't get enough of that girl," Sal said in a daze. "Tell me something, Charles, what really brings you to Vegas, other than gambling?"

"Nothing, just doing a little sightseeing," Charles lied.

"Is that why you're cashing chips in at every hotel you go to?" Sal said, causing Charles to do a double-take.

"You're not the only one washing money, you know. I've seen you at two other hotels while I was busy doing the same thing. I'm an arms dealer, Charles."

"What kind of arms?" Charles asked.

"Anything I can get my hands on. Mainly fully automatic weapons. They're the big sellers. In fact, I've got a big sale going on that's gonna force me to be out of the country for a while. But, if you need something, here's my pager number. Be sure to give me a call."

"Actually, I need a connect on something much different."

"Cocaine?" Sal guessed. Bingo. "How much are you looking to spend?"

Charles whispered the number in Sal's ear. Sal shook his head. "My people can handle that, but you have to find a way to smuggle it into the country. You see, it's coming from Afghanistan."

"I don't have a way to get it in the country," Charles confessed.

Sal thought about it, then said, "Let me sleep on this, and I'll get back to you in the morning."

Charles nodded and watched as Sal got up. He looked tired. When Sal kissed his wife on the cheek and let her know that he was going up to bed, Charles got up and approached her.

Once Sal was out of sight, Charles took a seat beside Brenda. "You having fun losing your money?" he asked.

"It beats being cramped up in that crappy hotel suite all day. Besides, it's not my money I'm losing," Brenda replied.

"Hey, that's no way to thank your man. I'm sure he did all this to impress you."

Brenda smiled. "You must not know my man. He's washing his money. The only reason I came along is because he promised to buy me a new fur coat. Other than that, I would be back in Philly."

"Is that so?" Charles asked smoothly.

Brenda looked at him and replied seductively, "Yeah."

She couldn't escape his handsome features: brown-skinned, carefully styled hair, brown eyes, and thick lips. His muscular build had Brenda wondering what he had under the hood.

"Let me ask you a question. Are you a woman who takes chances?" Charles asked.

"I guess you can say that. Why do you ask?"

"Because I want to take a chance with you tonight," Charles said, extending his hand.

Brenda looked at it for a second. She knew that she shouldn't entertain the thought. Her man was upstairs, getting ready for bed, and here she was, flirting with this man. But she couldn't resist taking his hand. Charles led her up to his suite, removed her dress and laid her on the queen-size bed. Before he entered her, she stopped him.

"Put on a condom first," she gasped passionately.

Charles pulled out a Trojan condom and poked a hole in it with his finger. He needed to feel the real thing, and a condom would only ruin it. He put the condom on in front of her, then entered her. Rocking back and forth until the condom popped, he gasped as he felt her wet, tight walls. He stroked her inner thighs until she climaxed. The sex was so good. Brenda had absolutely no regrets until Charles shot his load inside of her.

"What happened?" she asked as Charles looked down at his wet, exposed dick that had punctured the condom.

"The condom must have popped," Charles said, trying to sound concerned.

Brenda appeared to be a bit worried, but didn't say anything else about it.

A week later, Sal put Brenda on a plane back to Philly while he and Charles took a flight to Miami. On the plane, the two sat in first class. Sal explained to him what was going on.

"I've got somebody I want you to meet. His name is Verningo Castor. He's a big drug lord from Colombia. He's around my age and is the head of the Los Ra Strojos."

"What's Los Ra Strojos?" Charles asked.

"They're probably the largest cartel in Colombia. They're big, Charles. Believe me when I tell you."

Charles mulled this over as the plane landed at Miami International Airport. A white limousine awaited them to take them to a beautiful mansion in Golden Beach. Charles was impressed. The place was twice as big as the one the Russian mob boss had. Castor's mansion took up 32,000 square feet of green grass, surrounded by palm trees and golden sand. It was designed based on the 18th century English manor homes. Charles looked in wonder at the traditional red brick and white stone design as he climbed the left side of the limestone steps up to the front door.

Once they were escorted inside, Sal was greeted by a handsome Colombian who looked to be in his early 20s.

"Sal, it's good to see you again," Verningo Castor said, shaking his hand.

"You, too, Castor. I would like you to meet my friend, Charles White. Charles, this is the man who can make all your dreams come true," Sal said.

Castor chuckled modestly. "Come, Charles. Take a walk with me for a second."

Charles stood, and walked side by side with the Colombian, who was about his height. Castor laced his hands behind his back. "Sal tells me that you're looking to buy some cocaine. This true?"

Charles nodded, "Absolutely."

"And how much are you looking to spend?"

"$250,000," Charles replied.

Castor nodded his head. "And do you have the money with you?"

"Nah, it's in a safe location back home. If all goes well, I'll have my people send it to you."

Castor smiled. "Okay, Mr. White. I like your style. But before I can trust you, I have to have my people run a background check. There's a lot of undercover police running around, trying to catch big fish. One can never be too sure these days."

"That's understandable," Charles said.

"I'm gonna have to ask you to stay here with me for a few days until the process is over."

Charles looked at Sal. "That won't be a problem."

"Good, I have a room prepared for you," Castor said before having one of his maids escort him to the room.

Sal checked his watch. "Well, that's it for me. I've got a flight to catch out of the country."

"Big deal?" Castor asked.

"Very big," Sal said before heading out.

Charles stood at the window of his suite and looked out at the ocean. Even though he was now a hostage until his background came back, he wasn't at all nervous or worried. Soon he would have the drugs he needed to take over LA. This was the moment he had been waiting for, and there was nothing that would get in his way. At least, that's what he thought.

That night, when Charles came down to the dining room, he was surprised to see that Castor had guests. At the table were an older Cuban man with his beautiful teenage daughter seated beside him. She had to be no older than 17, Charles thought as he came into the room.

"Mr. White, your food is in the kitchen. You can take it up if you want."

Charles nodded and stole a glance at the most exotic beauty he had ever seen before going to get his plate.

Later on that night, as he lay on the bed and stared at the ceiling, he heard some sniffles coming from out on the terrace. Curious, he got up to investigate. He was surprised to see the young girl from the dining room standing on the terrace beside his, crying, with her face in her palms.

Charles climbed over the terrace and onto hers.

"Are you okay?" he asked, standing by the railing.

The girl looked up and was surprised to see him standing there. She shook her head no.

"What's wrong?"

When she didn't respond, he slowly approached her. She took a step back. "It's okay. I'm not going to hurt you," Charles reassured her, backing her to the end of the rail.

The girl looked up at the tall man in amazement. Her eyes were beautiful. Charles wiped her tears from her cheek with his thumb and said, "I'm Charles. What's your name?"

"Pearl," she responded with perfect English.

"Pearl. That's a beautiful name. Are you from Colombia?"

"No, my father's Cuban. I used to live in Canada with my mother until she was killed.

"Damn," Charles said as he leaned back on the railing. "I'm sorry to hear that. Is that why you're crying?"

"No. It's my father. He thinks he can run my life now that my mother is dead."

"Well, maybe your father just wants what's best for you. Did you ever think about that?" Charles asked.

"Yeah, right," she said. "My father only wants what can make him more money. He doesn't love me. He loves his wealth."

Charles admired this goddess. She was everything he dreamed of in a woman. Long hair, smooth, vanilla skin, and a great body. Within hours, they got lost in conversation about kids and other things that took Pearl's mind off her problems. After a while, Pearl felt at ease around this stranger. Charles was an adventurous man who loved to travel. This sparked her interest.

They sat out on the balcony all night until an unwanted shower of rain appeared.

"Where did this come from?" Charles asked.

"I don't know," Pearl said as her clothes began to get wet.

"Well, guess that's the end of our night. It was nice meeting you, Pearl," Charles said, extending his hand.

"You too, Charles," Pearl replied as she let him kiss the back of her hand.

As Charles turned to leave, Pearl stopped him. "Charles."

When he turned around, she said, "Is it possible that a man can lay with a woman and just hold her all night without any sexual relations?"

Charles smiled. "Of course, it's possible."

"Well, then, can you stay with me tonight?"

Charles nodded, following her back into the room. Even though it was possible that a man could sleep with a woman without having intercourse with her, that wouldn't be the plan tonight. Little did Charles know that not only was he gonna take Pearl's virginity, he was also about to break something far bigger.

Two days later, the word came back about Charles being on good terms and Verningo Castor sent out the shipment, which was 25 keys of Colombian cocaine. Castor only charged him $10,000 a key.

As Charles went to pack his bags, he noticed Pearl standing in the doorframe. "You're leaving?" she asked.

"Yeah, I have to get back to LA. I have a business to run."

"But what about us?" Pearl asked.

Charles stopped what he was doing to look at her beautiful eyes. He was used to womanizing females. It was so easy just to sleep with them and then dump them. But, Pearl was different. There was something about her that he couldn't let go of. Something made him want to hold onto her. Something kept him attached.

"Why don't you come with me?" Charles said.

"I can't. My father would be very upset if I left. He would disown me. I don't--"

Charles bent down and kissed her passionately, then stepped back. "Did that feel real to you?" he asked.

Pearl nodded.

"Well, then, come with me," he suggested.

"Give me a place where I can reach you. And when the time comes, I'll call for you to come and get me. Are you sure about this, Charles? I don't want to be a burden."

"I could never be more positive about the way I feel about you right now. And I will be back for you. I swear to God .I'm coming back for you, and with God as my witness, you will be my queen."

With that said, Pearl helped him pack the rest of his things and watched him leave. She didn't know why she felt this way about him, but she did. Most importantly, she trusted that he would come back for her. But, trust and destiny were two different things, and tomorrow wasn't promised.

When Charles got back to LA, there was a look in his eyes that none of the members in his group had ever seen before until now. Now that the Colombian cartel was backing him with an endless supply of drugs, Charles hit the streets aggressively in the form of a shark. Many people thought he was just at his old robbery tricks until bodies started disappearing. Months later, when they were discovered on ocean shores after being chewed on by sharks, people started to think otherwise.

It was the signature of an up and coming group of organized crime members. Members who took after Charles' last name and started calling themselves the Great Whites.

Charles, however, eventually took it to another level, gaining power. In the mansion, he bought in the hills of Los Angeles, he had a large aquarium built that held two adult great white sharks inside. The sharks were mainly fed humans, so instead of taking a stubborn hustler who didn't want to deal with him to the ocean, he would just throw them in the fish tank and videotape the attack. The footage would be sent to others as an example of his ruthlessness. It was then that fear was caused by rumor, so everyone knew that if you didn't deal with the Great Whites, then you were shark food.

As the bodies of those who didn't want to deal with Charles disappeared, new people were put in their place and soon word began to spread that Charles White was trying to take over LA. But, what they hadn't anticipated was that by the time they found out, it was already too late.

Car trunks of kilos quickly became truck loads, briefcases of hundred-dollar bills quickly became suitcases, and a pack of hungry wolves quickly became a pride of lions, with LA as their kingdom. It was a big, unexpected success, and with success comes arrogance.

CHAPTER 4

PEARL ELCANA

*A*fter Charles's departure, Pearl felt like she had said goodbye to the last bit of sunshine in her life. She was now a prisoner in Verningo Castor's mansion. Not once did Castor or her father come to visit her. It was as if they just locked her in a room and told a bunch of guards to keep an eye on her until the time came for her to be taken to Colombia.

Now that Pearl was confined, she had time to reflect on her mother. Her mother was a good spirit who didn't deserve to be murdered by a rival cartel in order to get back at her father for cutting them off. Pearl could still see the blood gushing from her head after she crawled out from under the bed.

Every time she thought of that horrible sight, tears trickled down her cheek. Her mother was the only one who really loved her, and that love was taken away.

The only good thing about being a prisoner was ordering out for food whenever she wanted. Pearl had been eating uncontrollably. Her favorite was the Chilean sea bass from Prime 112. Verningo Castor's reputation was so heavy in the streets of Miami, he had the restaurants deliver the food to the mansion.

Days went by like weeks, and weeks like months. Pearl grew tired and restless, so she tried to call Charles, but the number that he gave her was disconnected. She went as far as to use a maid to sneak out a letter to him. After a month or so, Charles still hadn't replied.

Two months later, Pearl had given up all hope of being with the man she fell in love with at first sight, until a package was delivered to her room. She opened it to find a wedding gown inside. She really began to stress now. Tears began to fall. She didn't want to open the card, fearing another order from her father.

Pearl wiped her eyes and took a deep breath. She opened the card and read:

Put this on, my queen, and walk to your window.
Charles

When Pearl saw that, her heart fluttered. She quickly got up, disregarding both the dress and the letter, and opened the slide window to walk out to the terrace.

There, standing by the railing, was her knight in shining armor.

"Charles," she gasped before running to his arms.

She buried her head in his chest as tears of joy flowed. "Why aren't you wearing your dress?" he asked.

"I'm sorry, I just got so excited. I've missed you so much," Pearl said, hugging him tightly.

Once they released each other, Charles went into his pocket and pulled out a huge, unusual colored diamond engagement ring. It was just a small piece from the large diamond he took from the Russians and sold to some South Africans, but on Pearl's finger, the 3-karat, reddish-orange diamond sparkled in a 24-karat gold setting.

"Charles, it's beautiful!" Pearl said before clasping his face and kissing him.

All of sudden, there was a knock on her bedroom door. The two quickly broke their romantic bond. "Charles, what are we gonna do?" Pearl asked.

Charles took Pearl by the hand. "Come on, follow me."

He led her to the railing and helped her over to the other side. He then climbed over himself. They snuck into the vacant room and out the door. Silently, they crept down the hallway. Pearl was so scared they would get caught, she started having slight pains in her stomach.

"Ouch!" she gasped, stopping to clutch her stomach.

"You okay?" Charles asked.

"Yeah, I'm fine."

"Hey!" one of the guards shouted, spotting them from the other side of the balcony.

Charles took Pearl's hand and rushed her down the steps. Pulling out his pistol, he spotted two guards at the door and quickly fired two shots, dropping them both. He and Pearl trotted down the steps as gunfire erupted.

Charles and Pearl rushed out to the mansion's open gates where two dead guards remained in the booth. On the side of the road was his red Ferrari. Pearl got into the passenger's side as the sound of screeching tires announced that cars were peeling out of the mansion's garage. Charles ignited the Ferrari's engine and roared off.

For a short while, they were under heavy fire, but when Charles got a clear lane, the henchmen's old Buick was no match for the foreign cars powerful, screaming engine.

Charles smiled at his cunning before looking over at Pearl, who was frowning. She was looking at something between her legs. Charles followed her gaze and saw blood.

"Oh, shit! Are you shot?" he asked.

"No, it's not that," Pearl said with tears.

"Then what is it?"

Pearl stared at Charles with sad eyes. "I think I just had a miscarriage."

Back at the mansion, Castor was led up to Pearl's room by the maid. The wedding dress was on the bed, and she was gone. Beside the dress was a card. Castor picked it up and read it with clenched teeth. Afterwards, he balled it up and flung it to the floor. When he turned around, he was staring at Diego Elcano, who was shaking his head in disappointment.

Castor had never been so humiliated in his life. He had proven that he wasn't worthy of being an ally to the Elcano cartel; therefore, their business relationship was no more. Charles White had made the ultimate mistake. He had wronged a vicious devil. But it wasn't over. From that day forward, Castor swore that he would unleash hell on Charles White and everyone he loved until that man was put in a casket.

CHAPTER 5

BRENDA SMITH

Three months after the eventful trip to Vegas, Brenda went to her doctor for a check-up. She hadn't been feeling like herself lately and needed to find out what was wrong with her. For the past few months, she had become cranky and temperamental. Her co-worker, Stacy, volunteered to keep her company. Stacy lived two blocks away from Brenda and was a good friend. No matter what, she always had Brenda's back at work.

Brenda didn't have many friends due to her split personality, but Stacy seemed to be the one who could tolerate most of her nonsense. As Brenda sat on the examination table, the doctor came into the room with her chart. "Well, Ms. Smith, I've tested your blood for STDs and it came back negative. However, you may want to start looking for baby clothes. You're pregnant."

"Pregnant?" Brenda repeated nervously.

"That's right. I recommend that you eventually get an ultrasound so you can see if it's a boy or girl."

After coming out of the hospital and getting into Stacy's car, Brenda was stone faced. "What happened?" Stacy asked.

Brenda looked at her. "I'm pregnant."

"Well, that's a good thing, isn't it?" Stacy asked.

"Stacy, if I tell you something, you have to promise me that you will keep this between us," Brenda demanded.

"Okay, Brenda, I'm not going to say anything to anyone. Besides, who cares? We don't have any friends. Now, what's going on?"

"That week I spent in Vegas with my boyfriend, well, we met this guy named Charles White and I--"

"Oh, my God, you slept with him!" Stacy exclaimed, wide-eyed.

"He was just so charming, so confident and sexy, I couldn't resist him, I swear," Brenda explained.

"Oh-my-god, so he's the father?"

"I think so. Me and Sal always use a condom."

"And you and this man Charles didn't?" Stacy asked glaring at her.

"It wasn't like that. The condom broke. God, what am I gonna do?" Brenda moaned.

"Just calm down. Where is Sal now?"

"I don't know. I haven't seen him since Las Vegas. He sends me love letters and postcards, but that's it."

"What about this Charles guy? Have you been in contact with him?"

"Once or twice. He lives in Los Angeles."

Stacy shook her head. "Girl, you've got some serious issues going on. And this Sal guy, how come you never let me meet him?" Stacy asked.

Because your ass is too flirty, Brenda thought to herself.

Stacy didn't know what to tell her. And, she also didn't know that Brenda was playing a dangerous game involving two men. Fortunately for her, Sal stayed away longer than she anticipated, and six months later, she had the baby. When Brenda saw the baby boy's features, she knew exactly who the father was. She named him Clyde Charles White. Once she summoned the strength, she called the baby's father. She kissed her son on the cheek, but she knew that she would never see her baby again. This would just have to be one more skeleton of the many that she would have to stuff in her closet and keep out of sight for good.

CHAPTER 6

THE BIRTH OF A PRINCESS
5 YEARS LATER

*I*t was a dark and surprisingly cool night throughout Los Angeles. The sky was clear and the moon was only a crescent. As a few homeless bums stood by a metal can, burning wood, a man's shouts of pain echoed down the dark and gloomy strip of warehouses. The homeless men paid the sounds no mind and continued trying to stay warm for the night.

In the depths of one of the abandoned warehouses, came the piercing cries of torture from a Colombian assassin, Chico. Two armed men stood in front of him as he hung from the metal pipes while they beat him with blackjacks.

"Ahhh!" Chico screamed before cursing them in Spanish while the boss watched with cold satisfaction.

Chico was an assassin, for the Colombian drug lord Verningo Castor and was sent to kill Charles White for personal reasons. However, Chico made the ultimate mistake when he got to America. He flashed White's photo to the wrong people, serious people. As Chico hung from the pipes, bruised and severely beaten, he laughed arrogantly in pain. Although he knew he couldn't take much more, his mouth kept firing away.

"You are a dead man, Charles. There is nowhere you can hide. Nowhere can you run. I no succeed, but someone will," Chico mumbled in broken English.

Before Charles could reply, another soldier with a white top hat and a black suit walked into the warehouse, along with three of his own assassins. His attire was almost as dapper as Charles' who dressed in a black suit with white pinstripes and a black top hat. The man whispered into Charles's ear, "Sir, your wife is having a baby. Would you like me to take over?"

"That isn't necessary. This'll only take a second," Charles replied, while pulling out his nickel-plated Colt .45 automatic.

He aimed it at Chico's beaten face before saying in Spanish, "I'll let Castor know that you're waiting for him in hell when the time comes."

Boom! Boom! Boom!

Walking out of the warehouse, Charles got into the back seat of a black Mercedes S500 and tapped his driver on the shoulder. "Take me to the hospital and step on it."

The Benz peeled off with two other vehicles following. This was probably the second happiest day of his life. The first was the birth of his five-year-old prince, Clyde. He took the boy from his biological mother as soon as Clyde was ready to leave the hospital. Now, his wife was delivering his second child.

Charles loved those three things: his son, his soon-to-be daughter, and his half-Cuban, half-Caucasian wife, Pearl. The two had a history together that many believed came right out of a Hollywood movie.

Pearl was by far the prettiest woman Charles had ever been in love with. She had long, dark hair, vanilla skin tone, great figure, and captivating brown eyes. Charles smiled as he thought about her. She was worth it all. When the Mercedes entourage pulled up to the hospital, Charles got out and headed for the entrance, with the rest of his henchmen on his heels. He walked up to the front desk, where a woman in blue scrubs sat. She was taken by this imposing group of men.

"Can I help you?" she asked to the group in general.

Charles stepped forward. "Yes, I'm looking for Pearl White. She's currently in labor. I'm her husband," he said smoothly.

This bit of news changed the woman's attitude, from cordial to cooperative. "Oh, Mr. White. Right this way, sir," she said, getting up and personally escorting him to the room.

Once they arrived, Charles walked in to see his wife cradling a beautiful, bright baby girl in her arms. Upon seeing her husband, Pearl rolled her eyes. He was supposed to be there to see his princess being born, but he was too busy running the streets, as usual.

"You're late," Pearl reprimanded him. "Well, since you're here, the least you can do is name her."

Pearl handed the quiet infant to her father, who was astonished by her light, glowing complexion. *Just like a jewel or a precious stone*, he thought. "I've got a name for her. We'll call her Diamond, because that's how she shines. Diamond Keyona White."

A broad smile spread across Pearl's face. "My Diamond," she said, with high expectations for her newborn. "Charles, I think we've got something special on our hands."

Charles looked down at his daughter and nodded, but said, "Worse, we've got an Aries baby on our hands. I just hope the world's ready for her."

CHAPTER 7

PHILADELPHIA, PA

*B*renda was disrupted from her bath by the knocking on her door downstairs. Looking at the clock on the wall, she saw it was only 6:45 AM. She knew it wasn't her girlfriend, Stacy, coming to pick her up for work. Stacy only lived around the corner, and they didn't have to be there until 8:00, so Brenda was at a loss. Pulling her gorgeous light-brown body out of the hot bubble bath, she wrapped herself in a towel and headed down the staircase.

Brenda lived in a two story 3-bedroom row house on an east Germantown block called Ardleigh Street. The house wasn't large like the ones on Chelten Avenue, but due to her good taste in interior decorating, she lived comfortably. The house had freshly painted whitewalls, and blue and gold wallpaper to match the finishing of her gold baseboards, banister and blue carpet. All her furniture was imported, thanks to her secret lover in Los Angeles.

There was a knock at the door.

"I'm coming. Jesus, who is it?" she snapped.

"Who do you think it is, woman?" a baritone voice responded, causing Brenda to flash a smile.

She recognized the voice instantly and quickly unlocked the door. As soon as she opened it, her man, Sal, stepped in to embrace her.

"Damn, you smell good, baby. It's been too long," he said soothingly.

Brenda buried her head into his chest and cried with joy. "Don't ever leave me like that again. Do you understand me?" she said, cupping his face.

"I'm sorry, baby," Sal replied, kissing her on the forehead.

He knew he was wrong for leaving without saying a word, but that was the life he led. He was a big arms dealer, the product of black and Saudi parents. His father was from Florida, his mother from Saudi Arabia. Raised by rebels all his life, selling illegal weapons was his mission in life until he met Brenda after making a big sale in Philly. Ever since that first encounter, he was mesmerized by the woman's style and grace.

Now, the two kissed and made love in the living room for what seemed like hours. The sound of the door began thudding once more. Brenda quickly broke their passionate embrace so they could put their clothes back on. "Can you answer that for me? That's Stacy," she said before heading for the steps.

"Stacy? Stacy who?" Sal asked.

"She's a co-worker of mine. She lives right around the corner," Brenda replied as she disappeared up the steps.

Sal headed for the door. When he opened it, he was stunned by the bad sister who was as thick as a Snickers bar. "Oh, I'm sorry. Is, ah… Brenda here?" Stacy asked with her eyes glued to Sal's sweaty six-pack.

"Yeah, she's upstairs. You wanna come in and wait for her?" he asked, undressing her sexy body with his eyes.

Stacy smiled and brushed by him with a sexy switch in her hips, aware that he was watching. Sal didn't take his eyes off of her until she sat down. Closing the door, he walked over to grab the rest of his clothes. He could feel her eyes all over him, and when he looked up, Stacy was gawking at him. Before he could speak, Brenda came down the steps in her scrubs, ready for work.

"You ready, Stacy?" she asked while digging in her bag.

"I sure am," Stacy replied, looking Sal dead in the eye. "Just waiting on you."

Sal caught her meaning, but quickly tried to hide his intentions by giving Brenda a kiss on the lips. "I'll be back at five. Please try not to get into any trouble. Okay?" Brenda said, giving him one last peck on the lips.

Stacy smiled. "Nice to meet you, Mister…"

"Salideen. Salideen Carter," he replied.

CHAPTER 8

LOS ANGELES, CA

*T*he entourage of expensive cars pulled up to the White's family mansion on a warm, cloudy afternoon. The White family mansion was like the White House of criminal organizations. Built in the hills of Los Angeles with a nice view of the city from certain rooms inside the white stone, the mansion was practically a drug dealer's monument. Not only was it one of the largest houses on the hills, constructed with the finest materials from around the world, but each room inside had a theme to it, from the chef's kitchen to the study room.

The butler ushered the men and women into the mansion, one by one. Each individual was a key member in Charles' Great White Organization. And each person had his own subdivision that was responsible for bringing in the profits of their illegal business. They assembled at the large rectangular table that Charles had in his conference room.

The first to walk in was a heavy-set, light-skinned guy with freckles and a thick beard named Reds. Reds' territory was Pennsylvania, New Jersey, and Delaware. Next was a tall, stocky, bald guy with dark skin and a thin chinstrap beard. His name was Gangwar. He supplied every major drug dealer in the DMV.

As he took a seat in one of the comfortable leather business chairs, a white guy with a black, lightly-trimmed beard, dark hair and green eyes walked in. His name was Michael Pharaoh, but everyone else called him Mickey Green Eyes. He was in charge of New York state and also had a few relatives in Congress. Beside him was a female African-American from Long Beach, California. She was accompanied by Whiskey, who was Puerto Rican and had Texas and Oklahoma in his pocket.

Last, but not least, was Charles' number-one enforcer, Sam. Two-Gun Sam. The reason for the name was obvious. Two-Gun Sam carried two big chrome Colt .45s and wouldn't hesitate to draw on a nigga. Charles couldn't ask for a better circle. For the past six years, they had been loyal to him and his cause, which made him a multi-millionaire. Not only did they get the cheapest prices on cocaine and heroin, they got the largest quantities.

As everyone settled down, Charles began. "I thank you all for coming out on this unexpected occasion, but there are a few things I wanted to address with you that couldn't be discussed over the phone. First, I want you all to know that there was another attempt on my life a few weeks ago, but thanks to Bonnie and her resources, we were able to eliminate him." Everyone glanced at Bonnie with approval.

"Now comes the big issue," Charles continued. "Verningo Castor. We all know why he wants me dead. And we all know how powerful he is, sitting in his mansion over in Colombia. He's untouchable. But, we aren't. We're within his reach. All it takes is one slip up, which is why we need to get stronger. I'm not just talkin' about more soldiers. I'm talkin' about money, as well. Yeah, we're one of the largest drug distributers in the nation, but we're screwed if government sharks like the FBI and DEA come after us. We need some white collar guys to protect us. And, I have a good friend that can help with that."

"Who might this friend be, Charles?" Bonnie asked.

"Carlton Butler," Charles replied. "Carlton and I went to school together here in California. He has a circle that is into prostitution, extortion, but not drugs. They go by the name of The Wolf Pack."

"The Wolf Pack. I've heard of that name. They're just like us, only they're a secret society, like the masons and the illuminati," Mickey Green Eyes recalled.

"And, I hear that they got a couple of federal judges in their pocket," Reds said.

"All, true. They also want to combine with us to make something really big," Charles added, which brought silence. "With all our talents combined, not even Verningo Castor can touch us."

"Yeah, but what about the Russians? There's been a lot of tension between us over the years. And I wouldn't be surprised if they tried something," Two-Gun Sam mentioned.

"You know, he's right. If we don't take care of the Russians now, people will doubt whether we can handle business," Bonnie said. "I think we need to get the Russian mafia out of California to show others that we aren't teaming up because we're weak."

Charles nodded in agreement. He knew that if he didn't deal with Sergei Zelinski and his Russian mob, they would eventually do the same to him. As much as he didn't want an all-out war after his wife had just given birth to his daughter, he had known from a young age that business was never personal.

Over the years since the death of his wife, Sergie Zelinski had gained power and created fear throughout the Russian mafia. His sick and twisted methods of elimination earned him the right to move up in the ranks. Before Charles could blink, Sergie Zelinski was running things and calling the shots. The worst part about it was that Zelinski was left with the memory of Charles killing his wife, which was something that he would never forget, nor would he forgive. That was a big problem that had to be dealt with before it was too late.

Looking around at the faces, he asked, "All in favor for a Great White, Wolf Pack connection?"

When he saw all the raised hands, he nodded. "All in favor for war against the Russians?"

He got the same reply-- agreement. He now knew what had to be done to stay on top.

He leaned over to speak to Two-Gun Sam. "Call Sal over in Saudi Arabia and let him know what the deal is. Make sure he delivers the best of what we talked about and prepare the shooters. There's gonna be a lot of fatherless children out there once this is over."

"A slight problem with that, Chuck," Two-Gun replied. "I called Sal the other day. He's in Philadelphia. So we might have a delay on that shipment. I suggest we use what we already have until he comes through."

Charles got upset at the news, but refused to let it get to him. There was too much going on right now for him to worry about the romance between Sal and Brenda. A war was brewing, and he had to be ready, physically and mentally.

CHAPTER 9

16 MONTHS LATER
EAST GERMANTOWN, PHILADELPHIA, PA

"*L*ook, you gonna have to tell her, or I will," Stacy warned with her arms folded as she stood on the porch of her mother's Blakemore Street row house. It was a regular evening and school had just let out. The streets were filled with children heading home to tackle homework. A swarm of dead brown leaves from the trees of fall circled in a whirlwind by Salideen's leg as he hissed and shook his head.

"Tell her what?" Sal asked, frustrated.

"Tell her about us. About my one-year-old daughter and hiding the fact that you are her father. What do you mean tell her what? She needs to know."

"Stacy, you know I can't do that to her right now. She's six months pregnant," Sal stated, as he walked up the steps to face her.

"Well, Brenda's gonna find out, eventually. Our daughter, Kia, has your last name and she has some of your most prominent features. It won't be long before Brenda puts two and two together," Stacy explained.

"Then let her find out on her own. I'm telling you, Stacy, this will break her heart. I can't risk that with my baby inside her. You know how I am about my kids. I'll tell her afterwards. How 'bout that?" Sal lied, cupping her face before kissing her lips. Within seconds, Stacy's hostility had melted away.

Yeah, she was stealing her girlfriend's man, but she had a right to. Sal was a good man, regardless of his lifestyle. He had a good heart and supported her and his child. There was no way she would let Brenda waste a good man like this because she wanted to fool around. Not only was Brenda trying to have her cake and eat it, too, she had dark secrets about her past that would change the way Sal felt about her, and Stacy knew it.

Stacy took Sal's hand and led him into her mother's house, up to her room, where they made love as if there was no tomorrow. As the two lay in bed together with Stacy listening to the beat of Sal's heart, she said, "Sal?"

"Yeah, baby," he murmured while stroking her long hair.

"Tell me something. You've always been so concerned about the welfare of others, but who's concerned about your welfare?"

Sal smiled before kissing her on the forehead. "I don't know, sweetheart. I really don't know."

"Well, if it's worth anything, through thick and thin, you can always count on me, no matter what. Just as long as you stay true to what you have right in front of you. And I'm not just talking about me. I'm talking about that little girl over there."

Sal looked over at the sleeping baby in the crib and knew what Stacy was asking for. A commitment. Although he agreed to her request, he knew that he might not be able to stick around long enough to see his kids grow up. There was no question: Papa was a rolling stone.

CHAPTER 10

LONG BEACH, CALIFORNIA

*R*eclining in a brown leather chair in the living room of his 30,000 square-foot estate, Russian mob boss, Sergei Zelinski, enjoyed a relaxing foot massage from his personal masseuse. Zelinski had some real stress in his life. For one, he watched his wife die in his arms, which he never got over. And ever since Zelinski and his mob migrated from Russia and established his criminal enterprise, his main nemesis was always Charles White and the Great White Organization.

Since the early '80s, Mr. White had been building an empire of his own, from Cali down to Texas. His reputation had rapidly spread across the Midwest to the East Coast, engaging in gun battles with some of the toughest mobsters around, burning down nightclubs, and extorting Russian bathhouses.

As Zelinski tried to relax and clear his head, one of his underbosses, Pete, from Chicago, entered the room, followed by a few other Russians. "Sergei, we need to talk," Pete said to the fat Russian man reclining in the chair.

Realizing that Pete had caught a flight from Chicago to talk to him in person, Zelinski told his masseuse to leave and had his eyes glued to her ass as she walked away. "What seems to be the problem?" he asked with a heavy accent, while circling his temple with his fingers.

"It's about the Whites, Sergei. Those bastards are outta control," Pete explained. "Not only do they have the DMV and the Tri-state, they're now moving in on the south. And their product is good quality. Now I'm hearing that they're uniting with the Wolf Pack in New York. I told you the minute he killed your wife to get rid of him because sooner or later he was gonna get too big for us."

"Who the fuck do you think you're talking to, huh?" Zelinski snapped. "I'm the boss. You don't tell me nothing. I tell you. Now don't worry about small potatoes, Pete. I've said many times that Charles White will be destroyed in due time."

"But that's just it, Sergei. The more we wait, the larger this man gets. It's not like he sends his army to do his dirty work and just sits on his ass. This guy is making major moves. I'm telling ya, if you sleep on this…"

"Pete!" Zelinski shouted, signifying that he had heard enough. "I said, let me handle it. Now, go make yourself useful while you're in LA and have your people pick up that money from Phillip at the warehouse. In fact, you go do it."

As much as Pete hated being told what to do, he nodded his head before getting up to exit the lounge. When the masseuse came back into the room, Zelinski had a job for her, as well. "Get, undressed," he demanded.

The woman looked at him with wide, frightened eyes. Before she could protest, he slapped her to the floor. Zelinski studied her like the predator he was and knew that after he raped this woman, he would see what she really tasted like.

ON THE OTHER side of town, it may have felt as if it never rained, but considering the heavy artillery that Mr. White and his accomplice were strapped with, it was damn sure going to be a very nasty lead shower. Sitting in the tinted limo with Mr. White were Bonnie and Two-Gun Sam. Together they watched an armored truck back into the warehouse loading dock that distributed ecstasy and other high-quality drugs. The place belonged to the Russian mafia. Mr. White had gotten this tip from a member who was responsible for trafficking women into America to work in Zelinski's whorehouses -- right before Charles blew the man's brains out.

After two big Russian guards guided the truck inside, Two-Gun Sam checked both of his semi-automatic pistols to make sure that there was one bullet in each chamber while Bonnie checked her M-16 assault rifle to make sure it was cocked and ready to blow.

Once the doors started to close, an army of Great White soldiers stormed the building. Two-Gun Sam, Bonnie, and Charles followed. Seeing this, the Russians inside reached for the Uzi's strapped around their necks. Bonnie fired first, as always. The others followed her lead.

Four armed Russians dropped to the ground instantly from the violent rapid fire that ripped through their bodies like razor blades. More Russian henchman emerged after hearing gunshots. They had no chance against the well-trained army of Great White soldiers.

Philip, who ran the warehouse for Zelinski, wobbled up the steel steps to his office, with two killers on his heels. "Holy shit!" the fat, crater-faced Russian shrieked, using the railing for support. He wheezed for air like a leaky tire, trying to make it to the top.

Once inside the office, he tried to jump down the fire escape out back. But, the men had a strong grip on his shirt collar. Philip tried oozing out of his $1,500 Versace shirt, but the goons had him surrounded. The gun battle inside the warehouse slowly came to an end as Mr. White walked through the office front door, his eyes burning holes through Philip.

"No, got-dammit!" Charles growled. He pointed to the fire escape.

"Please, Charles. Is it the money? It's in the truck," Philip said as the men ushered him out of the office, onto the fire escape.

"I already have money. Who gives a shit about yours?"

"Charles, please don't do this. I was just doing my job. Of course, you can see that."

Charles looked down at the long drop, then back at the Russian. "I can see. Well, carry on with your job. By all means, don't let me stop you," he replied, giving the men the signal to throw him over the railing, head-first.

Six stories down, Philip's body went splat like a bag of spaghetti sauce. Meanwhile, one of Sam's men wired the place with explosives. By the time they pulled off, the warehouse was erupting into a giant ball of flames. A few minutes later, Pete's limousine approached the burning warehouse and came to a complete stop when they saw the Los Angeles fire trucks massed, trying to put out a huge fire. Pete shook his head; he knew this wasn't an accident. He then picked up his car phone and dialed his boss's number. On the third ring, he answered.

"Hello?" Zelinski said.

"Yeah, Sergei, I'm afraid we're too late. White got to it before we could. I think it's time to drop this guy before he drops us."

Click.

CHAPTER 11

PHILADELHPIA, PA
1 YEAR LATER

*a*fter witnessing the birth of his baby boy, Rafeek, Sal headed for Brenda's house. This was his second child by Stacy, and Brenda still hadn't found out about his betrayal. Although Brenda had his oldest son, Kenneth, it was clear where his heart was. He was living two different lives; now it was time to set things straight with Brenda. When he pulled up to her block, he parked at the bottom, and took the alleyway to keep from being seen. When he reached the backyard of Brenda's house, he walked up to the door and knocked.

Seeing him, Brenda opened the door in a panic. "Oh, my god, Sal, I'm so glad they didn't get you. You got to get outta here before they come back," Brenda said frantically, while continuing to talk a thousand miles a minute. In her arms was his baby boy, who was reaching out for his daddy.

"Wait, wait, and slow down, Brenda. Now, who's been here?" Sal asked.

"The feds. They say they have a warrant out on you. Something about finding a bunch of unregistered weapons in one of your stash houses. They threatened to take my baby if I didn't cooperate with them. So you got to go," Brenda explained as tears trickled down her cheeks.

The tears weren't just because she was scared for him, but because her heart was broken. The feds had tried to goad her to talk by telling her about Sal and her girlfriend, Stacy, and the daughter he had by her.

Sal backtracked as he looked into his baby boy's eyes, wondering if he would ever see him again. He had no time to do anything but head back to his Jaguar. "I want you to get on the phone, call the federal agents back, and tell 'em I'm at your house," he instructed.

"Wh...What?" Brenda asked, confused.

"Just do it. It's the only way they'll let you keep the baby. Now do it," he said before taking off back down the alley.

Peeking out from the alley, he saw that there was no one around, so he quickly stepped out and headed for his car around the corner. As soon as he hit the next block, he spotted two federal agents, checking out his vehicle. Before they could reach for their hips, Sal had his Glock aimed and fired two shots without any reservation. Two bodies slumped to the ground. Sal didn't have an ounce of self-doubt about his aim. Growing up under rebels, being taught how to shoot a gun was like being taught how to ride a bike. Sal tucked the gun in his waistband, and headed for the driver's side door as both agents lay lifeless with a single bullet to their heads.

He quickly hopped in the Jag and started the engine. As soon as he pulled out of the parking space, several shots pierced the windshield and the vehicles fiberglass shell. Popping the car in reverse, he backed off the block, spun it around on Wister Street, and peeled off, leaving a murder scene that he knew had raised havoc with the feds.

Maybe he was done, but he wasn't going down without a fight. Pulling up to one of his stash houses, he jumped out. Just then, unmarked FBI cars screeched around the corner. Sal pulled out his Glock and fired a few rounds before dashing to the house and barricading himself inside.

Within minutes, the entire block was surrounded with more

government officials than a presidential election. A helicopter circled overhead, as well. Four agents approached the front door, holding a large metal battering ram, what the Philadelphia police department called the, *Key to the City*. Tactical officers in full uniform lined up behind those four, poised for an ambush with their modified Bushmaster M-4 assault rifles and .40 cal handguns. "On three," shouted one of the officers holding the door hammer.

"One...Two...Three!"

They slammed the ram into the door, busting it open. That triggered the pin to a homemade bomb hidden inside. Within seconds, the whole area surrounding the house was engulfed in flames.

Baboom!

CHAPTER 12

3 YEARS LATER

*P*earl peeked out of the master bedroom window of the White family mansion for the 15th time in 30 minutes. She was waiting for her husband. It was a very stressful time for her. Her husband's war with the Russian mafia was nerve-wracking. Her daughter, Diamond, sat on the bed with her brother's toy Nerf gun in her hand, watching her mother pace back and forth. At six years old, Diamond was way ahead of everyone else in her class at school. Her teacher advised Pearl that she should get bumped to the next grade.

"Damn it, Charles, where are you?" Pearl snapped, grabbing some folded clothes to refold.

"Damn it, Charles, where are you?" Diamond repeated as she shot one of the Nerf bullets at the mirror.

"You better watch your mouth, young lady, before I clean it out with some *mantequilla*," Pearl threatened.

Diamond frowned; she knew what *mantequilla* meant in Spanish. Butter. Diamond hated butter. "And what did I tell you about playing with those damn guns? You are a lady, and you need to act like one," Pearl said while reaching out to take the toy away from her.

Diamond snatched the gun out of reach, causing Pearl to jump back with surprise. "No!" Diamond said, jumping off the bed and holding the gun behind her.

"Oh, that's how you're gonna act with me, huh, little girl? I'm your mother," Pearl said disapprovingly.

Diamond pouted her lips and put on her award-winning sad face, the one that worked like magic with her father.

"But, mommy, Bonnie has guns. She's still a lady," Diamond whined.

"Girl, Bonnie is 27 years old. She can do whatever she wants. You're only six, and you have to listen to your mother. Now give me that gun," Pearl ordered, holding her hand out.

Diamond looked her mother straight in the eye and shook her head no. Not even the old butter trick that she had been using ever since Diamond first bit into a stick of butter, thinking it was a candy bar, would work anymore. Pearl didn't believe in spanking her children, especially after everything she had been through in the past. Looking into the sparkling eyes of the tan-skinned little girl with long, dark, silky tresses done up in curls, she couldn't push the issue. Once again, Diamond had won.

The truth was that she was Pearl's only peace and sanity. Pearl barely got to see her husband anymore, and when she did, they always argued. With her hands on her hips, all Pearl could do was shake her head.

"Well, I guess if you don't stand for something, you'll fall for anything, right?"

Diamond nodded and flashed a Shirley Temple smile. "Right," Diamond agreed just as Charles walked in the bedroom with a smile, two hands tucked behind his back.

Pearl jumped from her bad nerves. "Oh, Jesus, Charles. You scared me," she said as he rushed up and kissed her on the lips.

Diamond approached quickly. "Daddy!" she sang as she embraced him.

"There's my little girl," he said, removing the box from behind his back. "This is for you." He handed her a cops and robbers kit.

Diamond's face lit up when she saw the two guns inside. She took the box and headed for the bed to open it.

"Where's my gift?" Pearl asked, pouting like her daughter.

Charles reached in his pocket. "I didn't forget about my second favorite girl. This is for you," he said, handing Pearl a small box with a Cartier diamond necklace inside.

After opening it, she gave him another hug and a more passionate kiss.

"Daddy, I don't have anybody to be the cop," Diamond complained, breaking the romantic spell.

When the two looked over at her, she was holding up the cuffs and the guns. Pearl shook her head in disbelief. "I can't believe you bought that girl some guns. It's bad enough she runs around shooting everyone with her brother's guns. Why are you gonna go and encourage her?"

"Because that's what she likes, Pearl. What do you want me to do? You bought her over a hundred dolls and all she does is pop off their heads, arms and legs, tie them up, or set them on fire. How she knows how to use the stove is a mystery in itself," Charles explained.

"But Charles…" Pearl whined.

Before Charles could respond, the maid walked into the room. "Excuse me, Mr. White. You have an important call in your office," she said before walking back out.

Mr. White looked at his wife, who looked concerned. "It'll be alright. It's just a phone call," he said, heading for his office down the hall. Once inside, he closed the door and locked it.

"Hello?"

"Jeez, it took you long enough," the woman said from the other end.

"Sorry, I just got in the house," Charles whispered.

"Well, what time are you catching the flight? I've been dying to see you," she admitted.

"Just give me a second. I have to explain the shit to my wife. You know how worried she gets. I may have to bring my daughter."

The woman sucked her teeth and warned him, "Well, you better hurry up before you find me on your doorstep."

Charles smiled before hanging up the phone.

Taking a deep breath, he knew what he had to do when he got back to the master bedroom.

Before he could speak, Pearl hissed and walked over to her dresser.

"Baby, I really have to meet these people in Philadelphia. There's a big deal goin' down. I swear nothing's gonna happen. It's not that type of meeting. Everything's strictly legit," Charles explained.

"Oh, yeah, well, if it's not that type of meeting, then you won't have any problem taking your daughter with you. Since Clyde is staying over his friend's house, that gives me some time to myself. I'm tired of being the only one cooped up in this damn place." Pearl shouted as she began to pack some clothes.

"Pearl, you know I can't take--"

"I don't care anymore. We went half on this one, honey. You're the boss right? Well hire a babysitter, for all I care. I've been taking care of her for six whole years. It's time she gets a taste of what her daddy does for a living, since she wants to be you so bad." Pearl walked to the closet filled with all the shoes she never got to wear.

Charles made eye contact with his daughter, who shrugged her shoulders as she held two guns in her hand. Shaking his head, he thought, *what am I gonna do with you, little girl?*

CHAPTER 13

COLOMBIA

*I*n a country infamous for kidnapping, Colombia ranked fourth in the world in high-profile murders of politicians and drug lords. A large estate was hidden in the jungle of Cali, surrounded by four mammoth walls. Inside those walls, armed men patrolled the perimeter as their boss, Verningo Castor, dressed in white linen, entertained his guest.

Castor supplied almost twenty percent of the world's cocaine, thanks to his Cali cartel and paramilitary mercenaries who continuously waged war on the government in a long bloody conflict, making Cali the most feared spot in Colombia.

As Castor and his guest, Zelinski, walked through the botanical garden, Zelinski got straight to the point. "Something has to be done about this guy, Charles White. For six whole years, we've been at war, and for six years, we've failed to get this guy. He's killing my business in America. And if he's killing my business, he's killing yours. Now he's the head of something even bigger."

"To be honest with you, Mr. Zelinski, I'm not ready for Charles to die yet," Castor replied. Zelinski stopped dead in his tracks and glared at the tall Colombian with the dark hair.

"I'm sorry, but I thought we were on the same page. I thought you were the one who sent your assassins to kill him," Zelinski said.

"Those were amateurs just trying to prove their loyalty to me. And trust me, it would cost me more to keep them. Right now, I have a plan that doesn't consist only of Charles, but his whole organization, which they call the Underworld. Until my plan is complete, Charles will continue to breathe. I suggest you lay low for a while and rebuild your army. Don't worry, when Charles' time runs out, you'll be the first to know," Castor said, extending his hand.

Zelinski looked at it for a second. He didn't like the idea, but shook Castor's hand, anyway, before leaving. Castor watched Zelinski make his way towards the door and wondered if the Russians could be trusted. At that moment, he doubted it, but still continued to let them live.

CHAPTER 14

PHILADELPHIA

As the private jet touched down on the runway of Philadelphia International Airport and taxied to a hangar where the stretch midnight-blue Bentley Continental was accompanied by two Range Rovers. The steps descended, and Two-Gun Sam was the first to exit, followed by six other thugs who were licensed to carry. Mr. White and his daughter were the last.

Once they were in the limousine, the driver pulled out of the hangar and headed for the exit while the Range Rovers followed.

"Daddy, where are we going?" Diamond asked as she looked out the window of the vehicle, kicking her feet, taking in the huge City of Brotherly Love.

"We're going to a friend's house, but you have to promise daddy that this will be our little secret, okay?" Charles said.

"You mean, don't tell Mommy?"

"You want to be a big girl, right?" Charles asked.

Diamond nodded her head.

"Well, then, big girls don't go telling their moms everything. They keep the code of silence, which is never tell what you see. Okay?"

"Okay, Daddy, but are we still going to the zoo like you said," Diamond asked innocently.

Charles smiled at his beautiful little girl. "Of course, we are."

After a 30-minute drive from the airport, the Bentley pulled into a north Philadelphia area that was almost 65% Hispanic called The Badlandz. Diamond had never seen so much action going on. It was like watching adult TV. There were crackheads trying to cop some rock and dope fiends trying to buy some of the finest heroin in the city. Dope-boys of all races hustled on the corners. Hookers sold their bodies, while thieves sold stolen merchandise. Diamond had always been accustomed to the finer things in life, but now, being in such poverty, made her feel like she landed on another planet. Thus, came all the questions that a naïve six-year-old would ask. Mr. White answered her questions as honestly as he could. What he didn't tell her was that this was the zoo he promised to take her to, and his drugs were the cause of all that was going on.

Once they pulled up to a modern, two-story row house on Cambria, Mr. White had his driver pull over and park. When his two bodyguards stepped out of the car, Mr. White grabbed his daughter's hand. "C'mon, baby girl. Be good when you get in here."

Diamond took her father's hand, stepped out of the limo, and followed him up to the front door. After knocking twice, the door opened to reveal a pretty slim, brown-skinned woman with a short hairstyle. The woman smiled as she stepped to the side, allowing Mr. White to enter with his daughter.

"I thought you were lying when you said you were bringing your daughter with you," the woman stated.

Mr. White smiled as Diamond scanned the small living room, staying close to her father. She had never seen a place so small before. Her eyes stopped by the couch where a little boy was playing Nintendo's Super Mario Brothers on a 32-inch television. As Mr. White and the woman chatted, Diamond drifted over to the kid with the cornrows down to his shoulders. No sooner than he focused his eyes back on the screen, Super Mario was dead. Sucking his teeth, he looked back over at the girl who was quietly staring at the TV. He then scooted over.

"You can sit down if you want," he invited.

Diamond eyed him suspiciously for a moment, then sat down.

"You know how to play this?" he asked.

Diamond shook her head no. The boy quickly showed her what buttons to push, then handed her the rectangular joystick. Diamond smiled as she played the game that her brother never let her play while the five-year-old schooled her on what to push and what to watch out for. A half an hour later, the two were the best of friends.

"What's your name?" the little boy asked.

"Diamond, what's yours?" she asked as she played with his braids.

"My name is Kenneth, but everybody calls me Butter."

"Butter?" Diamond frowned.

"Yeah, what's wrong with that?"

"I don't like butter. My mother always threatens to wash my mouth out with it when I say bad words," Diamond explained. "I know. How about I call you Montega?"

"Montega? What's that mean?" he asked with a frown.

"It means butter in Spanish," she said.

What the boy didn't know was that Diamond had accidently butchered the actual word for butter in Spanish, which was *mantequilla*.

The kid stared at the little girl and paused. "How old are you?"

"I'm six years old, how old are you?"

"Five," Butter replied. "When is your birthday?"

"March 30th. What's yours?"

"July 14th. Hey, you wanna play Duck Hunt? I'll let you shoot," he offered, pulling out the red gun and handing it to her.

"Sure," Diamond said.

As he showed her how to shoot, Mr. White walked in with Brenda to check on them. When he saw the two having fun, he and Brenda snuck upstairs to finish what they had started in the kitchen. Bored with duck hunting, Diamond yawned and stretched her arms. "I don't wanna hunt ducks anymore," she complained.

"Well, what else you wanna do?" Butter asked, getting to his feet.

"I know, let's play house," Diamond suggested with glee.

Butter wasn't feeling the idea. "Nah, that's for girls and weak niggas. My mom said that a weak nigga would let a woman tie a noose around his neck and let him hang after she spent all his hard-earned money," Butter explained.

"Well, do you have any guns? We can play cops and robbers," Diamond suggested. Butter's face lit up.

He took off running out the living room and into the closet, where he kept his stash of guns: cap guns and water pistols. Diamond's eyes widened when he pulled the bin into the living room. "Okay, I'll be the robber and you be the cop," he said, pulling out two guns.

"I don't wanna be a cop. My dad said that cops are spineless cowards who hide behind a badge," Diamond protested.

"Well, I don't want to be a cop either. I hate cops."

Diamond looked around the room and searched for a solution. "Okay, since neither one of us wants to be a cop, then why don't we both be bad guys?" We can shoot at each other and not have to worry about the cops. That's how my daddy does it."

"Okay, you got the money, and I gotta get it from you," Butter stated, as he made up the rules.

For a whole hour, the two shot it out with each other downstairs. Butter chased Diamond back into the living room while busting his two guns. He tripped over the carpet and went headfirst into the corner of the coffee table, knocking himself out cold.

Diamond, who was busy giggling, turned around to see that her friend was no longer chasing her. "Montega?" she shouted, as she looked around for him. "Montega, where are you?"

When she walked back into the living room, her eyes got as wide as saucers when she saw the blood pouring out from the boy's head.

"Daddy, Daddy, Daddy!" she screamed.

Charles rushed down the steps, dressed in only his jeans, along with Brenda, who only had on a T-shirt.

When he saw the little boy lying still on the carpet, he tapped Brenda. "Call an ambulance, quick!" he shouted as he rushed to help.

"Diamond, what happened?" Mr. White shouted.

"I...I don't know. We...We were playing, and he just was laying here. Daddy, please don't let him die. He's my friend," Diamond begged as she watched her father work on the boy.

Once the ambulance arrived and the boy got placed on a stretcher, they headed out the door. "You need me to go with you to the hospital?" Charles asked.

"No, your daughter has been through enough for today. It's funny how kids are. Here they've only known each other for a few hours, and she's having a fit. Why don't you take her home? I'll call you when I know more about my son," Brenda replied.

Diamond watched as her first boyfriend was placed in the back of the ambulance and driven away. Tears trickled down her pretty face because deep in her heart she knew she would never see him again.

After a few hours in the hospital, Butter finally awoke in a strange place. Brenda rushed to his side, thankful that her son had revived.

"Ma...Mom," he mumbled as she stood over him.

"Hey, baby, mommy's right here," Brenda assured him.

"What happened?" he asked.

"You fell and bumped your head. The doctor said that you had to get stitches on your forehead."

Butter frowned. "How did I fall?"

Brenda thought that it might be best not to give him the details. Smiling, she said, "It doesn't matter, Butter. As long as you're alright, everything is fine."

Butter looked away from his mom for a second as something came to mind. "Mom, can you stop calling me Butter? I like the name Montega better," he said.

Brenda stared at her son. "Montega? Where did you learn that?"

Butter shrugged his shoulders. "I...I don't remember. I guess I just made it up. From now on, that's what I want to be called. Montega."

CHAPTER 15

GROWN AND SEXY
10 YEARS LATER

"*D*iamond, would you hurry the hell up, girl. I want to make it to the Doughnut Hole before it gets crowded," Mercedes complained as she anxiously waited for her best friend by the door of the classroom.

Diamond quickly finished the make-up test that she missed last Friday. She had never missed or failed a test ever, and she wasn't about to start now.

For 11 years, including a skipped grade, Diamond had gotten straight A's in school, which was why she could get into almost any college in the country. Finishing her test, she handed it to her teacher and strutted out of the classroom in a pair of tight, dark-blue Dior hipsters, a Prada blouse and black Giuseppe pumps to match her pocket book and Chrome Heart shades. Not only was she one of the smartest students in her high school, she was one of the prettiest. She was gorgeous from the moment her mother gave birth to her. Now, at 16, standing 5'5", and weighing 134 pounds, she was the epitome of the word alluring. She had curves in all the right places a 32D bust, a

24-inch waist, 39-inch hourglass hips and an apple-shaped ass that had all eyes on her whenever she walked by.

Her light, vanilla complexion could have been mistaken for tan in the summer and her long, silky, dark-brown hair was layered with streaks of sandy blond as it cascaded down to the small of her back, framing her beautiful, heart-shaped face. Like a diamond, she was flawless. No other girl in school could touch her style in any way, shape or form, because she carried herself with rare class and composure.

Once the two girls exited the school, as always, the eyes followed them. High school dismissal was always the shit. It was where ballers and players got a chance to kick it and hopefully try to scoop up a tender dime piece. JR was one of those ballers. He was a big drug dealer from the south side of LA. He was dark-skinned, tall, with wavy hair, a clean-cut face, a basketball player's physique, and a demeanor so cool he didn't seem like he was from the West Coast.

As the two mixed-breed females walked to the parking lot, where everyone was posted up in front of their low-riders and old-school Chevy's, JR's attention was arrested by the fine shorty who was walking with her girlfriend. The two girls oozed with confidence in every step they took.

Looking over at his homie, Calico, JR asked, "Yo, Cali, you see that?"

"See what? Oh, them bitches. They some high-class hoes. Fuck them. Now these bitches over here, they some old freaks," Calico said, pointing to a bunch of 'hood rats.

"Nigga, that's all ya fat ass look for in a bitch. If she ain't a freak, you ain't interested," JR grunted, leaving him.

"JR, where you goin', Loc?" Calico asked, but JR didn't respond.

It was no secret that JR was a lady's man. As he tried to catch up with the two foxy females, other women were eyeballing him. As Diamond and Mercedes approached their car, JR caught up with them.

"Hold up, pretty," he said. The two girls wheeled around.

Seeing the sun glint off his diamond link gold chain dangling from his neck, Mercedes smiled, already liking what she saw. Diamond, however, wasn't impressed.

"Can I help you?" she asked, eyeing him with suspicion.

JR looked her up and down and licked his lips. "For real, for real, you shouldn't walk so fast. Opportunity might pass you by and you might miss it. I ain't tryna waste ya time, baby. It's the first time I seen someone as fine as you around here, so you might have to bear with me. My name is Antwone, but everyone calls me JR. You look like you're in a rush, so why don't we exchange numbers and kick it later? That is, if you don't have a man already."

A small grin crept onto Diamond's face. Yeah, he was cute, but kicking it wasn't something she had time for.

Before she could offer a lie, Mercedes spoke for her. "No, she doesn't have a boyfriend. She sure needs one."

Diamond clenched her pearl-white teeth and shot her girlfriend a look of evil, then glared back at Mr. Handsome.

"Look..." she said while searching for a way to turn him down. "I'm gonna keep it real with you. I really don't have time for kicking it. I got a lot going on for me and I can't risk messing up my future. So, if it's destined for us to meet again under different circumstances, maybe I'll reconsider, JR."

JR looked shocked. Didn't she know who he was? It was obvious that Mercedes knew, but this one was definitely a tough challenge. He gave it one last shot. "Well, at least let me give you and your girlfriend a ride to where y'all gotta go."

Diamond flashed a wry smile at her girl. "Thanks, but I have a ride," she replied politely, opening the door of her burgundy S500 Mercedes Benz.

The smile on JR's face was priceless. As salty as he felt, he played it cool. He was in love and couldn't deny it. As Diamond started up the engine, queuing Ice Cube's, *Today was a Good Day*, Calico walked up on his homie to see the girls pull off.

"Damn, Cuz, you was right. That bitch is fine." he pointed towards the Benz. "Who you think lacin' her like that?"

JR felt like he had been touched by an angel. "I don't know, man, but I need her in my life."

Sitting across the street, watching him get into his silver Shelby GT 500, a South African drug dealer named Tanetche sat in the passenger's seat, next to the driver. "Is that the man responsible for stealing my diamonds?"

"Yes, boss. It was him. You want us to get out and tighten his ass up, right now?" Tanetche's soldier asked from the back seat.

"No, it wouldn't be a good idea to cause a scene like that in front of a school, but keep a close eye on him. He might have shooters around. One thing's for sure, you steal from me, you die. There's no other option.

CHAPTER 16

CAUGHT SLIPPIN'

*A*fter leaving the Doughnut Hole, Diamond drove to one of her brother's hangouts in the projects on the Southside. After high school, Clyde went right back to the streets with his foster cousin, Justin, and his home boys, Chavo, Shug, Tommygun, Polo, Reese Chubs, and Cheeko Raw. Together, they had the whole Southside jumping. Thanks to his father's muscle, he was the only cocaine supplier whose work wasn't stepped on.

Charles had instilled the game in his son at a young age. Now that Clyde was a man, looking like the spitting image of his father, he finally had a small piece of the family business and a team that rode harder than the LAPD. At the age of 21, he was well-respected throughout the 'hood. But, with respect came envy.

The two stuck out like zebras in a lion's den as they walked through the urban community that was full of gang violence, drug dealing, and prostitution. Besides the sound of loud music from the car systems and police sirens riding by every now and then, there was a musical vibration coming from inside the projects.

When Diamond and Mercedes arrived at the projects, one of the larger townhouses was staging a gangsta party. Females danced around in skimpy skirts, liquor got poured, weed got smoked, and music was thumping.

"Well, well, if it isn't Ms. Harvard," Polo said from a sofa where two chicks were lounging.

Polo was a fly-ass cat from NYC. He got the name because that's all he sported. He wore nothing without the man on the horse on it, not even his drawers and socks. Diamond stuck her tongue out playfully and headed for the kitchen, where Clyde, Shug, Tommygun, and Cheeko were playing cards with a pile of money in the middle of the table and a bowl of weed on the side.

Surrounding the guys were a few nice-looking females, most of whom were Spanish and dressed in skimpy, trashy outfits. They watched the guys pull out wads of hundred dollar bills until Diamond and Mercedes entered.

"You call this taking care of business? And what is that smell? This place smells like a skunk's been in here," Diamond said, holding her nose.

"Look, bitch, I own these projects. I can do what the fuck I want in 'em. You don't like it, you know where the door is," Clyde snapped as he gave Mercedes a wink to make her blush.

Mercedes had a huge crush on her best friend's brother. Clyde knew this and ran with it. He enjoyed toying around with the sexy young redbone, knowing that, one day, he would put dick up in her. He was getting so much pussy out on the streets, making Mercedes wait was more amusing than tempting. Mercedes smiled as she fluttered her eyes at the light-brown thug who resembled Chris Brown. Clyde was 6'1" and weighed 215 pounds, all of it rock-solid. He was blessed with his father's handsome features, along with the dimples and the arrogance of his mother.

"What are you doing all the way on the other side of LA, anyway?"

Clyde joked sarcastically. "You do know little girls like you who drive 500 Benzes get snatched up every day, don't you?"

"I look forward to that day," Diamond answered as she poured herself some orange juice.

"Did you make up the test?"

"Damn straight."

'Good. With your scores, you can get into any college in the country. You know, we need you to handle Pop's legal investments," Clyde said with a smile.

Suddenly, she spat the juice all over the floor and frowned. The guys busted out laughing. "What the fuck was that?" she asked with disgust while wiping her mouth.

"Gin and orange juice," Justin said, cracking up. "And I thought she was smart."

Diamond looked at the knife that was on the counter, then back at her brother's fake cousin by the overhead cabinet, who was still cracking up. With lightning speed, she picked up the knife by its blade and sent it soaring through the air in his direction. The loud thump that landed next to Justin's head silenced the whole kitchen. The only one laughing was now Diamond as she witnessed Justin curled up in a ball from the sound.

"And I thought you were a gangsta," she said sarcastically.

When Justin finally looked up to see the knife wedged in the cabinet, he shot his own daggers back at Diamond in a cold stare. She had punked him in front of everyone, including one of the girls he had his eye on.

Clyde shook his head as he played his hand. "You still fuckin' with that martial arts bullshit? That shit don't work for real, so don't think you can actually throw a knife at someone and make him go down. That shit only happens on the other side of town, in Hollywood."

"Hey, Clyde, if you think you can do better, try me," Diamond challenged.

"Wait a minute, you callin' me out?" he asked, as if it was the funniest thing he'd ever heard.

Diamond squinted at him. "Let me ask you a question, since you like jokes. I know you like to hang out in the 'hood and all, trying to be something you're not, but don't you think you could get a better spot to have your little whore parties?"

The women in the room looked at Diamond and rolled their eyes. "If I were your enemy, then you'd have something to pray on," she warned.

Clyde shook his head.

"I wish you'd just get the fuck out," Justin snarled.

"Mercedes, you ready? We're gonna be late if we stay in this shit-hole any longer," Diamond said, checking her watch.

"Where y'all goin'?" Tommy Guns asked.

"We got a date."

"Hold up. Not my little sister," Tommy said. "A date with who? And where? I'll get somebody to check him out."

Tommy Guns always played the big brother role with Diamond. He knew that Clyde really didn't give a shit about what happened to his sister, so he was always overprotective.

"C'mon, Tommy, don't pour gasoline on her fire. That's what she wants. The only date she ever goes on is to the shooting range with that piece a shit Smith and Wesson .9 mm she has in her bag," Clyde stated with a chuckle. "What she needs to do is get her weight up. I don't even know why she carries that shit. She ain't gonna use it."

"You keep thinking that, asshole. You'll be the first on my list," she warned before making her exit.

Clyde continued to chuckle as he refocused on the poker game. As Diamond slammed the door, Tommy's cell phone rang. He answered it and his eyes got wide. He hung up and said, "That nigga Ronny and them Crips done shot up our strip. Five of our pushers got smoked. We need to move out on this nigga. If he doesn't wanna deal with us because we serve the Bloods, then fuck 'em. Shit, it's bad enough them Ape Gang marks are tryin' us. Now this."

"Clyde, he's right. I think it's time we make a statement. The last thing we need is for someone to think we soft," Justin advised.

"Well, we gonna need some riders that ain't from 'round here to help us out. I got a plan," Clyde said, throwing his hand in.

"Yo, I got a couple thoroughbreds in Philly that move out without question. I'll give 'em a call and have 'em fly over here," Shug suggested.

"Alright, Cuz. Strap up, then. This weekend, we definitely gotta make a statement. Don't swim with the sharks."

CHAPTER 17

BODY SNATCHERS

On the other side of Los Angeles, Charles and his Great White committee were seated behind a table in the White mansion's situation room, discussing their next move. As Bonnie checked her watch, she excused herself from the meeting.

"Where are you off to?" Charles asked.

"Oh, I gotta get to the range. My students are probably already there, waiting."

Charles nodded with a satisfied smile, knowing just who her students were. Ever since Diamond was a little girl, all she ever wanted to do was play with guns. So, as soon as she turned 16, Charles asked Bonnie to teach her how to shoot. Diamond was excited because she finally had the chance to fulfill her dream. And, because she had Bonnie as a teacher, she was more motivated. Diamond looked up to Bonnie. The stories about Bonnie gave her confidence. She remembered sneaking out of her room at night, when she was too young, to be nosy in the doorway of the situation room. Although her mother couldn't understand why she adored all this,

Charles could. He knew that their blood ran deep, and when the time was right, his daughter would have to prove herself.

After leaving the estate, Bonnie drove to the range in East Los Angeles. She was so into her Mary J. Blige CD, she didn't realize she was being followed. Three cars behind, in a Lincoln town car, four Russians watched Bonnie's Jaguar. Underboss Pete Pachuskin sat on the back seat, calling the shots. His cousin, Rob, drove while the hit man, Mad Max, sat on the passenger's side, holding a 12-gauge, sawed-off shotgun. Also in the back seat, next to the Underboss, was a fat Russian who snored. Fatso.

Although he was slow and fat, Fatso was nothing to mess with. Pete kept these three by his side because they were loyal and ruthless. Even though the war against the White Family had been lost, Zelinski never forgot what Verningo Castor told him. And now, after the meeting in Colombia, it was time to execute their plan.

When Bonnie pulled up to the block, she parked four cars away from the entrance. Seeing Diamond's burgundy Benz parked a car away, Bonnie knew Diamond and her best friend were waiting. Diamond had become a skilled shooter at age 16, thanks to her teacher.

Bonnie got out of her car and popped the trunk to grab her bags.

While raising it, she heard footsteps approaching from behind. She quickly spun around to see who it was.

Whop!

She was clobbered with the butt of Mad Max's sawed-off. Before she hit the ground, Fatso caught her, then carried her to the trunk of their Buick and threw her inside.

"See, I told you the bitch would be easy," Mad Max bragged, slamming the trunk shut.

When he slid into the passenger's side, he admitted, "I gotta be straight up with you guys. I never tasted dark meat before."

Fatso chuckled, "Well there's a first time for everything, right?" he said as the car sped off.

Inside the range, Diamond and Mercedes got started without Bonnie. They couldn't understand why she hadn't called them. It was unlike Bonnie to miss her session. *Something isn't right*, Diamond thought as she walked out of the building and saw Bonnie's parked car. The trunk to the Jaguar was still open. She got on her cell phone and called her father.

"Hello?" Charles answered after the first ring.

"Daddy, I think something bad happened to Bonnie," Diamond explained fretfully.

"What are you talking about, princess? Didn't Bonnie meet you and your friend at the range?"

"Well, she was supposed to meet us, but she never showed. I'm standing in front of her car now. She left the trunk the wide open. There's no sign of her anywhere."

"Alright, listen to me, princess. I want you and your friend to get out of there, right now. Call me when you get to the house. I'll find out what happened," Charles assured her before hanging up.

After the phone call from his daughter, Charles put out a search for Bonnie. He didn't know what was going on, but he had to be cautious. If this was a hit from the Russians, he didn't want to be caught slippin'. Little did he know, rescuing Bonnie would be a failed mission.

CHAPTER 18

WAWA'S FOOD MARKET IN FLOUR TOWN, PA
(JUST A FEW MINUTES FROM PHILLY)

"Uh, Kenneth, can I speak with you in the back, please?" the Wawa manager said to 15-year-old Montega, who was standing behind the cash register, ringing up a customer.

After handing the customer his change and receipt, Montega followed the fat black woman to the back of the store, where he saw his book-bag on the desk, wide open, with five cartons of Newport 100 cigarettes inside. At that moment, he knew he was busted. He had been stealing cigarettes since the first day he was allowed in the store-room. He would take them around the neighborhood and sell them to the hustlers on the corner for $25 a carton. Now, his run had come to an end, and there was nothing he could say or do about it.

"Does this bag belong to you?" the manager asked.

"Nizzaw," Montega replied.

"C'mon, Kenny, I seen you come in with this bag today. Now, I'm not gonna call the cops and press charges which I should, but I am going to ask you to leave."

Montega didn't have to be told twice. Removing his apron, he headed for the exit, straight for the bus stop to wait on the number 96 that took him back to the city. Since he was 14, Montega had worked at five different jobs, from summer camp to fast food restaurants. Now, he had been fired again for trying to make some fast cash.

It was the only way to keep up with the guys in his high school who were looking fly and fucking all the bitches.

"What the fuck am I gonna do now?" he asked himself, as he watched the bus come to a stop in front of him.

Montega took in a deep breath of the night air as the long Septa bus pulled up to the stop directly in front of him. He stepped up and placed two dollars in the machine, along with some change, to get a pass for the next.

When he got it, he walked to the back, where he was surprised to see his best friend, Terrell, whom everyone called Razor, sitting by the window. Razor got the name for always carrying one under his tongue. He was dressed in his McDonalds uniform. "What the hell is you doin' off work so early?" Montega said, surprising him as he sat next to him.

"Montega!" Razor exclaimed. "What the fuck are you doin' off so early, nigga?"

"I got caught stealing cigarettes. They fired my ass," Montega explained.

Razor shook his head. "Why am I not surprised? See, nigga, I told you that shit don't last long."

"Last long, my ass. You janked me. Now I'm out of a job. How the hell am I gonna get money?" Montega said, frustrated.

"Shit, you ain't by yourself. I quit that job at McDonalds," Razor told him. "They only gave me $75 this paycheck. What the fuck am I supposed to do with that? Buy a Lo shirt and a pair of socks? Man, we need to holla at Mike and get a pack, like your little brother, Taliban. The other day I seen that nigga pull out like a nickel in all fifties. That nigga only 14, and he got more money than my teacher."

"Yeah, but I ain't tryna mess with no drugs, though," Montega confessed.

"Why not? Man, that's where the money at. Can you imagine us getting money like that? We both already two of the thoroughbreds in our school, and we got a little team that can move out. If we had money, we could have all kinds a shit. You feel me?"

Montega thought about that the whole ride to Chestnut Hill loop.

Once they got onto another bus, he asked, "Who's Mike?"

"You know Mike. He the stocky, brown-skinned bol around your brother and sister's way who be at the Chinese store," Razor explained.

"Oh, you talkin' 'bout the one who drive the Expedition?" Montega added.

"Yeah, that's him. He get weight from the bol, Million Dollar Moe. He the one who supply the whole uptown. Blakemore Street is his strip, and so is all the other blocks around there. We can't deal with Moe personally, but I know Mike will fuck with us," Razor said.

That night Montega decided not to take the train to his mother's house in North Philadelphia. Instead, he followed Razor to his old neighborhood, known as Summerville, where they spotted Mike's Expedition parked in front of the playground.

The playground was probably topside Summerville's capital. Only a block away from Kenny's mom's old crib, Lonnie Young was a big red and tan brick recreation center that stood strong on Chelten Avenue and Ardleigh Street. It was where the youth hung out, playing basketball, boxing, or just clowning around. Behind the recreation center was a playground for kids that was surrounded by two football fields, a basketball court and a swimming pool. All the hustlers played the courts at night, including their supplier.

"There he go, about to get in his truck," Razor stated.

Montega sped up his steps in order to catch Mike before he pulled off. As Mike started the engine, Montega knocked on the window. Mike looked over at the two young bucks standing outside of his truck and unlocked the door for them to get in. Mike was only 20 years old, but he carried himself in the 'hood like a real nigga. Like so many others, he had to wear his father's pants in his absence and take care of business. Everyone respected Mike, but that wasn't enough. He was in it to win it all.

"What's up, lil niggas? What ch'all got, some cigarettes y'all tryna sell?" Mike asked as Montega climbed into the passenger's seat while Razor got in the backseat.

"Nah, bol, I got fired today," Montega explained.

"Damn, lil nigga, I --"

"Montega," he corrected. "My name is Montega."

Mike raised his eyebrows at the young'un, sitting across from him. "Okay, Montega. What's up? What ch'all want from me?" he asked, amused.

"We need to make some money, dog. This job shit is for the birds," Montega admitted.

Mike looked over at the frustrated young'un, "Look, I got ch'all niggas, but y'all owe me for this, and one day, I'm gonna come to collect it. I'm a start y'all off with a five bomb, which is a $500 pack, and see how y'all work. If y'all fuck up, then that's it. I already got this nut-ass nigga Moe chargin' me up the ass for bullshit coke. I don't need to be gettin' burnt by no young bol, too." He went into his armrest and pulled out two clear plastic bags with stuffed caps of crack.

"I was gonna give these to Taliban and the others, but them niggas take too long to bring money back. These right here go for dimes. I want three hundred back off every five bomb you sell," Mike explained, handing them the packs. "Get with me when y'all finish. Y'all got cell phones?"

They both shook their heads. "Damn, you ain't got no cell phones? Alright, man, I'm a get ya some because y'all need it. If you niggas get caught up by the law, you don't know me. Y'all both juveniles, so you bound to get back outta jail. I'll see to that myself."

"I don't plan on getting caught," Montega replied, tucking away the five bomb.

"Yeah, that's what we all say, but mark my words, everybody gets caught slippin' sometimes. Now, go 'head, I gotta go outta town for a few weeks, so when y'all ready, I'm a have my man Reek hit you with the re-up," Mike said.

When the two got out of the truck, Mike pulled away.

"Damn, that was too easy," Montega said.

"Yeah, I thought we'd have to wait a few days while he checked us out," Razor replied.

The truth was that Mike had had his eyes on Montega and his homie Razor ever since he put his brother Taliban on. He liked how the two moved, and since Taliban was moving five bundles a day, he figured Montega and Razor would be millionaires in no time. He just hoped that their hearts were as big as their ambition to get money because there would come a time when they would be put to the ultimate test. In a game so slimy and a world so cold, they would have to learn a valuable lesson! Only the strong survive.

CHAPTER 19

NOTHING IS PROMISED

*L*A's club scene pulsed with life. Loud engines roared as expensive vehicles demanded attention. The front of the club looked like Christmas lights with all the jewelry that was out on display. The lines were thick and the bouncers were hard at work.

Men and women hit Century City in some of the most expensive outfits money could buy. Not only were their clothes and jewelry attracting attention, but their cars also made bold statements. Clyde and his boys pulled up in back-to-back different-colored BMWs with chrome rims. When they stepped out, their Versace outfits and dazzling jewels stood out from others in the club.

JR and his partner, Calico, also looked like heavy hitters, with their iced-out chains and Rolexes. They were in the club, popping Crystal as if it was going out of style while they grooved off of 2pac and Snoop's, *Gangsta Party.*

When Diamond pulled up at the valet stand in her father's silver and black Lamborghini Diablo, accompanied by her best friend, Mercedes, all heads turned as the doors lifted and the two stepped out, dressed in bodysuits. Diamond's was a black Gucci logo with high-heel knee boots to match, while Mercedes wore a red and green one.

The ballers in the club directed their eyes to these two sexy-ass underage females. No one would have guessed in a million years that Diamond was 16, going on 17. Her body was all grown up, and no woman in the club could match her, pound-for-pound.

When the girls walked up to the bouncer, they flashed their fake IDs that they had in their clutch bags and entered without the hassle of a search. The two strutted through the front entrance; envious eyes glared at them, wondering who they were.

"I can't believe I let you talk me into this," Diamond moaned as they scanned the club.

"Relax, you need this. Anything is better than being stuck in the house all night," Mercedes replied as they made their way through the crowd, heading for the VIP section.

Truthfully, Diamond would rather be home. There was too much going on and it was too dangerous for her to be out and about by herself. Her father still hadn't found Bonnie. And, no one knew what happened to her. This concerned Diamond. Bonnie was like an aunt to her. In fact, she was her mentor.

As the two females with eye candy figures strutted up the VIP steps, guys immediately tried to put their game down on the young tenders, but none were worthy. Diamond just didn't want to be bothered. That was until JR and Calico approached their table. This time was different than the last.

Diamond was admiring the man standing in front of her. His smile was seductive, and his attire was impeccable. But, most important, she was attracted to his smile.

"Is this seat taken?" JR asked with a grin.

"Maybe, maybe not. It all depends on the person," Diamond replied with a mutual smile.

Taking this as a green light, JR took a seat next to the sexy young lady as Calico eased himself down on the other side of Mercedes. JR soaked in her presence. She was gorgeous, stunning and irresistible.

As Diamond and JR introduced their friends, Clyde and Tommy

wandered over. "Ain't this a bitch? Can you believe this shit, Tommy? Do the bouncers know they got two underage girls in here?" Clyde chuckled.

"Damn, where they do that at?" Diamond said in disgust. "Don't y'all two have some tricks to tend to? This coupe only holds one passenger, so I suggest you go find somebody else to ride," Diamond replied.

"You hear this? She got jokes," Clyde weakly responded as he looked at both Calico and JR. Not giving a fuck about what his sister did, Clyde tapped Tommy on the side. "C'mon, Tommy, any place is better than being here," he said before stepping off.

JR looked at the two girls. "Y'all know them dicks?"

"Yeah, that's my asshole brother and his friend. Please excuse them, they're in a rush to stop breathing," Diamond explained.

"Oh, so that's your brother?" JR asked, looking over at Calico.

"Yes, it is, why? You scared or something?"

JR laughed. "Baby, you must not know me at all, but it's cool. If you give me a chance, you'll find out. You see, most women are attracted to me because of who I know or who I'm related to, but you, you somethin' special. And I be damned if I'll let you get away from me a second time," he said, putting his hand over hers.

Diamond looked at his hand, then back into his eyes. Had it been anyone else she would have removed her hand immediately. For some reason, her body wasn't functioning right.

"What's your plans after the party?" he whispered in her ear.

His breath was minty fresh and his Creed cologne was killing her softly. Her mind was saying, "Go Home," but her body was giving off a different signal. "I don't know. Why? Do you have some other place in mind, besides your house?" she asked, already hip to his game.

"As a matter of fact, I do," JR replied. "Oh, and I wasn't tryna take you home. Not just yet, anyway. Like I said before, you special, and you should be treated that way. Can we go, or would you like to have a few drinks?"

"I can't. I came with my girlfriend and she--"

"Oh, no, Diamond, go ahead. I'll be fine. Cali here said that he's gonna take me home. It's cool," Mercedes assured her, obviously with other intentions for the night.

Diamond studied her best friend for a second. She could easily detect a lie. Looking Mercedes in the eye, Diamond saw the Mercedes and her friend were up to no good. Mercedes might have been one of the most popular girls in high school, but she wasn't a saint, or a virgin. Nor did she mess with any males her age. Diamond knew this but never spoke on it. Diamond felt that Mercedes was her own woman; and if she wanted to fuck somebody, Diamond had no say-so in the matter. When Mercedes and Calico rolled out, JR and Diamond did the same.

"Where's your car?" JR asked as they walked out the front door together.

The valet pulled up in the $320,000 beauty and got out to let her in. JR was amazed by the foreign work of art parked before him. As much money as he made in the streets, he had never driven a Lambo before. Seeing the awe in his face, Diamond walked over to the passenger's side. "I hope you can drive a stick."

JR grinned from ear to ear. It was obvious that he wasn't dealing with some naïve, young girl he could easily impress. Diamond was rare to the point that she could almost be intimidating. After a nice drive across the city, the two ended up parked in a spot that JR recently found on the hills that overlooked the whole city, providing a spectacular night time view of Los Angeles. Diamond took it all in.

"So, how long have you been coming up here?" she asked as they sat on the hood of the car.

"For a few months now. This is where I come when I want to focus on my next move and get away from all the bullshit," he said, gazing at the crescent moon.

"You're not really from LA, are you?" Diamond asked while studying his face.

'How can you tell?" he asked.

"I don't know. You just don't fit the mold of the guys out here."

JR chuckled. "You right, Ma. I was born in Camden, New Jersey. Where I come from, there are no places like Hollywood or Rodeo Drive. It's more like Compton. My pops got locked up with a life sentence for murder, and my mom's was a crackhead. So, basically, I had to go into foster care when I was young. I got moved all over the east coast until I found a stable home. They moved me to Los Angeles when I was 12. That's when I realized that colors really meant something over here."

"So, you're in a gang?" Diamond asked.

"Not really. You see, my foster brother, Ronney, is a father to the Southside Crips. Me, I just get money and serve them work. I ain't into all that gang bangin' shit. And if a nigga ain't on my page, I don't even fuck with him. I think the two best things about coming to Cali was finding a connect to put me on my feet," he said leaning back.

"What's the second?" Diamond asked.

"Meeting you," he replied as he looked at her.

"Me?"

"Yeah, Diamond, I meant what I said about you. You special, for real. I've been with a lot of girls since I've been down here, I ain't gonna lie, both young and old, but none has the swag you have. Whoever raised you must have big plans for you. I don't wanna get in the way of those plans; I just wanna be there to see you make it," JR confessed.

Diamond blushed at the man beside her. She didn't like the fact that someone else had plans for her in life, but didn't speak on it. She decided not to ruin the moment. She could feel genuine respect coming from JR. He was nothing like the guys in high school, who just wanted to add her to their list of bitches they fucked or the dopeboys who just wanted her as a prized possession on their arm. He was unique. He was cut from a different cloth.

After they summarized their lives growing up, Diamond dropped JR off at his condo on Sepulveda Boulevard near Manhattan Beach. She headed home, sure that her parents would be worried sick if she stayed out any longer.

When she walked into the mansion's foyer, the sound of weeping coming from the cigar room caught her attention. Trying to avoid being questioned on her whereabouts, she quickly slipped out of her boots and tiptoed past the cigar room, where her father and his friends were grieving over an opened box that was on the table. When Diamond stopped and saw the box, she frowned, then entered the room to get a closer look.

The second she stepped in, Two Gun Sam tapped Charles on the shoulder as Whisky quickly blocked her off while trying to explain.

"Baby, this isn't the time. You shouldn't be here right now."

His nervous demeanor only gave way to more curiosity and before one of the men could remove the box, Diamond walked up to it and removed the top. "Diamond, no," Charles said helplessly.

The first thing that hit his daughter was the faint smell of cooked meat. She never blinked as she held the box in her hand. Once she realized that the cooked head in the box was Bonnie's, tears rolled down her cheeks and she buried her face in her father's chest.

"It's alright, princess," Charles said stroking her long hair as she cried.

"Wha…What happened to Bonnie, Daddy?" she kept crying.

Charles looked up at Two-Gun Sam as if to ask, Should I tell her? Two-Gun Sam nodded. It was always best to tell a child the truth. In the long run, the child would respect you more.

"Baby, Bonnie was kidnapped by the Russian mafia. These sick fucks are no ordinary people, they're cannibals. They believe that if they eat the flesh of their enemy it will make them stronger. That's what they did to Bonnie," he explained while hugging his daughter.

Diamond's emotions were in overdrive. She had never seen something so gruesome in her life. Her mind was filled with so many emotions that not even her high I.Q. could answer them. The sight of Bonnie's bloody, decapitated head was tattooed in her memory and would haunt her for the rest of her life. The image was so indelible, it was as if Diamond had witnessed the execution. What really haunted her was the way the scene repeated itself, over and over, casting a terrible shadow over her innocent, beating heart. The worst part of it all was that she wasn't dreaming. This was real.

All the memories of her life with Bonnie flashed in her head. It was a crazy world. One day a person was there; the next, she was gone. What happened to Bonnie told Diamond that nothing in life was promised but death. When her time would come, nobody knew.

CHAPTER 20

STREET WAR
(MONTHS DOWN THE LINE)

"Yo, pass the Dutch," Shug said to his homie, Kev, as they rolled four deep in the black Grand Marquis with dark, tinted windows.

Kev was from Shug's neighborhood in South Philadelphia. He and Shug grew up together and always stayed true to each other. They rode around South Central LA, accompanied by one of Shug's cousins, Mike, and his shooter, Maniac, who was in the backseat, playing with his short dreadlocks with one hand, while holding his Beretta in the other. Trailing them was another set of shooters.

Once they got to Crenshaw Boulevard, their targets were outside a small house, smoking sherm sticks, without a care in the world. Before they noticed the car approaching, Kev slammed on the gas while Shug's shooter hung out the window, blazing away with his fully automatic Beretta .12 submachine gun. Within seconds, he riddled the victims with slugs, turning their clothes to the color red, like the rags in their back pockets.

ON THE OTHER side of Compton, Tommy Gun and Cheeko were causing havoc throughout Ape Gang and Crips territory like a rampaging tornado. No one had any idea that the hits were coming from Clyde, which caused rival gangs to turn on each other. Before they knew it, a vicious street war began, courtesy of Clyde White.

JR followed Diamond inside Neiman Marcus as she made her final stop in the mall after a five-hour shopping spree. JR watched as she went into a shopping frenzy throughout name brand stores like the mall was closing down. She had so many bags, five of his soldiers had to carry them while he and Diamond strolled around the mall like royalty. For six months, they had been dating. JR had done nothing but treat Diamond like the underworld princess she was. He took her everywhere and showed her off to everyone. When he wasn't out in the streets, he was with Diamond, schooling her on the drug game that he was so heavy in.

TALKS like that inspired her to do what she wanted. Everyone was pushing for her to go to college and Diamond decided that she wanted to be a doctor. She took medical classes five hours a day with one of her father's good friends as her teacher. Not only was she book smart, she knew how to weigh cocaine, cook crack, and bag it up. There were plenty of occasions when she would stop by JR's condo to find him bagging up work for his crack houses.

Once they were done shopping, JR took her back to his condo, where they just kicked it all evening until it was time for Diamond to go home. As they sat on the couch, bussing it up about life, Diamond looked over at him.

"Can I ask you a question?"

"Anything, baby. What's up?" JR asked with his arms around her.

"We've been going together for months now. All that time, you never took our relationship any further than making out with me. I know you're a man, and you have needs. I also know that you probably have some chicks on the side, and I'm not upset about that. I just want to be the one to please you more than anyone else. I know I'm a virgin; all I ask is that you teach me."

JR's mind was blown when he heard that. The truth was that he actually did have a few chicks on the side that kept him satisfied so that he didn't have to put any pressure on Diamond. She was special to him, and if he had to wait for her, so be it. Now, she was ready to experience the most important part of their relationship.

JR gently placed his hand on the right side of her beautiful face and stroked her soft cheek with his thumb. He then gave her a slow passionate kiss before taking her hand and leading her to the bedroom. There, he undressed her, down to just her thong and bra. "Lie back on the bed, while I get undressed," he instructed her as he removed his T-shirt.

His eyes never left her shapely body.

Diamond lay back nervously. Her heart thumped, but her eyes gazed at the muscular figure who climbed into bed and slowly kissed her again to relax her. Sitting up a bit, he looked her in her eyes to see if the fire and desire still scorched within her.

"Before teaching you how to please me, I'm going to please you first. The reason is because you're the prize, not me. A real man will always recognize that before they make love to you," he whispered before lightly kissing her neck.

He savored her smooth skin and her sensual scent. Overwhelmed by her perfume, he sucked on her neck while working the clasps apart to her bra. JR tossed the bra to the floor and Diamond's nipples instantly got hard as stones.

JR paused briefly to admire her perky breasts like a connoisseur would when he studies a work of art. Diamond breathed deeply as she locked her gaze on him, but then her eyes slowly rolled to the back of her head with pleasure. JR squeezed her breasts and feasted on her nipples like a starving infant. Diamond wrapped her arms around him, heaving deep, passionate sighs. JR's hands explored her sexy body. Not only was she fat in the ass and titties, she had succulent thighs, and her pussy was trimmed and juicy. Diamond's mouth widened with delight when JR went downtown on her and tasted her juices. As his tongue probed her slot and circled her pearl, she felt as if she couldn't breathe any longer.

"Uhhhh!" she panted breathlessly, lost in the heat of the moment.

She was soaking wet and didn't know what to do but moan. Then a weird feeling came over her; she felt like she had to pee. She was too afraid to ask what was happening to her body and what happened next almost drained the life out of her. JR felt the vibrations of her trembling legs and knew she had had her first climax. Diamond exploded her sweet juices into his mouth. Huffing and puffing with sweat pouring down her face, she watched as he rose to his knees on the bed.

"Come here, baby," he murmured as he faced her.

Diamond rose to her knees while watching him stroke his dick.

"The key to oral pleasure is the technique," he told her, cupping both sides of her face.

With one hand wrapped around the base of his dick, Diamond began sucking the head. "Try not to use any teeth, and always give me eye contact. I want to know that you enjoy pleasing me just as much as I enjoy getting pleased," he instructed as he eased her back and forth with his hand on the back of her head.

Diamond quickly got the hang of it and moved her warm mouth up and down his shaft until he was rock-hard. Once she stopped, he strapped on a condom. There was no turning back for Diamond, now; she was about to leave her childhood for good and become a woman. When JR plunged inside of her and tunneled into unexplored territory, she gripped the nape of his neck and scraped her manicured nails across his chocolate skin.

"Sssss-ow," she gasped as he rhythmically pumped her full of dick.

He knew she wasn't used to penetration; she pressed against his chest, so he eased up. After a couple of light strokes, the pain began to subside, allowing him to go deeper down her tight pink hole. Diamond started to move her hips in unison with his. JR cupped his hands under her firm, round, apple-shaped ass and fed her pussy more and more of his manhood until she had all 8 1/2 inches inside of her. Her soft moans had him reaching his own moment of truth.

Their body fluids blended together. This was pure bliss for both of them.

JR lay beside his Snow White princess and silently studied her beauty. Never had he felt this way about anyone. He actually found someone to love, and it scared him because he knew that this wouldn't last forever. That was the reason he had hesitated with her. Diamond had a spell on him. And, from that day forth, he didn't want any other woman. He hoped that destiny would keep her in his life until he left this world. Little did he know, there were some very angry South Africans who wanted to make that happen.

CHAPTER 21

SOUTH CENTRAL LA
(ONE YEAR LATER)

*A*s Steel sat in front of the steps of one of his drug houses, surrounded by his homeboys, Vicious, C-4, Buck, Sid, Poke, and Iceman, he mapped out how he would exterminate the Crips on the other side of town. Steel and his boys were a part of the notorious Ape Gang run by the Agugbo Brothers.

"Listen here. I just got off the phone with Tanetche and he gave the green light on the mark that stole his diamonds," Steel began. "He also thinks that his foster brother Ronney and them Crips are responsible for all those drive-bys. We gonna let the streets know that we serious, and we ain't nothin' to be played with. I say we take out the head, and the body will fall."

"Well, if we gonna go at this mark, we need Iceman to handle the job," Sid suggested. Iceman was the king of ruthless hits.

Iceman nodded his head and flashed a crooked smile. It was definitely about to go down.

"A'ight, Iceman's got the job, but I still want him to take a few apes with him." Steel instructed. "Buck, you can also tag along. Don't fuck this up. We got big hitters depending on us. I want the streets buzzing about this tomorrow morning, and I want those bitch-ass Crips hiding when they find out that their supplier is dead.

$\sim$

MERCEDES ROLLED her eyes when she recognized the number on her cell phone.

She pressed talk. "What do you want, Ronney?" she hissed.

"Damn, that's how you gonna carry me?" Calico replied.

"No, but I told you that I'm in a relationship now. Why can't you honor that? You didn't want a relationship, remember?" Mercedes told him.

Mercedes cut Calico off the minute Clyde made a commitment to her. It was no secret that she had had a big crush on Clyde since junior high, so when he came at her, she was delirious. She was now 19 years old and looking bad as ever. Seeing how happy she looked, Calico just couldn't let her ride out on him like that.

"Look, I understand all that, but I need to talk to you. It's very important," Calico pleaded.

"Well, what are you waiting for? Speak."

"C'mon, Mercedes, the shit I got to say can't be said over the phone. Why don't you meet me somewhere, where we can talk face-to-face?" he suggested.

"Look, Ronney, I don't have time for your bullshit--'

"Just meet me. Please," he urged, cutting her off. "At least you can do that. Then we can go our separate ways."

Mercedes remained silent for a whole 60 seconds to think about her choices. After realizing that there wasn't any harm in finding out what he had to say, she relented.

"Okay, Ronney, after this, though, you have to stop calling me. If my boyfriend catches us, he'll kill you."

"Yeah, whatever. There's a restaurant on Avalon Boulevard. Meet me in the parking lot," Calico instructed.

"Okay, I'm on my way," she replied before clearing the line.

When Mercedes arrived at the spot, Calico was already awaiting with three of his soldiers, who were standing nearby. Mercedes got out of her two-door Saab and approached him.

"Okay, Ronney, I'm here. Now, what's this all about?" she asked, looking around at the rough neighborhood she was in, a far cry from her condo in Hollywood.

"A'ight, it's like this; I know it's none of my business what you do since we're no longer together, but you need to check your boyfriend," Calico warned.

Mercedes frowned. "What are you talking about?"

"I'm talkin' about how that Buster be doggin' you. I watched this nigga every night at the club, leaving with some new pussy, and all I can think about is you. You may feel like I don't deserve you, but you sure as hell don't deserve that type of shit bein' done to you," Calico explained.

Mercedes couldn't believe what she was hearing. She had suspected Clyde of cheating, but she wasn't sure. Until now. She didn't realize how much Calico cared for her. At that moment, Mercedes reacted with her heart. She was suddenly drawn towards his lips. As soon as they kissed, they were massacred by semiautomatic gunfire from men wearing red bandanas over their faces. His partner fired a Mac-10 while he held a Tec-9 sideways with no remorse for the woman that caught a wig shot next to Calico, who was next to feel the heat.

Calico plopped down on top of Mercedes. The ambush happened so suddenly that Calico's soldiers couldn't retaliate. They drew fire from two heartless Bloods who lurked behind a parked car. When their magazines were empty, instead of fleeing, the Bloods simply reloaded their 50-shot magazines. The ambush continued as they both put one in the chamber, then popped back up, blazing.

They didn't stop until the three men were injured. The shootout didn't end until the last Crip fell dead on the ground. The fallen and wounded were finished off with head shots before the shooters headed to the car, where Steel was waiting. Removing their red bandanas and tossing them to the ground before they got in, they greeted their boss with wicked smiles. They had just given the Bloods the charge before the car peeled off.

CHAPTER 22

BLOOD DIAMOND

*A*s JR drove Diamond to her family estate, he popped in his favorite Machiavelli CD and cranked it up. The dashboard started vibrating, so Diamond quickly turned it down.

"That is way too loud for my ears," she griped, staring at him like he was crazy. "And where are we going tonight?"

"There's a little outdoor movie theater where everyone takes their shorties. I figured we stop by there and make out or something."

"Make out, huh? You are too much," Diamond said, adoring his style of trying to be romantic. "You know what? I've been meaning to ask you something. Why did you really wait so long to take my virginity?"

JR smiled as he thought of how smart and ambitious she was. She never let one thing pass her by without addressing it. "You don't miss anything, do you?"

"Only when a loved one dies," she smirked.

"Okay, to be honest, the reason I fell back for so long was because I knew you had me, so I was a little shook."

"Had you-- like what?" Diamond asked, puzzled.

"You don't even know, do you? I'm sprung over you, baby. I can't deny it. And nothing is more powerful and controlling than what you have between your legs. My weakness is you, and that's what scares me," he confessed as they pulled into the White family's mansion gate.

Clyde and Justin had just walked out the glass double doors, but they stopped when they saw the blue BMW pull up to the front entrance. At first, the two thought that their plan to have rival gangs at war with each other had backfired. They started to reach for their guns until Diamond stepped out of the passenger's side.

Clyde was surprised to see his sister still with the Crips supplier.

"Is this bitch crazy?" he mumbled.

When Diamond approached, Clyde began with his sarcasm. "Damn, you still fuckin' with that nigga?" he asked.

"Yeah, so? Why do you care?" she snapped, as she brushed by the two and stepped inside. Clyde and Justin followed her.

"I don't, but that nigga is affiliated with them Crips in Compton," Clyde stated as if she didn't know already.

"So, what does that have to do with me?" she asked.

"You brung him here. That's a problem. I'm telling you some real shit. You need to fall back off this nigga. It's a crazy war goin' on out there in South Central, LA between the Crips and the Ape Gang," Clyde warned.

"News flash, Clyde," Diamond said sarcastically, her hands on her hips. "I think it's a little too late to try and be a big brother. I'm a big girl now, all grown up, so you can save that dramatic shit for one of those dumb hoes you be doggin' my girlfriend for."

Justin's eyes narrowed in on her perfectly-shaped body. It was as if she was getting thicker, and her runway model walk wasn't helping his hunger subside either. She was right about one thing. She was definitely a big girl now. Little Diamond had become a number-one stunner.

"Yo, Cuz, you think we need to check that nigga?" Justin asked as he stared at Diamond's ass.

"Nah, I'll let him live," Clyde answered. "I ain't startin' nothin' over that hard-headed bitch. I'll let them Agugbo Brothers eliminate him like a contestant on a game show that gave the wrong answer. Feel me?" he said as they made a detour to the garage.

"Yeah, Clyde, I feel you," Justin replied, but his mind was somewhere else.

Meanwhile, upstairs in the master bedroom, Charles and Pearl had their own little domestic dispute.

"Why must you always leave the minute you get here, Charles? You never stay home anymore, and I'm sick of it!" Pearl shouted at him.

"Pearl, I told you before. I got a meeting with one of my good friends in New York. I can't keep arguing with you over some petty bullshit like this," Charles replied as he fixed his tie in the mirror.

"Bullshit, Charles? That's all bullshit. I know where you're going. I'm not stupid, okay? You're going to see that girl, aren't you?" she asked, glaring at him.

"I don't know what you're talking about. I'm--"

"How long has it been, Charles?" she blurted as tears streamed down her cheeks. "How long have you been sneaking around on me?"

Charles looked at his wife and shook his head as he put his suit jacket on. The sound of the door down the hallway slammed shut as Diamond stood behind it in her own room, shaking her head with disgust. She was fed up with all of her mother's complaints. If it wasn't about his cheating, it was about his line of work. Charles had become a star in the criminal underworld. He and Carlton Butler's Underworld organization handled about 15% of the drugs coming into the country. And on the streets he was known as the Snow White King.

As her mother continued to complain about the woman Charles was cheating on her with in Philadelphia, Diamond thought back to when she was a little girl. She still remembered seeing the blood coming from the little boy's head and wondered if he ever survived his accident with the coffee table. She never asked her father about it because he made her swear never to bring it up again. Diamond got dressed and headed back outside. When she got into the BMW with her boyfriend, she beamed like a searchlight.

"You ready, boo?," she asked before kissing him.

"Don't ready boo me," JR said, before pulling off. "What took you so long in there?"

"You know I had to find something to wear. I thought you knew how picky I could be when I want to look cute for my man," she replied, stroking his ego.

JR couldn't counter that. When they arrived at the drive-in movie theater, he parked up and reclined back in his seat. Diamond just sat there like a mannequin.

"You okay?" he asked.

"Yeah, I'm fine. Why do you ask?" Diamond asked impatiently.

"Because you look like a white girl in a gang-related neighborhood," he said, which wasn't too far-fetched. "Why are you so uncomfortable?"

"I'm not uncomfortable. I'm just watching my surroundings. A lot of dumb shit happens in these type of places," Diamond explained.

JR chuckled. "You can't be serious."

"What? What's so funny?" Diamond frowned.

"You, girl. Let me tell you something. You ain't got shit to worry about. This my 'hood. I run shit around here. Now, relax, this time is supposed to be about us," he reassured her.

Diamond knew that he was right. He was calm, cool, and smooth. So she relaxed a little. He was a big drug dealer in this neighborhood and beyond it. In fact, he was supplying far more people than she knew. She looked at the handsome thug who stared at her and smiled.

She wanted to kiss him, but just then someone rushed up to the driver's side door. Instead of being dramatic, her reactions were totally opposite. Survival shot through her veins. JR saw horror in her face and how fast her hand reached into her Fendi bag for her gun, but it was too late for him.

Boom!

A shot slammed into JR's head from the open window.

Diamond watched JR's brains burst from his head like a watermelon. In a flash, she pulled the gun from her bag, aimed, and with no hesitation squeezed the trigger.

Boom! Boom! Boom!

The bullets struck the assassin, sending him stumbling into a vacant parked car while innocent bystanders who were stuck in the parking spaces got out and ran for cover. Blood spurted out of the assassin's neck like a faucet. Even his chest was leaking with two big holes. After hitting the car, he fell to the ground, shaking.

Diamond glanced in the rear view mirror and saw another man sneaking up from behind. She hit the ignition, pressed her foot on the brake pedal, and shifted the car in reverse. The vehicle backed into another parked car, sandwiching the gunman. He squealed in pain like a woman having a baby. Then two more goons swooped in. Diamond peeped the blitz and started blasting for her life, shattering the side window from the inside. The two thugs stopped in their tracks and took cover behind another car. Seeing this, Diamond got a chance to seize the opportunity she needed to get away. She fired three more cover shots at the two assassins. Iceman then popped up, ready to fire. Diamond fired a single shot into his skull. On seeing their top Ape Gang assassin go down, Buck tucked his gun and sprinted off for his life. Diamond jammed the car back in park, then got out to inspect her work.

She walked up to the assassin who was sandwiched between the two cars. He was moaning in pain. Diamond pulled his ski mask from his face and snarled at him.

Pressing her gun to his temple, she asked with clenched teeth, "Who are you?"

"I...Ugh, Ape Gang...I...Please, don't kill--"

Boom!

One side of his head splattered against the asphalt.. She then walked over to the one who was shot in the chest and neck. With no remorse, she executed him, as well. She then gazed over at JR's lifeless body slumped on the passenger's seat. It dawned on her; they had taken away her happiness. Her sanity. And now there was no turning back.

Her emotions began to crumble inside of her. Tears welled up in her beautiful brown eyes until they streamed down her cheeks. Diamond slid down the side of the car until her ass hit the ground.

Dramatically, she held her head in her hands. *What have I done?* she thought. She had just killed not one, but four, men. That amount of blood on her hands was something she couldn't confess to in church. It weighed too heavy on her heart.

Just then, the sounds of police sirens wailed in the night air from a mile away. When her mind finally registered to what those sounds meant, her emotions stopped at a standstill. Wiping her eyes, she got back on her feet and quickly looked around for an escape route. As much as she wanted to run, she refused to leave her boyfriend behind. Once she found the courage and strength to move him to the passenger's seat, she got into the car and made her getaway.

That night she lost her virginity a second time. That innocent, little girl was completely gone. The Agugbo brothers had flipped on her switch. The cold-blooded killer lurking inside her was now awake.

CHAPTER 23

PHILADELPHIA, PA
(EAST GERMANTOWN)

*O*n one of the longest blocks in Summerville, Montega waited on the corner, at the Chinese store on Blakemore Street, where he hustled, for Mike to re-up on the half-ounce he was copping every three days. Hustling crack wasn't at all what he had expected. Yeah, he was making big money, but the hassle of waiting for the re-up irritated him. Mike would always tell him to meet him somewhere and never show. Montega hated missing out on money because he always ended up spending what he had saved. As he sat on the steps of the store, watching his brother, Taliban, and a few other hustlers run down the crackheads to serve them, his cell phone rang. Hoping it was Mike, he answered without checking the caller ID.

"Yo, bol!"

"Yo, what's good, Tega? What chu doin'?" Razor asked.

"Waiting for Mike's fuckin' ass. It's been two days Dog, and he still ain't hit me off with that. Where you at?" Montega asked.

"I'm with J-Rider, Nino, Killa, Tank, and Gutta. We at the mall, tryna cop them new Jordans so we can stunt at the chick Brandy's party tonight," Razor explained.

"Damn, I almost forgot about that party. Yo, pick me up a size nine, and I'll give you the bread when you get here."

"I got chu, bol. Holla at chu when I get back," Razor said before hanging up.

As Montega stood up and dusted himself off, a silver Porsche 911 slowly rode up with Million Dollar Moe inside, slouched to the side with a phone in his ear. Montega frowned when he saw his sister, Kia, get out of the passenger's side and shut the door. Moe ice-grilled the young hustler for a moment before pulling off.

"Where the fuck you comin' from?" Taliban interrogated her.

"Nigga, I'm grown. Don't be asking me no questions, boy," Kia shot back as she approached Montega. "What's up, brother? You alright?"

Montega nodded as he scanned his older sister's outfit from head to toe. She had on some tight Sergio Jeans, a V-neck shirt and a pair of Tory Burch sneakers. Besides her bangin' body, Montega realized that she was one of the prettiest brown-skinned chicks uptown. Her silky, shoulder-length dark hair was her mother's contribution to a package of beauty.

Montega hugged his sister. "I know you gonna do you, regardless of what I say, but be careful messin' around with dudes like that. You're a jewel to me, but to others you might be just a possession worth showing off."

Kia smiled before she kissed her brother on the cheek, and headed down the block to her mom's house.

"Man, that bitch is outta pocket. I can't stand that nigga Moe," Talban said with a sneer.

Taliban was Kia's and Montega's opposite. He was high-yellow in color, like his father, but also resembled his mother. He was overprotective with his sister and let every cat know it.

"Ain't shit we can do about it, bol, but hope he don't do her dirty," Montega said.

"Oh, there's something we can do about it, a'ight," Taliban stated.

"Just the other day, I overheard Mike and Reek talkin' about taking over uptown and rockin' Moe to sleep."

"Yeah?" Montega asked with surprise. "But I thought Million Dollar Moe was his old head."

Taliban shrugged his shoulders, giving Montega something to ponder on. That night, Montega met up with his crew at the corner of the block, where the party was being held. His homie, Tank, who was a light-brown skinned smooth thug, was there. Tank swore he was God's gift to women. With him was a dark-complexion guy named Nino, who was at least 6 feet 2. Nino made his money installing stolen car stereo systems and doing tint jobs. When they were younger, he was the one who always fixed up the bikes for everybody.

Next up was Gutter, a flashy, light-skinned nigga with curly hair. Gutter loved to wear fly clothes and bust on all the dirty niggas who couldn't afford what he had. Then there was J-Rider, who had Montega's almond complexion. Instead of cornrows, like Montega, he wore strands that stretched past his shoulders. His cousin, Killa, looked like his twin, except for their different skin tones. They both lived in North Philly's Blumburg projects, but had originally migrated from LA, before J-Rider's mother died. Razor was a high-yellow, half-black, half-Colombian gangsta who was the same height as Montega, 5 feet 9, weighed 160 pounds, soaking wet. He rocked thick, straight, back braids, and could almost pass for a skinnier version of Montega's brother, Taliban.

Last, you had Montega's homie who lived around the corner from his mom's house in the Bad Landz of North Philadelphia, Beeto, who everyone called Lil Man. Lil Man was 100% Puerto Rican, with a Napoleon complex. He was a hothead, but he could back up his mouth. His brother, Skimask was a skilled street robber who had an impressive collection of guns. Lil Man's weapon of choice was the fully automatic AK-47, which he would use on a nigga if he got out of line. He was the only one in the crew who had a body under his belt.

The crew was greeted at the party by thumping rap music, flashing strobe lights and neighborhood chicks with glorious, fat asses. The house was packed with fellas and ladies. Their red cups reeked of spiked punch.

"Damn, look at shorty over there. She got a fat ass," Montega marveled in Lil Man's ear.

"Yeah, but look at that bitch-ass nigga dancin' with her," Lil Man replied, causing Montega to do a double-take look at his homie.

Montega shook his head in disapproval and stepped off on Lil Man to get some punch. As he poured himself a drink, Brandy appeared. "Hey, Kenny. I'm glad you and your friends could make it because my girlfriend was bugging the shit outta me about you."

"Me? What she buggin' you about me for? And who is she?" Montega asked.

My girlfriend, Tasha. She just graduated from Dobbins High School and is on her way to college somewhere in Atlanta soon. She said that she always see you around the 'hood, but never said anything to you.

"You sure she ain't talkin' 'bout Tank?" Montega said, making Brandy frown.

"Boy, stop playing. Don't nobody want Tank's conceited ass."

"See for yourself. She's over there, dancing with some dude," Brandy said, pointing to the chick he had seen first with the fat ass full of Jell-O and hair like Beyoncé. She was a shade lighter than him and moved like she practiced dancing everyday in her mirror at home.

Montega couldn't recall seeing shorty anywhere. Maybe it was the weed fucking with him, but he knew he had to have her.

"What's her name again?" he asked as his eyes undressed her.

"Tasha. And don't think you just gonna get in them drawahs, 'cause you not. She's a virgin," Brandy informed him before walking off to entertain other guests.

Montega tossed down the whole cup of punch, then approached Tasha as she rubbed her hips on some freshman from LaSalle University.

Calm and nonchalant, Montega eyed the football player. "Beat'cha feet, homie, I need to talk to her for a second."

The guy paused, then when he saw who it was, he walked off, leaving Tasha standing there, confused.

"Dag, if you wanted my attention, you could've just asked to dance with me," she proclaimed to the young hustler with the long braids.

"I ain't tryna dance. I'm tryna talk, so what's up?" he asked.

"I don't know," she said innocently, shrugging her shoulder. "You tell me."

"A'ight, I see what type time you on, so here's how this is gonna go. You rollin' with me now, so all these niggas in here who think they got a shot at poppin' your cherry before you go to college can forget it," Montega said matter-of-factly.

Tasha's mouth dropped open. She had never heard anybody so boldly talk to her like that. She was used to telling boys what to do, and here was this guy. Not only was he bold, he was cute as shit. "So, you're saying you want me to be your girl?" Tasha asked.

"No, I'm not saying it. I'm telling you. Now, let's ditch this dumb-ass party and go somewhere where we can talk in private," he said, reaching out to grab her hand.

Tasha didn't know why she had even entertained the thought of going anywhere with him, but she couldn't find it within herself to tell him no. He was so blunt, before she knew it, he was popping her cherry and calling her his. That night, when Montega stepped into his mom's house, it was close to midnight, but his mom, Brenda, was coming down the steps, looking fabulous in a mini-dress and heels. Montega almost didn't recognize her.

"Where you think you're going this time of night?" he asked with a frown.

"Do I look that good?" Brenda asked, twisting from left to right.

"Yeah, Mom, you look beautiful, but that wasn't my question. Where are you going this time of night?" Montega repeated.

"I have a date with an old friend of mine, baby. Let me ask you a question. Do you remember Charles?"

"Who?"

"Charles. Remember he came by when you were little, with his little girl? You don't remember how you got that scar on your forehead?"

Montega couldn't recollect. He had no memory of what had happened before he bumped his head. He thought he had gotten the little scar in some scrap as a kid. Brenda saw that he had drawn a blank.

Montega watched his mother grab her pocketbook and leave. Something in him told him not to let her go out that night, but he couldn't spoil her happiness. Little did he know that he might never see her happy again.

CHAPTER 24

DEATH WISH

*L*ater on that night, Two Gun Sam and Whisky accompanied Charles as they rode to a little bar in south Philadelphia. The place was big on the outside, but from the looks of the guys hanging around, it looked to be nothing but trouble. Hookers pranced by the dealers in tight little outfits, looking to make ends meet. Even the stray alley cats were on the move, searching for a late-night meal. One of the drug dealers who had a fish platter from inside, tossed the bones near the curb and watched as the cats fought for them.

When they arrived, Two Gun Sam put the car in park. "You need us to go with you, Chuck?" Sam asked.

"Sure, why don't you and Whisky come have a drink? I'm supposed to meet with Carlton Butler." He looked over at the appointed spot.

"I still don't see why we didn't bring more protection with us. This place looks grimy," Two Gun Sam stated.

Charles chuckled. "Carlton said that it was best not to draw too much attention. Besides, the hotel is only a few blocks down the

trying to say something. "WA...Watch...O...O...over my...family." Then came the blank stare with glassy eyes.

With Charles dead, Two Gun Sam and Whisky knew they had to get out of that bar. They grabbed Charles's gun and cautiously walked out the door.

When Mad Max got to the car, he had a big smile on his face as he dialed Zelinski's number. "Hello, boss? It's done. We got him."

"Excellent," Zelinski said. "You done a good job. Keep me posted."

'Sure thing, boss."

In Miami, Florida, Carlton Butler sat on the sofa in a Fisher Island mansion with the notorious drug lord, Verningo Castor. Castor was the Russian mob's main cocaine supplier. He also supplied a number of big-time drug syndicates. He was infamous for putting out hits on anyone who tried to muscle into his territory. But with Charles, it was different.

"So, tell me, Mr. Butler, now that Charles is out of the way, how do you plan on getting rid of his son," Castor asked.

"I know Clyde will come for his father's share of the underworld. I also know the Great White committee won't listen to anyone but one of their own, so I plan to let Clyde have his father's share. I'm getting old in this business, so I want to keep everything simple. This is why I'm putting my son in charge of the Wolf Pack."

"So I take it that with Deshawn and Clyde running the business, you're gonna play the puppet master?" Castor asked.

"Your exactly right Mr. Castor, because I fear the consequences if you're wrong," Castor said before walking to the table and grabbing his briefcase.

He brought the briefcase over to Carlton and sat it in front of him. "Here's your ten million for helping me set up Charles. I guess you can buy your son Stephon a new sponsor now," Castor joked. "I saw his fight the other day on DISH. He's very talented."

"Of course, he is. He's a Butler," Carlton said.

"Can I ask you a question?"

Butler stopped. "Speak."

"You still haven't said anything about Charles's associates. I'm sure they'll try to get revenge."

Butler chuckled arrogantly. "You know, for a man that is like a God in his country, you worry too much. I'll tell you what. I'll talk to Clyde personally. By the time I finish with him, he'll think that it was all Charles's associates' fault. And then you know what happens after that."

CHAPTER 25

DEATH OF THE SNOW WHITE KING

MONTEGA SAT in the empty pew in the first row of the empty church, silently staring at his mother's casket. The church was quiet, dark, and gloomy. The wooden pews were so hard, his ass felt numb. Montega looked up from the casket to the statue of Jesus, hanging from the cross and wondered why God had dealt him such a fucked up hand in life. He didn't cry because there was no one he could lean on.

Only a handful of people were there; Brenda never had many friends. However, an anonymous someone had been generous enough to pay for the funeral. Among the few who did come to pay their respects were Lil Man, his little sister, Faith, and his mother, Stephanie, Stacy, her two children, Kia and Taliban. Brenda's parents and her nephew, Rodney, came all the way from Atlanta. Seated in the last row were two homicide detectives.

Montega didn't show tears, nor did he show anger. He knew that his mother was in a better place. Now he was looking for answers. All he knew was that she was a victim of a shootout between three men, and now she was dead, just like his father, 16 years ago. Now he was all alone. After the funeral, as Montega got up to leave, he spotted Stacy talking with his grandparents just before his sister, Kia, came up to hug him.

"I'm sorry, boo. My mom just talked to the detectives. They said that your mom's killers got away. They don't even have the description of the guys," Kia explained.

"So, my mom's killer is still out there somewhere?" Montega asked.

Kia nodded. They both knew there was nothing anyone could do about it. For now.

As Montega hung his head, Stacy approached. "I talked to your grandparents. They want you to come stay with them in Atlanta. But I figured you wouldn't want to leave everything behind. Plus, I don't think it's right to break up a family that's already established so you can stay with me if you want. That is, until you find an apartment," Stacy said before hugging him and kissing him on the forehead.

His mother had schooled him so much in the past about how to move and how to be a man. Even though it was hard for a mother to teach that, she still did her best with what she knew. Now it was time for her son to be the man of the house. That was harder than it sounded; he felt like the weight of the world was on his shoulders. And the only way to survive in that world was to make it his own.

THROUGHOUT THE CITY OF LA, an almost endless line of cars crowded the streets as people from all over the country came to pay their respects to the White Family and remember the Snow White King. Diamond sat in the Catholic church next to her family, dressed in a black Donna Karen dress with matching shades and shoes and she listened to the priest speak. It was tough to pick up on what he was saying while her mother engaged in hysterics.

Pearl broke down at the news of Charles' death. She didn't know what hurt her more-- that her husband was dead or that he had cheated on her. This despair had led her to a suicide attempt. She was only still alive because Diamond had found her in the tub, trying to slit her wrists.

Diamond sat quietly and hid her face behind the veil. Had it not been for the black satin gloves she wore, her sweat would have dripped from her closed fist of anger. Inside her, a storm was raging. She was too angry and too proud to cry. What she wanted was revenge.

But no revenge was as sinister as what Clyde had on his mind. Clyde not only wanted the blood from those responsible for his father's death, he also wanted it from the people who didn't save him. Before the funeral, he had a serious talk with the chairman of the underworld, Carlton Butler. After listening to him, he made up his mind.

At the cemetery, Clyde couldn't take his eyes off of Two Gun Sam and his cronies. He felt that they were to blame; they were there to protect his father, and yet, not one of them had a scratch. Pearl's hysterics also had him flaming. Clyde had always accepted Pearl since he didn't know his real mother, but now that his father was dead, he decided to cut his ties as soon as he got back home.

As he continued to stare at his father's so called friends, someone moved through the crowd of people gathered all the way up to the casket. Diamond thought maybe the guy was mourning, until she saw him go into his pocket and pull out a grenade. Her eyes got wide. She wanted to stop him as he pulled the pin and tossed it into the grave, but instincts told her to push her mother to the ground and cover her. Clyde, too, saw the man, but couldn't believe his own eyes. As the man made a run for it, Charles's casket exploded. The Russian whipped out a mini AR-15 and started firing on the stunned crowd, sending everyone in a panic. Diamond, who was covering her screaming mother, looked around and spotted the man running. She quickly went for her bag to get her gun. Even from the distance where the Russian was running, she had no doubts about her aim. But before she could get to the gun, a hail fire of bullets ripped into his back. The Russian fell face-first to the ground, just before another Great White henchman walked up on him and shot him in the head. Pearl pushed her daughter away from her and looked to where Charles's casket once sat and saw nothing but body parts. At the sight of that, she passed out. Clyde shook his head as his new business partner, Deshawn "Scar" Butler, and his father, Carlton, approached.

"I don't believe this shit," Clyde said, looking at the scene.

Carlton Butler placed his hand on his shoulder. "See what happens when you don't have tight security?"

Carlton looked at Two Gun Sam.

Clyde followed his gaze. Carlton whispered in his ear, "Keep your circle tight, Clyde. Don't make the same mistake your father did."

After the tragic event, just before Sam left the cemetery, Tommy stopped him. "Yo, Sam, Clyde wants you to ride with me to pick up a package."

Still in mourning, Sam couldn't believe that Clyde insisted on work at a time like this, but out of respect for Charles, he got into the car and rode off with Tommy, with no idea where he was going.

CHAPTER 26

CHANGING THE GAME

When Diamond got home from the funeral, she headed straight up to her bedroom, where she flopped down on her bed and stared at the ceiling in silence. Instantly, her emotions broke through the barrier of her strong will. She was devastated. All her life, she had been shielded by the horrors of life. Now, they were coming at her from every angle. Eventually, her sorrow transformed into anger, and anger turned into rage.

Diamond sat up, grabbed the crystal ball on her dresser, and threw it at her mirror. The glass shattered into tiny pieces. Seeing the damage she'd done, she fell back to the bed and sighed. Her mouth felt dry, and her stomach started to growl, but she ignored it. She was too exhausted and hurt too much inside to eat. Not only had she lost her father, but her best friend and first love was also gone. What left a bad taste in her mouth was the simple fact that none of their killers were brought to justice. A teardrop swelled in her eyes for the 20th time. This time, she let it roll down her cheek as JR's cell phone rang; it was still sitting on her nightstand.

Wiping her cheek, she sat up, picked up the phone, and answered it with a raspy voice. "Hello?"

"Que pasa?" Someone with a Spanish accent spoke on the other end. "Is JR there?"

"No, he isn't. May I take a message?" she asked coyly.

"Can you tell him that I'm ready to see him?" he asked.

At first, Diamond thought about telling him about JR's murder, but then she got an inspiration. "You know what? Can I call you right back?" she asked.

"Yeah, mommy. Sure," he said before she clicked over to the other line.

The man's name was Spud, and his intentions were the same. Diamond put him on stand-by, along with five other guys who had called within 10 minutes. Diamond quickly figured out that the cell phone was used for drug transactions.

Once she put all the clients on stand-by, she searched through the phone for the Russian man she once met with JR at a restaurant on La Cienga Boulevard. She remembered it being a business conference. And now her boyfriend was gone, and yet his old clients kept calling. She remembered the lessons that JR had taught her about the drug game.

As she searched through the list of numbers she recognized a name: Semok Budinov. She then made a call. Three rings later, the Russian answered.

"I was wondering when you would call," he said.

"Um, is this Mr. Budinov?" she asked nervously.

"Who is this?" Semok wondered.

"Mr. Budinov, I believe we met once at a restaurant on La Cienga Boulevard. I accompanied my boyfriend, JR," she said, hoping to jog his memory.

"Oh, yes, I remember. Why have you called me?"

"Well, if you didn't know already, my boyfriend was murdered a week ago," she lamented.

Semok got quiet for a moment. "I see. I'm truly sorry, my dear. JR was a good business man. He will be tough to replace in LA."

"Well, you see, Mr. Budinov, that's actually what I need to talk to you about," Diamond hinted.

"What are you saying?" Semok asked.

"I really don't want to discuss business over the phone, but we can meet up at the same place, at, say, 3:00 PM?" Diamond asked, checking her watch.

"Listen, miss..."

"Diamond. My name is Diamond," she said.

"Yes, well, Diamond, I'm a very busy man and I--"

"I know," she interjected. "I've been around busy men all my life. One thing I learned about them is that they never turn down anything worth their while," she said, tossing him the bait. She wanted to convince him that she was serious.

"Okay, be at the restaurant at precisely 3:00. If you're late, you must never call my phone again," Semok warned.

"Yeah, I understand," Diamond said before hanging up and rushing to get herself together.

She knew what she was about to get herself into, so she had to look the part. She wanted to project pure business. So she dove into her walk-in closet, searching for the right outfit: a charcoal Armani two-piece form fitted skirt suit.

Diamond thought she would never dress like a business woman, being as though she had her heart set to tackle the medical world. Today was different. Today she was set to tackle a totally different world that was far more dangerous than anything she could ever imagine. Today she wanted Semok to know just how serious she was. Not only was her suit a perfect fit on her immaculate curves, but her black pumps and blouse set it off. She strutted to her burgundy S500 Mercedes Benz. It was time for the princess to take her place as the queen. What she was about to do would change the game.

WHEN TOMMY and Two Gun Sam arrived at the spot in Compton, they both got out of the car and headed for the door. Tommy knocked twice but no one answered. He knocked again; still no answer. Tommy then tried the knob, which was surprisingly unlocked, allowing them to enter. The house was empty, and none of the light switches worked. Once inside, Two Gun Sam searched for the package.

"I think he said it was in there," Tommy said, pointing to the bedroom.

Two Gun Sam pulled out one of his Colts, just in case someone was behind the door. Cautiously, he turned the knob and swung the door open and pointed his weapon at an empty room. What he saw sitting in the middle of the floor was a large wooden box that he had mistaken for a chest. Two Gun Sam frowned as he approached it. "What the hell is that?" Tommy asked, following his tall, skinny partner.

Two Gun didn't speak. When he got to the box, he squinted. It wasn't a box at all, nor was it a chest. It was a casket, his casket. As he shook his head in disappointment, Tommy's Desert Eagle opened up the back of Two Gun's head, dropping him face-first into the casket. Tommy lifted Two Gun's legs over the lip and into the casket before closing it. "Good riddance to you, you old fart," he said before strolling for the exit.

CHAPTER 27

THE SIT-DOWN

When Diamond entered the restaurant, she found a nice spot in the back where she could see the entrance and everyone inside. It was an old trick her father used whenever they went out to eat as a family. She checked her watch: 2:58 PM. She pulled her mirror out and checked her appearance. She snapped the case shut as a white Mercedes limousine pulled up and five Russians got out and entered the restaurant, each monitoring an area outside. In came Semok, who spotted Diamond already seated and approached looking like a mobster from a movie. He was stocky, with broad shoulders and short, spiked hair. He stood 5'11" and was over 200 pounds of solid muscle.

"Did you order yet?" he asked, while taking a seat across the booth from her.

"No, I was gonna wait until you got here," she replied.

"Very good. I could eat a horse," Semok said, opening his menu.

Once he ordered his meal, he got down to business. "Okay, tell me what it is that would interest me."

Diamond removed her sunglasses and made direct eye contact with the Russian mob boss. "I mentioned over the phone that my boyfriend is dead. And from what I understand, you might need someone to replace him," she began.

"And you want his spot, I assume," Semok said, eyeing her precariously.

"Well, Mr. Budinov, that's exactly what I want," she said, gazing right at him.

Semok grinned with admiration at this woman. She was brave and ambitious. Easing back into his seat, he replied, "I should remind you that JR moved more than 200 kilos for me a month. That's a helluva lot of coke to handle, especially for a woman to handle all by herself. Pardon me for perhaps discriminating against you, but do you actually think you can handle a big shipment like that every month?"

Diamond smiled with confidence. "No, I don't think I can. I know I can. Look Mr. Budi--"

"Semok," he said, cutting her off. "Just call me Semok."

"Well, Semok, it's like this: I've been around long enough to know how to handle myself. In fact, I know all of my boyfriend's clients, who are currently on hold and awaiting my call. The game is in my blood, Semok. All I ask is for a chance to prove myself."

Semok's amused grin turned into a full-blown smile. This female in front of him had not come to play games. "Well, Diamond, if you are serious, I'll charge you the same price JR once had. Fifteen a key, but--"

"Excuse me Semok," Diamond interrupted, "but I'm well aware of the prices JR paid, and it's not $15,000. Now, do you want to make money or not? Or do you want to keep playing games?" Diamond asked.

"Playing hard ball, eh?" he grunted.

"My father didn't name me Diamond just because I was beautiful."

"Okay, Diamond, $7,000 a key. But I should warn you that taking your boyfriend's place means assuming the debt he left behind," Semok emphasized.

"I understand. In fact, I stopped by his loft and collected the

Bruce. Then there was Sunny Black, who controlled a few projects in Englewood, Tom-Tom, Buddy, and six other major drug dealers. Each man was used to buying at least five or more keys a week. Diamond knew she had her work cut out for her.

When she spoke, she spoke with such confidence and passion, everyone around her paid close attention. That day, she made the group an offer they couldn't refuse--15 a key.

Sput raised his hand. "What about the Ape Gang?"

Diamond clenched her teeth when she heard the name.

"That's a good question," Tom-Tom- agreed. "If the Ape Gang killed JR, won't they be looking to strike again?"

Diamond addressed these worries. "Let me handle the Ape Gang. You guys only have to worry about making money. And Lonnie, I know JR was family, but don't let his death cause you to lose your head and fuck up what you got going. I promise you by next week, you guys will have it your way," she said, looking over at Butch.

He already knew what she had in mind.

"OH, YES, FUCK ME, DADDY!" Rachel moaned as she rode Buns' dick like he was Seattle Slew. "C'mon, hit it harder, Ssss, oooh!" she screamed in bliss.

Bun was a vicious sugar daddy. He loved to fuck young girls and had a fetish for fat asses. That's how he got the nickname: Buns.

As Rachel bounced up and down on his dick, there was a knock on the motel door. "I'm busy, come back later," Buns grunted.

The knocking got louder.

"I said I'm fuckin' bu--"

Boom!

A 12-gauge shotgun door buster shell blew the door open. Buns quickly pushed the broad off his dick. She fell to the floor, only to leave his chest wide open for the next shot.

Click! Clack!

Another shell got loaded in the chamber.

"You can't make it to your friend's funeral, but you got time to fuck underage bitches, you pervert," Reese Chubs said, pulling the trigger.

Boom!

Buns' chest caught a slug like a pass from Michael Vick. He flipped off the bed onto the floor. Rachel looked up in mortal terror. Reese showed no emotion, but then smiled as his dick got hard. Shug's cousin, Mike, walked in the room with Chavo. Mike pulled out his revolver just as Reese started to unzip his pants. He beat Reese to the punch and put a bullet in her skull.

"What chu do that for?" Reese asked.

"Bring ya freak ass on. Ain't none of that shit goin' down while I'm here," Mike stated before he walked out the door.

Reese looked at him and frowned, but Chavo just shrugged his shoulders as if to say, "He's right."

Chavo got on his phone and called Clyde. "Yeah, the job is done."

"That's the best news I've heard all day. I tell you what. Let's go out or something. I need a drink," Clyde replied.

CHAPTER 29

KISS OF DEATH

*W*hen Diamond got home, the first thing she did was take a hot bath in her jet water spa. She was still coming to grips with the loss of her father, her best friend, and her lover, all in one week of mayhem. Such tragedies should have knocked her right off her pins, but Diamond was driven by dark forces: anger and vengeance. She was ready to unleash both of them. Once she got out of the tub, she grabbed a fluffy towel to dry off with, and got dressed in a pair of YSL jeans, a Louis Vuitton shirt and a pair of Prada sneakers. She pulled her long hair back in a bun, then grabbed her cell phone to dial Butch's number. After the first ring, he answered, "What sup, little cuz?"

"Get some guys together. I'm coming to get you. Oh, and Butch, make sure they're heavily armed," she told him, looking at the black Uzi automatic gun with the two extended clips on her bed.

"Cuz, I swear, you must have read my mind," Butch responded.

"I'll see you when I get there," Diamond said before hanging up.

Suddenly, she heard her mother screaming somewhere in the mansion. Diamond dashed out of her room to see what was going on.

When she got to the second-floor balcony of the U-shaped double staircase, she saw four white males in white scrubs, trying to stick her mother with a needle. Clyde was standing close by.

Diamond darted down the red carpet covered steps to see what was going on. "Clyde, what the hell are they doing with my mother, and why are you just standing there?" she snapped. "Why the hell do you have your hands on my mom?" she asked one of the men in white.

"Relax," Clyde said casually.

"What the fuck do you mean, relax? Where are they taking her?" Diamond demanded.

'Someplace where she'll be safe and they can keep an eye on her," Clyde explained, his arms folded.

"I'm not understanding this. I thought she was safe here."

"And whose gonna watch her? You? C'mon, Diamond, all you do is run the streets all day long. What your mom needs now is constant care," Clyde pointed out.

"No, she needs to be with her family. This family," Diamond replied indignantly.

"And, what might happen while you're gone? What'll happen the next time she cuts her wrists? Are you ready to deal with that?" Clyde asked, trying to reason with his sister.

Diamond watched her mother mellow out from the tranquilizers. That gave the medical people the opportunity to put her onto a gurney and into a van out front. She then looked at an administrator, who had legal papers for Clyde to sign. "Gimme that," she snarled, snatching them before Clyde could sign. "I'll sign these. That's my mother. And, if anything happens to her, I'll hold all of you responsible," she threatened. She hastily read and signed the document, then shoved the paper and pen into the man's chest and stormed off.

Clyde smirked devilishly. He didn't care how his sister felt about his actions. All he knew was that the White family mansion, and every other big asset, would eventually be his.

As he stepped outside to watch the van pull off with Pearl, Mickey pulled up just as Shug stepped outside.

"Well, well, well, we're right on schedule," Clyde mumbled.

Mickey had to confer with Clyde about Charles's business interests. As Mickey stepped out of his Lexis, Clyde said, "Mickey, I need you to ride with my men to pick up my stepmom."

Mickey frowned, "Where is she?" he asked.

"She went shopping by herself. She keeps calling me to send someone to get her. My friend, Shug, here and his partner, Kev, will join you if that's not a problem," Clyde said.

"No, not at all," Mickey replied, then turned to walk back to the car.

When Mickey got in the driver's seat, Kev got into the back seat while Mickey drove all the way to a supermarket in Long Beach. He couldn't understand why Pearl had gone so far to do food shopping. He knew she was undergoing a lot of stress, but this was ridiculous.

Once he pulled into the parking lot and parked, Kev pulled out his .357 revolver and placed it at the back of Mickey's head.

Boom!

Mickey's brains were all over the front windshield and the dashboard. "Fuck, Kev. You almost got that shit on these Pradas," Shug joked. "Next time let me know when you're gonna shoot."

The two exited the car, walked out of the parking lot, and saw Polo and Cheeko Raw, sitting in a blue Buick Regal. As they got in, Polo asked, "Did y'all get him?"

With a deep voice, Shug asked, "What'chu think?"

IN COMPTON, Diamond, Butch, 4-5, and Butta sat behind the tinted window of a white Chevy Suburban, watching Vicious, C-4 and Poke loitering out front at one of the Ape Gang's main coke houses, surrounded by six other gang members.

"Are you sure these are the guys?" Diamond asked, staring at Vicious and C-4, who were walking into the house.

"Yeah, I told you Cuz, word on the street is that these dudes are vicious. They're known for hitting Crips on their own turf," Butch explained.

"Alright, let's see how they react when the tables are turned," Diamond replied, cocking back her 50-shot Uzi.

The team did the same. "You sure you ready for this Cuz? You know we can handle this from here," Butch said, uneasy about putting his cousin in danger.

"Save your worries, Butch. I'm not the little girl you think I am. Besides, if you want something done right, you gotta do it yourself. Right?" Diamond asked.

She wrapped a white bandana around her face and tied another over her freshly-braided hair.

The other three did the same before getting out. Diamond had already picked out Poke to be the first victim. Poke spotted them, but before his hand reached the handle of his gun, a hail of bullets took him down. Instantly, an enormous wave of bullets rained on the porch and steps. The loud crack of gunshots echoed through the neighborhood, ripping up chunks of wood. Mothers rushed outside of their homes to get their children back in the house. Crackheads stood close by, hoping to find a couple of dollars on a dead body, so that they could cop more drugs, while the LAPD turned in the opposite direction of the gunshots.

Diamond and her three wolves stood in the middle of the street, ripping bodies to shreds. When there was no one left standing, she and the others stepped over their corpses and went into the house. From the kitchen, Vicious and C-4 started blasting their handguns back into the living room. Diamond took cover behind the safety of a sofa. She peeked out to see where the two were. Instantly, Butch dashed through the door, firing a Mac-10. Seeing he was outnumbered, Vicious made a run for the back door, while C-4 provided cover.

Diamond snuck out from behind the sofa, pulling the trigger as the Uzi vibrated her arms, tearing up tables and furniture. C-4 couldn't dive for safety fast enough and got hit. When his body hit the floor, Diamond had a clear shot at Vicious' head before he could escape. She took a precise aim and pulled the trigger.

Click!

"Shit!" she hissed, watching Vicious run out the door.

When Butch joined her, she turned and said, "Go get the truck started and give me your gun."

After trading guns, Butch followed orders. Diamond watched C-4 crawl to grab his gun. She slowly moved in for the kill. She stood over him as he turned onto his back to witness the face of death. Diamond pulled the bandana down to blow him a kiss before aiming and firing.

Boom!

CHAPTER 30

BLOOD MONEY

*I*n east Germantown, Philadelphia, outside on the basketball court at the Lonnie Young Recreation Center, Montega sat on a park bench surrounded by the seven young up and coming stars of the 'hood. Razor, Tank, Lil Man, Killa, Gutta, J-Rider, and Nino. They all listened intently to Montega. As the other guys played basketball and kids swam in the pool, the seven looked to Montega for guidance.

"So, what are we gonna call ourselves?" J-Rider asked, with his hands behind his back.

"How about Dangerous Villains?" Razor suggested.

"Fuck, no. That was a long time ago. We grown now," Montega stated before leaning forward. "Look, we can't be representin' shit that don't pertain to what we after. You got to look at it this way. What are we all after here?"

"Money." Gutta stated the obvious.

Montega nodded. "Okay, and what would we do for money?" he continued.

"Anything necessary," J-Rider replied emphatically.

"Would you kill somebody for it?" Montega asked.

"Fucking real," Killa retorted.

"Would you rob a nigga for it?" Montega inquired.

Everyone nodded with serious faces. That's when an idea came to mind. "How about...BMM?" Montega suggested.

"BMM? What the fuck is that?" Razor asked as someone approached.

"Blood Money Mafia," Montega revealed.

Everyone thought about the name for a moment before nodding their heads in approval. That decided, Montega cracked open a Heineken and took a sip, then passed it around to his homies to formalize the decision.

The meeting was interrupted when a chick with honey-brown skin and micro braids walked up with a look of urgency. "Which one of you guys is Kenny?" she asked.

"Ay, look, shorty, I'm a little busy right now. Tell them that--"

"No, you look," Breezy interrupted, posing with one hand on her curved hip that was shifted to one side. "You need to get down there and see who put their hands on Kia, because she got a big-ass handprint on the side of her face."

"What?" Montega vented while quickly rising to his feet. He followed Breezy down the block and over to Stacy's house.

As soon as he walked in, he spotted Kia sitting on the couch with her girlfriends, Gi-Gi, Crystal, and Jasmine. Taliban hovered over her, trying to get a name. "Kia, who fucking hit chu?" Taliban repeated for the seventh time. But Kia didn't respond.

As soon as Montega walked in the house with Breezy, Kia looked at him dead in the eyes. The two had a bond that no one could understand but them. It was like Montega could read her mind. So, instead of asking her who had hit her, he headed down the steps to his room in the basement.

Going under his bed, he pulled out a Timberland shoe box where he hid a Mac-11 fully automatic submachine gun with an infrared tracer beam and a 31-shot magazine filled with dum-dums. Montega had purchased the gun from a crackhead for $200 and five dimes of crack. He had never had a chance to use it until now. Taking the gun out of the box, he attached the extended clip and cocked it back, sliding a bullet into the chamber. Sticking the gun in his waistband, he went searching his drawer for the old costume he wore on Halloween, the night he and his homies went on a robbing spree around the 'hood.

Montega tucked the black Phantom mask into his pocket, along with the black bodysuit that came with it. He went out the basement door and headed up the alley. Million Dollar Moe had just pulled up to the corner of the Chinese store and gotten out with two of his soldiers, Kali and Kyree. Million Dollar Moe was a big bruiser with an intimidating stare and a humungous chip on his shoulder. Everyone knew that upsetting him could be perilous. Moe was only 28 and had already earned close to $2 million. Kali and Kyree were Moe's two ruthless goons; everyone knew that they meant business. Million Dollar Moe spotted Reek by the mailbox and approached him. "Yo, where that muthafucka Mike at? That nigga ain't check in with me in two fuckin' weeks," Moe snapped.

Reek shrugged his shoulders. "He probably outta town or something," Reek replied.

"He ain't tell me," Moe shot as if Mike had to.

"And, he shouldn't have to, frontin'-ass nigga," Reek said under his breath, but replied aloud, "I don't know what to tell you, Moe."

Moe shook his head in disgust. "I put that nigga in charge and he skips town on me. First, I gotta smack the shit outta my little bitch, now this. You know what? Everybody, get the fuck off my block, right now."

Everybody looked at him like he was crazy. "Oh, y'all think this a game? Ay, Kali and Kyree, get these niggas off my strip. I'll hustle my own coke if niggas can't be out here"

"Y'all heard what he said," Kyree shot back, approaching the guys on the corner with intimidation.

While the hustlers started to walk off feeling like suckas, a figure in the alley crept out and cautiously approached. Before Kyree could turn around, a red dot was on the back of his head. Montega's heart pounded with fear. He really didn't want to kill anybody, but he knew that there was no other way. And, like going down a one way street, there was no way he could turn back.

Kali peeped game and quickly tried to warn his boys. "Ay, Kyree, watch ya--"?

"BOOM!"

The Mac sprayed from Montega's hand, ripping Kyree's head apart. Montega's ears rung like crazy as everything seemed as if it was all in slow motion. When Kali witnessed his homie fall to the Phantom killer, he froze in shock, giving Montega just the time he needed to target him. Kali tried to duck, but the rapid fire of the bullets were much faster, ripping him to shreds.

As soon as Montega looked up, Million Dollar Moe was making a run for it down Woodlawn while all the other hustlers ran for cover. It didn't take long for Montega to catch up with Moe and spray his back red. Moe stumbled and fell out in the middle of the street while everyone in the swimming pool screamed and ran out for their lives.

As Moe rolled over onto his back in pain, the Phantom figure stood over him. "Please, don't do this. I'll give you anything," Moe squealed in agony.

Montega ignored Moe's pleas for help and thought about his sister's bruised face. Clenching his teeth, he pulled back on the Mac, emptying out the rest of the clip into Moe's body. He then stood over the corpse, watching it twitch for a few moments before taking steps back and turning to head for the alleyway.

Inside Stacy's house, everyone besides Kia ran to the porch to see what had transpired at the top of Blakemore Street. Kia couldn't care less what was going on. She was too hurt and heart-broken. Suddenly, she heard a door close in the basement, which made her curious as to what her brother was up to.

Kia got up and headed down the basement steps and unexpectedly witnessed her brother slide a box under the bed and stand up to face her. His face looked white as if he had done something he shouldn't have.

"Kenny are you al--"

"Kia!" Gi-Gi said, rushing down the steps. "Guess what just happened. Oh-my-God, you're not gonna believe this. Somebody just shot Moe and his two young bols. I think they're dead."

When Kia heard that, she turned her attention to her brother, who was now lying on his bed with his hands behind his head, looking up at the ceiling. He couldn't get the face out of his head, nor could he speak at the moment. That day, a monster had been created.

CHAPTER 31

ACT LIKE A LADY, MOVE LIKE A GANGSTA

*D*iamond watched from the back seat of the SUV as her team followed Vicious' Impala to the outskirts of Compton. Once he parked, they did the same, five cars away. The team observed the Ape Gang lieutenant jump out of his car and rush into a house that had a black screen door. Diamond popped another 50-shot ladder into her Uzi, cocked it, and swiftly exited her car, with Butch at her heels.

Butch was amazed at how gangsta his little cousin had become. She rode harder than most killers he knew. He had heard the saying about a woman scorned, but Diamond was way past that. She was a rider.

When Vicious got inside the crib, his pregnant girlfriend was on the couch, doing his mother's hair. His father sat in the recliner, a 40 of Old English in his hand, watching "Cops" while his 17- year-old younger brother had just come down the steps, ready to head out the door to a basketball game. Vicious quickly got on the kitchen phone to call Steel and let him know what the hell just went down.

As his little brother opened the door, he stopped in-stride before taking a step back as guns were pointed in his face. Once Diamond and Butch entered, Vicious's mother screamed in fear. His father spewed a mouthful of beer onto the screen, causing Vicious to drop the phone as Diamond pointed a gun at his pregnant girlfriend's head. "Oh, shit!" Vicious gasped in desperation.

"You might as well come out," Diamond said coldly.

Seeing that he had no play, he walked out with his hands up.

"What the fuck do you want with me?" he asked as his eyes scanned the room.

Butch fired a warning shot at the ceiling, making everyone jump, including Diamond. "She's asking the questions, not you," Butch snapped.

Diamond took over. "I want to know who was involved in killing JR, and you better not lie to me," she warned.

"Man, I don't know," Vicious grumbled.

Diamond aimed at the pregnant girl and pulled the trigger.

The woman howled in pain as a hot bullet plunged into her arm. Vicious' eyes became as wide as manhole covers at the sight of her falling to the ground, holding her bloody arm.

"What the fuck?! OK, OK. I'll tell you. Just don't kill her," Vicious pleaded. "It was the Agugbo brothers. Tanetche gave the order to Steel to kill JR. He said something about JR stealing his diamonds."

"Who's the Agugbo brothers? And who the fuck is Steel?" Diamond questioned.

"The Agugbo brothers live in New York. They are head of the Ape Gang, but Steel, he's their lieutenant," Vicious answered, quickly glancing over at the wounded girl crying on the floor.

"Where can I find this Steel?" she asked.

"He be round Lawndale, near Alondra Park. That's his main spot."

Diamond looked over her shoulder at Butch, then back at Vicious. "Now I know." She aimed her gun at his head and pulled the trigger. Butch drew his weapon on the wounded girl, but before he could squeeze off a shot, Diamond stopped him.

"Stop. We have no beef with them. Let's move out,'" Diamond instructed before she turned and walked out.

Butch smiled wickedly before spraying up the whole house.

When Diamond arrived back at the White mansion, Justin was emerging from the kitchen. As Diamond picked up the few envelopes of mail in her name, she looked up and glanced at him before heading up the steps. She had other things on her mind. But first, she hopped into the spa tub to relax a bit. She had seen a lot of death in the last few days, more than most police officers saw in a lifetime. Once she was washed and at ease, she wrapped herself in a towel, then walked over to a full-length mirror, where she dropped it to stare at her naked body. Suddenly, there was a knock at the door. She abandoned the mirror and put on a robe. When she answered the door, she saw Justin standing there.

"What?" she asked irritably after cracking the door.

"Can we talk?" he asked calmly.

Diamond frowned. "Talk? Talk about what?" she asked cynically while she brushed a strand of her hair behind her ear.

Justin slid into her room as she was tying the belt to her robe. He couldn't help but notice her pretty, painted, pedicured toenails and her wide, hour-glass hips, which left little to the imagination behind the silk fabric.

"Can you make this fast? I kinda want to be alone right now," Diamond mentioned.

"Alone for what?" he asked, pausing to study her a moment, circling her to get a glimpse of her apple bottom. "You know I care about you, Diamond, regardless of our differences. I don't want to see anything bad happen to you. I don't know if you've heard, but your brother is now in charge of your pop's business. A lot of people are gonna test him to see what he's made of, including Castor- - your pop's arch enemy. Castors already taken out all of your pop's organization. You need protection. I can protect you."

Diamond looked up at the tall, light-skinned man with braids.

"So, you want to protect me? What's in it for you?" Diamond asked seductively.

"I don't know," he lied, closing the gap between them. He fondled the drawstring on her robe. "Whatever pops up fir --"

Before he could make another move, Diamond kneed him square in the nuts. Justin let out a loud oomph, before curling up on the floor in the fetal position. She then pushed him out of her room, causing him to fall in the hallway in pain. Banishing him with a warning, she said, "If you ever try to pull some weak-ass shit like that again, I swear, I'll cut off your balls and feed them to you!" She then slammed the door and locked it.

CHAPTER 32

DEVIL IN A TIGHT DRESS

*I*nside the fabulous Supper Club that entertained the rich and famous of LA, Clyde threw one of the biggest parties that the city had ever seen. Everybody who was blessed with wealth showed their faces for this mega event. Men and women were dressed in outrageously expensive designer outfits. Movie stars, real live gangsters, rappers, athletes and divas were there. DJ Khalid was bangin' "The Game" and 50 Cent' "This Is How We Do." From the balcony, Clyde and his boys watched as some of the finest ladies in LA sat at the bar, gyrating their hips on their stools, enjoying shots of Patron.

"Yo, have somebody call those bitches up here," Justin ordered.

Once his soldiers walked downstairs, Clyde smiled. "Damn, cuz," he said, popping open another bottle of champagne, "we got enough bitches around us already. How many more do you want?"

"It's never enough bitches, cuz," Justin replied before snatching the bottle out of Clyde's hand and taking a long swallow. Besides, I want the VIP room to be packed with so many hoes that by the time we leave I'm a be swimmin' out this muthafucka."

Clyde looked at Shug, who had two women sitting on opposite sides of his lap while rubbing his large belly. No doubt, they were tripping off of ecstasy; every now and then, Shug would get them to kiss each other. Clyde chuckled because he'd pick out two women himself later that night to take home. There were so many sack chasers running around, he didn't know which one he wanted. As Mike strolled into the section with Deshawn Butler and his brother, Stephon, Clyde snapped out of his fantasy.

"Clyde," Deshawn greeted him before shaking his hand, "what's been goin' on, son?"

The two embraced, looking like two true bosses. Both were dressed in Armani and Gucci and had jewelry that was so expensive that Jacob the Jeweler himself would have been impressed.

Deshawn had an introduction to take care of before they proceeded. He gestured towards a well-built man behind him who could almost pass for his twin. "Clyde, this is my brother, Stephon."

"Oh, shit, I know who you are," Clyde said, shaking Stephon's hand. "You're gonna be the next middleweight champion."

Stephon smiled. "Scar, I like this guy already. Word."

"C'mon, y'all, have a seat. We were just about to politic. How's everything goin' in New York?" Clyde inquired.

"Everything's smooth," Deshawn replied. "I'm tryna get my brother a Nike endorsement deal. They wanna wait and see if he can beat the middleweight champ. So we're on hold right now."

"Well, you know how that shit goes. Hell, I wish I had a brother that was in sports. Instead, I got cursed with a spoiled brat for a sister."

Deshawn chuckled. He had never met Diamond, but from what he had heard from Clyde, he knew she must be a problem child. Just then, a big commotion erupted near the club entrance. All heads turned as three African men in immaculate clothes walked in with a group of men. They parted the throng of people like they were Hollywood's biggest stars. They headed up the lighted staircase, onto the balcony, where Clyde and the others sat.

Deshawn was the first to stand. He extended his hand and the shorter African with a short goatee shook it first. "Simon, Hillary, Tanetche, it's good of you all to come on such a short notice," Deshawn said, stepping to the side. "This is the man I've been talking about. Meet the head of the Great White Organization, Clyde White, and these are his homies."

Once the men shook hands with everyone in Clyde's circle, they took a seat. Clyde had his soldiers remove most of the women, so the men could discuss business.

"I want to get right to the point," Tanetche said, dismissing a waitress who was trying to pour him a drink. The woman rolled her eyes at the man's ignorance. Tanetche was very imposing. He was pitch-black, with the face of an angry bull. He had dark, sinister eyes and nostrils almost as wide as the Lincoln Tunnel. "You run this city, right?" Tanetche asked.

Clyde nodded confidently. "Yeah."

"Well, tell me, then. What do you know about a bitch who calls herself the black kiss of death?"

Clyde was confused. "I'm sorry, sir, but I've never heard such a name," he replied.

"Well, she's right here in LA, and she's been killing some of my top lieutenants. Surely, you gotta know something."

Tanetche's brother, Hilary, quickly intervened. He knew what a hothead his brother could be and wanted no quarrel with any of the men at the table. Hilary was a shade lighter than his brother, with short twists in his head, a trimmed mustache and glasses. He stood 6'4" and was brilliant. "I apologize for my brother. This woman has caused him a lot of stress."

"I understand. And, yo, I can promise you that I'll look into it. But, chances are this kiss of death broad is just hype," Clyde said naively.

"No, Clyde, that's not the case at all," Tanetche countered. "Please let me know if you find anything pertaining to this woman. I want to be the one to look her in the eyes before she dies."

Stephon was getting bored listening to the men bickering over some renegade broad who was made out to be some type of devil in a tight dress. She sounded like some nasty slut you'd meet in a strip club. As he peered over the balcony, he spotted someone with exquisite beauty. She stood out in a crowd of fine woman. She wore a black, strapless, Burberry dress that looked like it had been melted onto her perfectly curved body like candle wax. The Bottega Veneta shoes on her feet made her look almost half a foot taller. Her hair was pulled back into a long tail, and her skin was almost as lustrous as the diamond choker she had around her neck.

Excusing himself from the table, Stephon headed down the stairs to meet her. When he finally saw her, sipping on her drink, he approached. Catching a whiff of his Hugo Boss cologne, Diamond turned to see him standing in front of her: 5'10", nice build, and looking rather sexy in a navy blue Armani suit. "Can I buy you a drink, beautiful?" he asked smoothly.

Diamond was drawn to his magnetism. But, before she could accept his offer, her three targets were now coming back downstairs. She had no idea why they were there or whom they had come to see. All she knew was that, regarding the Agugbo brothers, revenge was about to be in her favor.

Stephon frowned when her attention had drifted from him. He wasn't used to getting the brush off. He was used to being in the spotlight, the showstopper, the main event. "Hey, I'm over here, sweetheart. Something wrong?" he asked, fighting to get her attention back.

"I'm sorry, I gotta go," Diamond replied while grabbing her clutch bag and getting ready to walk off.

"Wait, can't I at least get your name?"

"Look," Diamond said, "don't take this the wrong way, but I have some unfinished business to take care of. However, I believe in fate, so if we're destined to meet again, maybe things will be different next time."

Stephon watched her gorgeous ass walk away. He didn't know what he liked better: seeing her coming, or watching her leave. From that day on, he was committed to finding out who in the hell she was. And when he did, he would make her his.

When Diamond stepped outside, she thoroughly looked in both directions to see where the three brothers and their entourage were headed. When she spotted them heading for a stretch Expedition in the parking lot, she quickened her pace. She was anxious to snuff out the men responsible for JR's death, but she also didn't want to break her ankles strutting around in heels.

Clutching her bag, she approached her target. "Excuse me," she said softly. Six hostile men turned around, ready to draw their weapons, but when Hillary saw that it was just a woman, he stopped and smiled. Diamond put on her Hollywood smile. "Are you gentlemen the Agugbo Brothers?"

Tanetche sneered, "Who wants to know?"

"The Kiss of Death, you ugly bitch," Diamond coldly replied, with a screw you look, pulling out a compact 9 mm and aiming it at Tanetche's head. One of his men leaped between them just as Diamond fired. The soldier slumped to the ground, with part of his head blown off.

Tanetche and his two brothers dove for cover.

"Kill that bitch!" he ordered.

Diamond quickly scrambled behind a parked car and took aim at the five remaining shooters. Gunfire exploded out in the parking lot, sounding like a small war. Diamond popped another clip in her gun and fired away. The brief pause gave the Agugbo brothers just enough time to jump into the limo and peel away. Diamond dropped the last goon and fired her gun in vain at the fleeing limousine until the clip was empty. Raking her hands through her head in frustration, she cursed herself for letting them slip away.

At least she had three faces etched into her memory. Not even her brother could stop the onslaught to come. The Black Kiss of Death had gone public, and now there was no turning back. The Snow White princess had become the devil in the tight dress.

CHAPTER 33

MILLION DOLLAR MIKE

*A*s the loud sound of Beanie Sigel, Freeway, and Jay-Z's "What We Do Is Wrong" blared on large speakers out on Blakemore Street, neighbors squatted on their porches while the smell of barbeque grills lingered in the air. Females of all shapes and sizes hung out at the block party in hopes of finding a new sponsor. Kia and all her girlfriends loitered in front of her mother's house, while her brother, Taliban, did his thing at the top of the block with Mike and the rest of the hustlers from Blakemore.

Blakemore Street stretched downhill with over fifty row houses on each side of a one-way street. And, even though drug sales were plentiful, the long strip was a hustler's nightmare when it came to running from the police.

Mike was now the crowned king of uptown, thanks to the mysterious masked Phantom whom the detectives were out to nab for the deaths of Million Dollar Moe and his two enforcers.

Everyone thought that it was Mike who iced Million Dollar Moe, since his cousin Shug had declared war against Reds and Gangwar, but Mike had no clue about those murders. However, he thrived off the rumor that he had offed Moe and his boys. He even had a new nickname: Million Dollar Mike.

As Mike sat on the step, surrounded by his lieutenants, lookouts, shooters, and hustlers, he stressed the importance of getting Red and Gangwar out of the picture, for good. Even though Charles White was dead, Reds and Gangwar still managed to find a line and keep the city stocked with cocaine, heroin, weed, and syrup. Not only that, their names were ringing in the streets. Shug wanted to put an end to all that. Clyde White was now in control of the Underworld and had put him in charge of Pennsylvania. Clyde had put a price out on Reds and Gangwar for failing to protect his father. That didn't help matters.

While Mike discussed inventory and prices, a loud four-wheeler came roaring up as Montega whipped around the corner on a black Yamaha Banshee.

Tasha sat behind him with her arms wrapped around his waist. Mike looked up and shook his head in disgust as Montega got off the Banshee to approach the boys. "I'll be right back," he said to Tasha who hated that he hung around with criminal types.

Tasha had been accepted into a small college in Atlanta. She wanted to take up criminal law so that one day she could become a cop and fight crime. She tried to steer her boyfriend away from the street life, but there wasn't much she could do. She was already in too deep to leave him.

"What's good?" Montega asked, giving his man Razor some dap, along with his brother.

"Damn, dog. I called you like an hour ago. But, you wanna be ridin' around with bitches all day, instead of getting money, like you suppose to," Mike complained.

"Man, if you can give me some work on time, I wouldn't be ridin' nowhere. I'd be hustlin'," Montega replied. Everyone looked at each other.

No one spoke to Mike that way, especially after what happened to Million Dollar Moe. But, Montega was defiant and cold-blooded. He knew the truth about the murders and wasn't scared of Mike or anyone else. He was afraid, though, of meeting God one day and explaining to him why he had three bodies under his belt. Seeing that the young goon wasn't going to back down easily without having to smack the shit out of him, Mike just shook his head and continued to talk to the group. "If y'all see the nigga Reds or Gangwar, don't go at 'em yourselves. Let me know, and I'll handle it. As far as the work, like I said earlier, I'm not fuckin' with no quarter-coppin' dudes. If that's the case, y'all might as well take bundles. I'm only selling halves or better." Montega had already heard the lecture from Mike a hundred times before.

He was already copping two halves from him every week and didn't need to hear anymore bullshit, so he got back on his four-wheeler and rode down the block, where his sister and her friends were sitting at tables out in the middle of the street, eating barbecue, and drinking liquor and Smirnoff coolers. "You hungry?" Montega asked Tasha.

She shook her head, but Montega didn't believe her. "Man, c'mon," he insisted, grabbing her hand.

When the girls saw the pretty brown-skinned chick with the curly hair and the bubble-shaped ass, they became envious. Tasha looked cute in a Christian Dior jean miniskirt, with white Adidas shell tops, a white B. Fly halter and oversize, square-frame Ralph Lauren sunglasses. "Who that girl with your brother?" Breezy asked as she sipped some vodka.

"Oh, that's his little girlfriend. She supposed to be in college or going to college," Kia explained as she watched her brother make the girl a plate of food.

"Aww, that's sweet. He making her a plate," Gi-Gi said, causing Breezy to roll her eyes with jealousy.

As she watched Montega sit on the porch with his shorty, Kia got up and moved towards them. "Kenny, can I talk to you for a second?" she asked, opening the door to go inside the house.

Montega got up and followed her inside. When Kia checked the house to make sure no one was around, she turned to look at her brother long enough, to make him feel uncomfortable. "What sup, Kia? Why you starin' at me all crazy?"

Kia glared at her brother. "Did you kill Moe?"

The look on Montega's face gave him up. "WA...What are you talking about?" he asked nervously, but Kia had already got the answer she expected.

The truth was she suspected him as soon as it happened. Montega had changed after that. The playfulness in him came to a shocking end. His laughter almost disappeared. He was now more serious and mysterious. Kia turned towards the door. "Kia, you ain't answer my question," Montega said.

"It doesn't matter. You already answered mine," Kia responded before walking out.

Realizing he had been busted, Montega sat down on the couch, with his hand on his forehead. He didn't know how his sister knew, but he promised himself that he would never freeze up under pressure like that again.

GANGWAR AND REDS sat in Peter Luger's in Brooklyn, discussing business with their new connect: none other than their good friend's daughter, Diamond. The three had been doing business for a few months now, and Diamond had treated them like family. "Diamond, I gotta admit, you have grown to be a stunning woman. Not to mention you have your father's ambition," Reds complimented her while finishing his porterhouse steak.

"I appreciate that," Diamond said modestly.

Gangwar shook his head in frustration. "I don't know how your brother ended up the way he did. He's a different breed. I mean, to actually think that we had something to do with Charles' death. That's crazy. Maybe he gets his genes from that bitch your father used to- -"

"Cool out, Gangwar. You're getting in your feelings," Reds said, cutting him off.

"Nah, it's true, though. I ain't gonna bite my tongue. I never did. Charles' whole circle is gone because of Clyde. Two Gun Sam,

Whisky, Buns, they're all gone. And if we don't play it smart, we're next," Gangwar predicted.

Diamond listened calmly, but there wasn't much she could do. She didn't want her brother to know what she was up to, let alone try to pick a fight with him. Folding her hands on the table, she said, "Can I ask you guys something personal? Off-the-record, that is?"

Both men looked at each other before nodding. "How did my father end up beefing with Verningo Castor?" she asked.

Gangwar looked back at Reds as if to say, Should I explain? But, Reds spoke first. "A year before your brother was born, your father was in business with Castor. In fact, he was the one who put your father in the game. If you want answers, I might as well start at the beginning. Your father was always a robber, probably the best I've ever known. There was nothing he couldn't steal. However, he had very bad addictions. One was fucking with women who didn't belong to him. It first started with this Saudi guy we met, an arms merchant. He was the one who plugged your father into that line. His family was supposed to be some rich opium suppliers. However, he was a big arms dealer and stayed in motion.

"The two met in Vegas after a big sting we did on the Russian mafia the night before. Charles was introduced to the man's girl and instantly drawn to her. He felt he just had to have this women. So, one night, when the man went up to bed early, Charles and this woman went to his suite. And, a little down the line a baby popped up."

Diamond's mouth dropped when she heard that. She knew exactly who the outcome of that union was.

Gangwar took over. "It was a miracle the guy was out of the country the whole time the woman was pregnant. As soon as she had Clyde, she called Charles and had him come get the child. Now, at that time, Charles had already plugged in with the Saudi's family, just in case the man ever did find out about him and his girlfriend. But, he never did. In fact, your brother still deals with the Saudi to this day."

"So, what happened with Castor?" Diamond asked, constantly checking her watch.

"Well, it was the same thing all over again," Reds explained. "Castor brought Charles to his mansion in Miami, where he stayed a week. During that time, a very wealthy Cuban met with Castor regarding his beautiful daughter. This Cuban was big, and he and Castor had a mutual respect for each other. So much so, he wanted Castor to marry his daughter."

"Oh, no," Diamond said with her hand over her mouth.

"Somehow, your father got into Pearl's head and her panties. She got pregnant quick. But it wasn't you. The baby never made it because she ended up having a miscarriage," Red answered.

"When she first got pregnant, she and Charles went on the run. Pearl was traditional. She was a virgin before Charles got to her, and that hurt her father. He disowned her after that. And, Castor put a hit out on Charles when he found out, which had Charles looking over his shoulder all the time. One day, Charles got into a big gun battle while Pearl was in the car. She had the miscarriage, right there on the spot," Reds said, shaking his head.

Diamond checked her watch again, "Look, I gotta go. There's something I have to take care of while I'm in New York. But, we'll finish this conversation next time," she said, getting up.

"Oh, before you go. There's one more thing you should know. It probably doesn't mean nothing, but there's a possibility that Clyde may have a sibling out there somewhere," Gangwar said.

Diamond stopped in her tracks when she heard that, but then just nodded her head and headed for the door, bewildered. However, she had no time to ponder all this; there were other things on her mind, far more important.

CHAPTER 34

A LIFE 4 A LIFE

On an early morning in Jamaica, Queens, Tanetche Agugbo lounged in his living room, discussing business with his brother, Simon and Hillary. All three were vicious killers, and for a whole year, there had been war between the Ape Gang and the Black Kiss of Death. No one knew where she came from, but with all the mayhem she had spread throughout the area, it was obvious that the war wouldn't end anytime soon.

As the three sat on a wrap-around white sofa, Tanetche slammed his fist into his palm. "Look, we gotta do something about this problem we're having over in LA. This Kiss of Death bitch has threatened our whole operation. Her army is systematically wiping out our brothers."

Hillary agreed. "Let us also not forget just last year, she almost put a bullet in your head, right before she put down six enforcers, single-handedly. Can you get any information about her identity?"

"We still don't have any address, but I have my sources working day and night on this," Simon explained. "Hilary's right, who is this bitch to declare war on us? We need to stop sitting on our asses and find her before she brings the beef to our doorstep. If our people see that we're not handling business, they'll start to doubt us. We need to start making examples of people -- and fast."

Tanetche's wife, Shelly, walked into the living room with her purse, ready to go. "Are you ready?" Shelly asked irritably, with her arms folded.

"Go ahead to the car. I'll be right behind you," Tanetche said as his phone rang. Shelly sneered at him as he listened to the voice at the other end. After he hung up, Shelly rolled her eyes and stormed off.

Tanetche looked at his brother. "We lost ten soldiers and a lieutenant at our warehouse, here in New York. That bitch is too close for comfort."

"Wait a minute. If she hit the warehouse in New York, you don't think anybody opened their mouth to her..." Simon said looking at his brother Tanetche nervously.

Tanetche raised an eyebrow at the hint, then thought about his wife, who had walked down the hall. "Baby! No!" he shouted while running out of the living room and down the hall to stop her before she walked out the door.

He was too late. Shelly had already left the building. As soon as she pulled on the car door handle, a huge explosion erupted.

KA-BOOM!

The bomb blew the two glass double doors off their hinges and sent Tanetche flying onto the marble floor. Glass and debris rained onto him like an evening shower. When he finally staggered to his feet, the limousine out front had been obliterated and his wife was no more.

"You bitch, I'm gonna kill you!" he bellowed.

BACK IN CALIFORNIA, Diamond's fury ignited throughout the state. Butch's army of wolves were ruthless; they showed no mercy to the enemy. From firebombing to deadly drive-bys, they muscled out the competition until Diamond slowly gained control. Her main target was the Ape Gang.

Each week, Diamond pointed to a new spot on the map that she wanted. Butch and his boys then swooped in like birds of prey. And, just as she promised in the beginning, as she rose to power, so did they all. Within a year, she was copping more bricks of coke than any client Semok ever had, a thousand key's a month. And, while the Black Kiss of Death was making big noise, the Great White Organization was building a new empire throughout the United States. Clyde wanted it all. With Deshawn and the Wolfpack on the other side of the Underworld, money came in like never before.

They had heroin coming in from Afghanistan. Cocaine and ecstasy from Nicaragua. Marijuana from Jamaica and meth, straight from the labs in LA. Sure, the money was good, but Clyde's biggest worry was the Russian mafia. They were cold-blooded and would always be a threat because they had succeeded in killing the Great White's biggest boss: Charles White.

As Clyde and all the heads of the Great White Organization sat at the table in his father's old situation room, he brought up a subject that was starting to become a concern. "What's up with this crazy chick that's warring with the Ape Gang? Who the fuck is this bitch?"

Chavo shook his head with no knowledge. "No one knows who she is. All we know is that she's called the Kiss of Death."

"Kiss of Death?" Shug repeated.

"Yeah, dudes say she blows a kiss before she drops your ass," Chavo added.

Shug found that amusing. "Man, that's some ole movie type shit. Where y'all hear this crazy shit?"

"It's true, Shug," Chavo emphasized. "She almost took out Tanetche at the club last year. But that's not the big worry. I'm hearing that she's taking over operations all over California and moving her boys in. When people start hearin' shit like this, they get scared, and join up with her to avoid getting squashed."

"You mean, they're down with that crazy bitch?" Shug asked.

"Hell, yeah. Especially when they hear all the stories of big players getting whacked."

"And, she's out there, icin' dudes herself?" Shug asked.

Chavo leaned forward. "She don't just sit around, givin' orders. She likes to get her hands dirty."

A cloud of fear was displayed on all their faces. It was no question that something had to be done. And fast.

CHAPTER 35

THE BLACK CLOUD

Kia and her girlfriend, Breezy, sat in a local bar on Germantown Avenue, enjoying some down time, before they went to the afterhours. While sipping on Grey Goose and pineapple juice, listening to songs they had picked out on a jukebox, Kia spotted a familiar face entering the bar. "Ain't that Kev from south Philly?" she asked, tugging on Breezy's sleeve.

When Breezy looked up, she spotted a tall, handsome, dark-skinned man with a thick beard and wavy hair stepping inside, accompanied by two of his boys. As soon as Kev noticed them, he put on his mack face and approached.

Breezy pretended to look away, but it didn't matter. Kev had been wanting to holla at her for the longest, but had never gotten the chance. Kia and Breezy were perhaps unaware that they were considered the baddest bitches uptown. If you didn't know them, you weren't a major nigga.

Kev pulled up a stool beside Breezy just as the bartender appeared. "Can I get you anything, Sweety?" the woman asked pleasantly.

"Yeah, get me whatever they drinkin'. And get them another

round," Kev replied before turning his attention to Breezy. "Yo, what's good, pretty thing? It's about time we ran into each other. You a hard person to find."

Breezy batted her eyes. "You say that like you were anticipating this moment," she replied modestly.

"To be honest, I was," Kev admitted.

"And why is that?" Breezy asked, swiveling her stool around to look at him while crossing her legs, which certainly got Kev's full attention.

Kev glanced down at her succulent thighs framed by a mini-skirt. "Because I wanna take you out, that's why."

"Where you taking me?" Breezy asked, baffled.

"Just put your number in my phone. I can't tell you, I'd rather surprise you," he replied, handing Breezy the phone just as a group of guys walked in.

When Kev looked up and saw Gangwar, accompanied by a few of his shooters, his eyes ballooned. Once Breezy put her number in his phone, he stored it, then dialed Mike's number. "Excuse me one second," he said, stepping away.

Kia elbowed her girlfriend, then cocked her head towards the group sitting across from them. Breezy raised her eyebrows when she saw Gangwar and his goons. "Oh, shit," she gasped.

"Oh, shit, is right. I think something's about to go down. We better roll out before we caught in the middle of it," Kia suggested.

Breezy took another look at the men and nodded. "You know what, Kia? I think you're right."

Once Mike got off the cell phone, he shook his head in disappointment. Lying on his bare chest was his Spanish girlfriend, Jennifer, whom he had just made love to for the third time that night.

"Who was that, baby?" she asked innocently while tracing her hand across his stomach.

"That was my man. I gotta make a run," Mike replied.

"No, don't leave me. I need to feel you next to me tonight, daddy. Can't it wait?" she whined before sitting up to stare into his eyes.

Mike stroked her hair and kissed her forehead. The truth was he really didn't want to get out of bed. Instead, a better idea came to mind: he needed a guy with heart. Picking up his phone again, he dialed Montega's number.

After the second ring, he answered. "Yo," Montega said impassively.

"Yo, you wanna make two ounces?" Mike asked, seeing if he would bite.

"What chu need me to do?" Montega asked.

Mike explained the situation with Gangwar and where he could find him. "So, what's it gonna be?" Mike questioned.

"Just watch the news and have them ounces ready. I ain't tryna be waitin' all day for you to bring 'em, either," Montega said before hanging up the phone. He dashed to the drawer to grab his Phantom mask and his Mac-11.

"Where you going, nigga?" Razor asked while puffing on a Dutch of weed, lying on the couch.

"Yo, you wanna make an ounce?" Montega asked.

"Hell, yeah, what sup?" Razor responded, sitting up.

"Look, don't ask no questions. All I know is we goin' out to hurt somebody. Now grab your burner and ride with me," Montega instructed before making his way to the back yard to get his Banshee.

Razor threw on a black scully hat and wrapped a black bandana around his face while Montega slipped the Phantom mask over his face. Kicking on the twin 360 engine, the two bright fog lights beamed to life as Razor got on back. Once the clutch was pulled and he got it in first gear, the Banshee roared out of the alley like a bat out of hell.

As Kia and Breezy stepped out of the bar and strutted towards the car in the parking lot, the sound of the Banshee's roaring engine caught their attention. When the two villains on the four-wheeler rode up, Kia stayed cool and just stared. Breezy quickly got into the passenger's side, hoping that she and her girlfriend weren't spotted by the masked men with guns.

As Montega got off the four-wheeler, he clutched the Mac that was strapped around his neck with a shoe string. Razor had a small Tech 9 with a 50-shot ladder. "Look, bol, I'm a go in here and soak this nigga. You play the side, just in case dudes start drawing," Montega said before turning to enter the building.

Razor's heart was thumping. He had never shot anyone, let alone killed someone. But, Montega was his brother from another, and there was no way he would let him ride by himself. As soon as Montega entered the bar, his eyes scanned the room. The music was blasting and everyone was drinking, dancing, or chatting. No one even noticed him. He figured that this was the same way his mother and her friend were before they were killed. Kev, over in the corner, watched as the two masked men entered. He slipped into the bath-room before any shots were fired.

As soon as Montega spotted Gangwar with his men, he aimed his machine gun and fired. Loud shots rang out in the bar, causing everyone to dive to the floor or sprint for the exit. Gangwar spun around to face the shooters. Several bullets ripped into his abdomen, then his face. He slumped on the counter top. His bodyguards flung themselves on the floor, pulling out automatic weapons.

"C'mon, man, we out," Razor advised, grabbing Montega by the arm as bystanders made a run for the door.

Montega snatched away from his homie and shot back at the men, wounding them in the process. When he was out of bullets, he and Razor crouched low as bullets whizzed around the bar. Kia watched in horror as people spilled out the door in panic.

Just when she thought it was over, the two gun men emerged. They jumped on the Banshee and sped off. After the four-wheeler whipped around the corner, Kia started her engine and drove off.

Kev came out of the bathroom. The music was still blasting, but the place was almost empty. As he walked by several wounded men, he spotted Gangwar, on the floor by the counter. There was no life behind those eyes. His face and stomach were smothered in blood. Whoever had come, got the job done fast and got out.

He then got on the phone and called Mike. "Yo," Mike answered, anxious to know what happened.

"One down, one more to go," Kev said as he walked away from the bar room massacre.

"It shouldn't be long now. There's a black cloud in our city. Make sure that the last gets caught in the storm," Mike said before hanging up.

CHAPTER 36

A PRIZE WINNER

Clyde threw a big party for his cousin Justin. Rodeo Drive was filled with expensive cars, and high society from all over California came to celebrate: a couple of basketball players from the LA Lakers, NFL players and entertainers of all sorts, including the new middleweight champion, Stephon "Babyface" Butler.

The huge ballroom jumped when The Game took the mic to sing his latest song. Clyde and Justin sat with their circle in the VIP, enjoying the company of some of the finest women in the city. Diamond and her people also made an appearance. When Clyde saw his sister, accompanied by his cousin Butch, and all his homies, he stared in confusion. He saw Butch as a grimy nigga who only had time for his family if money was involved. Clyde made a mental note to see what was going on behind his back.

Diamond strutted over to her booth, dressed in a tight, low-cut Chanel dress with a belt wrapped around her 24-inch waist to match her five-inch Anaconda platform pumps that cost a small fortune. Heads swiveled to gaze at her perfect, round ass. Men drooled at the vision inside that tight, white dress.

Stephon might have been the one most stimulated by her magnetism. Diamond dazzled him, from head to toe. Once she and the boys were seated, a waiter immediately brought their most expensive bottle of champagne. "The gentlemen over there sent this," he said, pointing to the dark-skinned man standing beside his seven-foot tall bodyguard.

Stephon raised his glass, and Diamond smiled and mouthed, "Thank you" to him. She bought five more bottles of the same champagne and had one sent to his table, along with her phone number. Diamond admired the man's smooth, dark complexion and his burly 5'10" body. He had a baby face and a sparkling smile. He sported a low fade and a dapper-looking Canalli suit.

She had no clue who he was, but she would soon find out. Stephon pulled out his cell phone and dialed her number. Diamond watched him intently until her cell phone buzzed in her pocketbook. Trying not to smile, she said seductively, "Hello?"

"I see that you're the type of lady who doesn't like to be outdone," he said,

"I'm an Aries. What do you expect?" she replied gazing at him from across the room.

"How about we take this conversation out to the balcony where it's a little more private," Stephon proposed.

"Sounds good to me," she replied and hung up.

Stephon grabbed a bottle and two glasses, then headed towards the balcony. His bodyguard followed. "Bain, stay by the door for me while I talk to this pretty lady. Make sure nobody comes out to disturb us," Stephon commanded.

The seven-foot bodyguard nodded his head and held the door. Stephon leaned on the balcony that overlooked a beautiful shot of Wilshire Blvd. as Diamond joined him.

"Is that your bodyguard?" she asked as she stood beside him and looked out at the scenery below.

"Yeah, that's Bain. He's very reliable. He used to be a correctional officer, but he's too soft-hearted when it comes to women, if you ask me. He doesn't speak a word, a mute. I think he lost his voice after a car accident, which caused him to lose his wife. He's good at his job, I'll tell ya that," Stephon explained.

Diamond listened with sympathy. "Are you from LA or somewhere else in California?" she asked.

"Nah, I'm from NYC." He looked at her strangely.

"Oh, really?" And what is a New Yorker doing all the way over here, on the west coast?" Diamond inquired, now leaning on the railing to look at him.

Stephon frowned. "You don't recognize me -- do you?" he asked.

"I'm sorry. Was I supposed to know you from somewhere?"

Stephon saw that she wasn't a typical groupie. "My name is Stephon Butler. I'm the middleweight champion of the world. I'm scheduled to fight in three days at Mandalay Bay in Vegas," he said proudly. Diamond didn't seem all that impressed. All he got was a lame, "Congratulations."

Diamond picked up the champagne bottle and poured them both a glass. At that point, Stephon's mind was made up. He had to have this enigmatic woman. While they talked about their lives, he told her about his big fights and overseas trips while Diamond listened and smiled. Even though she wasn't impressed, she was still attracted to him.

While the festive party proceeded inside, the two laughed and talked outside. The night was winding down, and Stephon didn't want it to end without taking the next step. "I'll tell you what. Next Saturday night, why don't you come to my fight in Vegas? I'll pay your way."

"Go to Vegas, just to see you get knocked out? I don't think so," she answered before sipping her drink, giving him a smirk.

Stephon just stood there, stunned. "I'm just kidding," Diamond giggled. "And, for the record, you don't have to pay my way. I'm not one of those money-chasing bitches you always run into. To them, a million dollars is a come-up. To me, it's just toilet tissue. If I like a guy, I like him. Nothing more, nothing less."

Stephon was quickly falling for the unique treasure. "Well, then, I guess I'll see you after the fight," he said suavely, grabbing her hand to kiss it.

"You better win, or I'll never come to another fight of yours again," she joked.

"Trust me, with a beautiful lady in my corner, I'm already a winner," he replied. He left the balcony while Diamond watched him glide through the crowd as if he was walking on air.

CHAPTER 37

SHE THE BEST

*I*n Inglewood, California, in a room buried under a race track, Tanetche Agugbo and five henchman surrounded one of Diamond's team members, Silk. He was tied up to a chair, brutally beaten by Tanetche's men. "I will ask you again -- where does the Kiss of Death live?" Tanetche inquired, gripping him by the back of his head.

"Fuck you, you fucking dirtball," Silk replied before spitting in his face.

Tanetche lost his temper and started pounding on Silk's face. The dull thuds of fist on bone echoed in the dark basement. When he finally let up, Silk's face was unidentifiable. Tanetche pulled out his Glock .40, aimed it at Silk's head and squeezed the trigger.

Boom! Boom!

He glanced over at his men. "I want his body to be dumped out in public as a warning. I want that bitch to see what happens when you do battle with us. I want her to realize that she's next."

It was Saturday night in the city that never sleeps. Vegas was ablaze with lights. Tonight, the Mandalay Bay was where everyone wanted to be. Fight night.

When Diamond arrived with her crew, the security up front knew exactly who she was. They escorted her all the way down to ringside, next to actors Brad Pitt and Denzel Washington.

As she took her seat, looking fabulous in a Piazza Sempione dress and Jimmy Choo heels, someone behind her tapped her on the shoulder. "I didn't know you were into boxing, my dear," Semok said with his heavy Russian accent.

Diamond got up to give him a hug. "Semok, so good to see you," she greeted him warmly. He then introduced her to all his Russian friends and family, including his boss, Zelinski. "So, you're a Babyface Butler fan, I assume?" he asked.

"He's a friend of mine," she replied before turning back around to catch Stephon's grand entrance.

Bain was the first to come out of the tunnel, followed by Stephon and his entourage. Pulsating music accompanied the appearance of the champ in the black hooded robe wearing the title belt.

Diamond had never been to a prize fight before, but she had to admit that the electricity that raced through the crowd was exciting. Once the fight began, she watched in awe as Stephon beat blood out of his opponent for five rounds, finishing him off with a hard right that sent him down for the ten-count.

"The winner and still middleweight champion of the world, the undefeated Babyface Butler!" the ring announcer shouted.

When the fight was over, Diamond was escorted to Stephon's penthouse suite. She walked in to find Stephon seated on the couch, talking to his brother, Deshawn. Both stood when she entered.

"Ah, here she is. I was beginning to worry that you didn't come," Stephon said as she approached.

"I'm a woman of my word. So here I am," Diamond said, extending her arms.

Deshawn was mesmerized by her peanut butter complexion. "Scar, this is the woman I've been chewing your ear off about.

Diamond White. Diamond, this is my brother, Deshawn," Stephon said.

"Nice to meet you," she replied, shaking his hand modestly.

"You're Clyde's sister, right?" Scar asked. Diamond nodded. "Wow! Clyde never said that his sister looked like an angel."

Yeah, right, the angel of death, Diamond thought as she blushed. She couldn't help but notice how much alike the two were. Only the scar on Deshawn's face was different. "Do you mind if I ask what happened to your face?"

"Not at all. I got this on Riker's Island. The guy that did this didn't live to brag about it."

"Yes, well, Deshawn, don't you have something to do?" Stephon asked, trying to coax him out of his suite.

"Yeah, right. I have to be going. It was nice to meet you, Ms. White."

"The pleasure was all mine," Diamond replied before he walked out the door. As Stephon went to close the door, Diamond went to inspect the hotel suite. When she got to the window to look out at the bright city, she said, "I think I need to come here more often."

Stephon got up to join her. He had on a gray Ralph Lauren sweatsuit and some sneakers. Diamond frowned at his attire; he picked up on it. "I'm sorry. Did you want to go out, because I was hoping we could chill here. The press is like a pack of hyenas, and I just wanted to have a quiet evening," he said.

Diamond was actually relieved. My type of guy, she thought.

"No, here is good," she replied.

That night the two had room service delivered to the suit while they watched "The Long Kiss Goodnight."

During the movie, Diamond got comfortable as she sipped on Belvy and cranberry juice. Once the alcohol caught up to them, Stephon's eyes explored every inch of Diamond's figure as she sat next to him in a stunning red dress. Diamond could feel his eyes undressing her, but stayed focused on the movie.

The movie became an afterthought when he gently swept her hair out of the way so he could kiss her neck. Diamond closed her eyes and sighed as his lips caressed her neck. She hadn't had sex since the death of her boyfriend. She just couldn't seem to connect with the men that she came across. Most were jerks, while many were too scared and intimidated to approach her. Seeing no resistance, he began licking all over her sweet skin.

His tongue traveled down the bust line of her spaghetti strap dress. He then unzipped the back and slowly slid the dress off her body. Her perky breasts were now fully exposed. The chill from the AC and his touch caused her ripe nipples to harden. Stephon stood to remove his clothes, then kneeled back down to suck on her titties while he played with her tight love box. His finger slowly plunged in and out of her, making her anxious to feel something much bigger inside her wet pussy.

Diamond pushed him back on the couch and reached in her clutch bag for a condom. Stephon allowed her to roll it onto him. He licked on her clitoris. The smell of her juices had a hint of strawberry. Stephon came up for air, then spread her legs wide on the couch. With his knees on the floor, he went inside her.

Diamond moaned softly as her pussy engulfed all eight inches of his pipe. Stephon grabbed her by the waist and began sliding in and out of her, serenaded by her steady gasps of excitement. Even the thick, black, tuxedo condom he wore couldn't diminish the pleasure of ravishing the best pussy he'd ever had.

Six months without sex was definitely worth it. Before he busted, he pulled out and turned her around, bending her over the couch with her ass spread in the shape of a heart. The view from behind drove him crazy. Her ass was just too phat to pass up. He plunged in and out of her pink, swollen lips while tightly holding her waist. Diamond went buck wild on his dick. Before she knew it, she felt herself on the verge of cumming. Stephon tried to hold back a bit longer, but to no avail. The pussy was just too good.

Grabbing a handful of her plump breast, he exploded. From that moment on, Stephon knew that she was the one. Diamond wasn't going anywhere, if he had anything to do with it. She would be his, no matter what he had to do.

CHAPTER 38

THE CITY IS YOURS

"Ummmm, Kennnny...that's right, baby. Fuck me good!" Tasha cried as Montega crushed her from the rear on the living room floor of her mother's crib on Chelton Avenue. Looking at himself in the large mirror, he put on a show as he watched himself fuck Tasha's brains out, doggy-style. "You like that?" he asked as he watched his dick flush out her pussy with a creamy, white ooze.

"Yes, I love it!" Tasha screamed as she erupted with her second orgasm. "Ummm!"

Montega fed her all nine inches of his dick and spasmed as he shot gobs of cum into her. He wasn't worried about getting her pregnant because he knew Tasha was on the Depo shot. Montega pulled out of his shorty; he knew he would miss her sexy ass when she left for college in a few hours.

"I love you so much. You know that? Tasha beamed as she lay on her side and gazed at him.

"Yeah, I know," he replied nonchalantly as he got to his feet to clean himself off.

"Well, if you know, then how come you never tell me that you love me back?" she implored.

"Because I'm too young to know what love is right now," he replied honestly. Just then, his Nextel went off.

Tasha rolled her eyes as she tried to turn his phone off, but Montega was faster, snatching the phone from her grasp. Smirking at her, he pressed talk and answered. "Yo."

"Yo, I'm outside. I need you to ride with me to handle something," Mike stated.

"A'ight, I'm getting dressed now," Montega said before pressing the end button.

Tasha hissed. She hated when Montega left her alone. "Where are you going now? Did you forget I'm supposed to leave in a few hours?" she reminded him.

"I know, and I'll be back before you go, so stop trippin'," Montega said, slipping into his jeans.

"Kenny, you need to stop with all the gangster business before something happens to you. If it's not that light skin boy asking for you all the time, it's Mike."

"That light skin bol's name is Razor, and that's my brother. So fall back. Look, don't tell me how to walk, Tasha. I've been doin' this shit since I was a kid. If I need some help, I would have brought a cane. Now, I'll see you when I get back," Montega informed her before heading for the door, with Tasha glaring at him all the way out.

Montega stepped outside and found Mike sitting out front in a black Buick Regal with tinted windows. As Montega approached, Mike got out of the driver's side and walked around to the back seat. "You drive," Mike instructed before getting in.

Montega looked puzzled for a moment, then got in. Mike's enforcer, J-Black, was in the passenger's seat with his Smith and Wesson 10 mm on his lap. Montega put the car in drive, figuring out what the trip was about. "Where we goin'?" he asked nonchalantly.

"DRIVE TO T&J's BAR," Mike commanded.

T&J's bar was a small hole in the wall, located directly around the corner from Tasha's crib on Boyer Street. They say one man's trash is another man's treasure. Well, T&J's was the place to be when the hustlers needed a drink and a little piece of mind. Since everyone and their mom hustled in Summerville, the bar was packed.

Montega slowly stopped at the stop sign on Boyer and Woodlawn, looking at the bar on the corner that was illuminated by the bright spotlights. Beside the crackheads that hung out, drinking cans of 211 malt liquor, there was a small group of people in conversation.

"Park at the corner," Mike instructed.

When Montega did as told, Mike tapped Black before they both got out of the car. Standing at the street corner of Woodlawn and Boyer were a few old heads, trying to make a dollar. An outsider named Smoke was the only one able to steal sales from the size of his dimes. But when he saw Mike approaching with his enforcer, he quickly got out of the way. Mike wasn't at all worried about Smoke trying to hustle. Mike walked into the bar and spotted Reds kicking it with a few of his people. By the time Reds looked up to see what everyone was staring at, Mike and Black were standing directly in front of him.

"Don't make a scene, nigga just --"

Before Mike could get out another word, Reds jumped up and hit him with a hard right. Mike stumbled over a stool, and as Black went to grab him, Reds elbowed him in the chest and hauled ass out of the bar.

Montega watched through the rear view mirror as Reds broke out of the bar, full speed. Mike fired without blinking. The bullet struck Reds in the back, causing him to spin around and fall to the ground. Reds quickly tried to stagger to his feet, but Mike nailed him again.

BOOM!

The second bullet hit Reds square in the chest. Mike calmly walked up to Reds and iced him with a head shot. Smoke witnessed the whole scene. Mike and Black quickly jumped into the back seat of the Regal and ordered Montega to head for Mike's shorty's crib. As soon as Mike got there, he handed her the gun and told her to put it in the safe where he kept his serious cash. Jennifer did as she was told. When Mike got back into the car with Montega and J-Black, he whipped out his phone and called his cousin. When Shug answered, Mike smiled and said, "Yo, cuz, the city is all yours."

CHAPTER 39

MURDER, INC.

$\mathcal{M}$iles off the coast of California, the blue-green waters of the Pacific had invited some explorers to plunge in. The sunlight sparkled across the ocean. Sea gulls continued to glide in the clear blue sky, hoping to catch a school of fish off-guard. As dolphins shot out of the water like missiles, at the bottom of the sea bed, Diamond swam in full scuba gear, enjoying the beautiful world of marine life. Hundreds of sharp fin barracudas swam about freely amongst large sea turtles and stingrays.

Diamond explored the sea bed for any type of sunken treasures. After an hour of exploring, she headed for the surface, where the yacht awaited. Climbing onto the deck, she spotted her boyfriend, on his cell phone. Exhausted, she removed her goggles, air hose, and tank, then began shaking out her long, wet hair.

When Stephon saw her, he quickly got off the phone and approached her. "Hey, sexy, I was beginning to worry about you. You almost had me slipping into one of those wet suits to find you," he said before kissing her soft lips.

"That's sweet. I'm glad you didn't, though, because the sharks are starting to prowl around," she replied while pulling off her flippers. "Did I get a call?"

"Nope. I guess nobody loves you," he joked.

Diamond threw a playful jab at his chest, which surprised him and was too quick to dodge. "Damn, boo, I didn't know you could throw 'em like that."

"There's a lot of things you don't know about me," Diamond replied mysteriously, flashing a devilish smile.

Stephon closed the gap between them. He pulled on the zipper of the wet suit, exposing her luscious breasts and her washboard stomach. Diamond knew where this was headed and let him proceed. "I didn't know you had a thing for scuba divers," she joked.

"I don't, but I love when my seafood is fresh out of the water," he replied as his hand wandered to feel her goods.

The ring of Diamond's cell phone interrupted this sexual tryst. "C'mon, now, you don't have to answer that," he said, watching her slide her arms back into the wet suit. Once she zipped up, Diamond walked over to the table and picked up her phone. "Hello?"

"Dee, what up, cuz?" Butta said.

"Hey, fat ass, what's up?" Diamond answered.

"I need you to come check something out for me. Angel's on some other shit and I think he might be fuckin' with the police," Butta suspected.

"The law? What makes you think that?" she asked while ringing her hair out.

"I just got that feeling, ma. I asked him could I check out the safe. That pussy talkin' about he busy. Then he calls me back, talkin' reckless over the phone. Askin' for shit he never asked for. I'm telling you, Dee, I don't trust him with our money. I suggest you look for another accountant, and let his ass stick to the music side of things."

"Okay, Butta, I'm on my way. In fact, why don't you do me a favor and come get me?" she asked before giving him her location.

"A'ight, I'm on my way. I'm pullin' out of Burger King right now," Butta said before hanging up.

Stephon looked over at Diamond, who was walking towards the

bow of the boat. After giving the captain the order to take them back to shore, Stephon approached her. "What's going on? I thought this was our time together," he mildly complained.

"Baby, it was. And I'm sorry, but I have to handle a situation. Business comes first, you know that." She gave him a passionate kiss on the lips. "Don't worry, boo, I'm gonna make it up to you, I promise."

Stephon nodded reluctantly. When Diamond got to shore, Butta was waiting for her in a dark gray Range Rover. He and Stephon made eye contact, but neither spoke to each other.

Stephon didn't feel threatened by Butta's 450 pounds. Butta rocked a bald head with a thick Rick Ross beard with nappy hair bumps under his chin. Once she was inside, he pulled off. "Yo, what 'sup with main man? He starin' at me like me and you fuckin' or somethin'," Butta told her.

"He gets a little jealous at times. He's harmless, though," she replied with a grin, as if Stephon was her pet, rather than her man.

"A little jealous? You got that nigga pussy whipped or something? You done fucked him so good, you turned him into a weak-ass nut. Fuck he jealous for? He can get any bitch--"

Diamond shot Butta a look that could kill.

"My bad, shorty."

"Tell me more about Angel," Diamond requested.

"Man, this nigga is in the fuckin' way. I think that he be dippin' in the stash or something. For one, he got this big-ass mansion in the hills, like five different foreign cars, and they say he be in the club, frontin' like he own the joint. He don't even sell drugs. He's a fucking accountant," Butta snapped as he banged his fist against he steering wheel.

Diamond sighed. "I told that asshole to stay low-key. The last thing we need is for him to get us caught up with the feds."

"I knew somethin' wasn't right with that dude. The other day, he asked me for a half a brick of coke and told me not to tell you. The bad thing about it was that he wanted it cooked up."

When Diamond heard that, her jaws clenched shut. Once they pulled up to the big studio that Angel ran, they got out. Butta looked both ways to see if anyone was being nosy. He then pulled the Mossberg 12-gauge from his back seat and followed Diamond inside. The two disregarded the security booth and got on the elevator, heading for the third floor. When the doors opened, they were met by the sound of loud music. Butta was the first to step. What he saw made him shake his head. Diamond looked around his wide body to see Angel dead, slumped back on the couch with his dick still in his hand.

"Maybe he wasn't workin' with the law," Butta said, cautiously approaching the dead girl beside him.

The knife was still lodged in his chest and in his lap was a bloody note: "Kiss my black ass."

There was no doubt that this was an Agugbo brothers hit. "There's another one dead in the booth," Butta stated, shaking his head.

When Diamond looked through the engineer's window, she shook her head when she saw Carrie. She was Diamond's top singer and probably would have made it to the top.

"Dee, we need to check that safe out at Angel's crib," Butta suggested while waddling back to the elevator.

Diamond took one last look at Angel, then followed Butta. When they got to Angel's million-dollar mansion, Diamond strapped up with her Ruger and headed inside. She had to admit, Butta was right ... Angel's crib was like some fancy pad on MTV. Although it wasn't as big as the White's family mansion, it was huge -- especially for an accountant/record producer.

As they headed through the elegant dining room, she asked, "You know where he keeps the safe?"

"Hell, yeah, and I know the code. He got the shit in the basement," Butta said, escorting her down to the wine cellar.

Diamond was amazed to see so many old vintage brands of wine. She concluded that there was no way he could have afforded all this luxury without tapping into the stash. Butta pulled back another door to expose the large six-foot safe; it looked like a miniature bank vault. Butta punched in a code on the electronic key pad. The red light turned green, indicating that the door was unlocked. He then began unwinding the lock.

When he pulled the heavy titanium door open, his eyes bulged.

"Nooo! That nut-ass nigga got us," he shouted as he walked inside.

Diamond took a deep breath before silently following him.

Butta's huge bulk collapsed to his knees. All the money was gone. Diamond stood there impassively. She would show no emotion, even though she was dying inside.

"Get up, Butta. We're leaving," she said turning to walk out. She had a pretty good idea who was behind this whole thing.

"What the fuck are we gonna do now?" he asked miserably.

"Start over. That's all we can do," Diamond replied.

"Oh, yeah?" Butta asked bitterly as he got to his feet. "And how we supposed to do that? Those fuckin' Africans got our bread and butter."

Diamond turned to look at him. "Surely you don't think I would actually leave my re-up in the same spot as the money we made, do you?" she revealed, before walking out. "There is another safe."

It took a few seconds for Butta to register what she just said. "Another safe? Wait a minute, we got another safe?"

"Of course, we do. Always remember whenever you plan something, think of all contingencies. That's what I do. So, I'll go to my back-up."

When the two got back in the car and pulled off, another car followed at a distance. "Do you want us to burn her?" one of Tanetche's shooters asked.

"Not at all," Tanetche's captain, Raymond, stated. "I want to see where this bitch is going first. Keep at a safe distance. I don't want her to spot us because I'm not sure who she is."

When Butta pulled up at Stephon's mansion, he parked out front. "You good, ma? That nigga don't be puttin' his hands on you, do he? Because I'll bust his ass."

Diamond laughed. "Boy, please. It's not that type of party. Besides, any man who thinks he has the balls to put his hands on this girl must not wanna live long."

"Oh, yeah? And what type girl are you?" Butta taunted her before she stepped out.

Diamond opened the door and replied, "Royalty."

CHAPTER 40

THE SET UP

"C'mon, Clyde, shoot the ball," Polo said out of frustration, breathing heavily.

"Nigga, stop whinin' and stick Dee," Clyde taunted as he dribbled the ball between his legs and passed it to Cheeko for a lay-up. "That's game, muthafuckas." Cheeko came over to give Clyde some dap.

"Good shit," Reese Chubs replied as they sat down on the bench by the basketball courts. They were sweaty and tired.

"Next time, nigga," Polo warned before popping a bottle of spring water.

"Damn, yo! It hasn't been the same since the squad expanded. Chavo's in Vegas, Shug's back in PA, and Tommy Guns is up in ATL. Maybe I should find a state to wreak havoc in," Cheeko Raw said as Polo's cell phone broke up their conversation.

Polo saw that it was his sister, Tina, on his caller ID. "What chu want, yo?" he asked.

After listening for a moment, he said, "I'm on my way."

"Something wrong?" Clyde asked, seeing him disconnect the phone.

"Nah, it's my sister's baby father. The nigga don't know how to keep his hands to himself," Polo said, seething.

"Who? That nigga, Sid?" Clyde questioned.

"Yeah, man," Polo said, grabbing his gym bag.

"Yo, you need me to ride with chu?" Mook asked.

"Naw, I can handle his bitch-ass," Polo returned.

"I don't know why you gave that nigga a pass, anyway. He fuck with them Russians heavy," Reese said before chomping on a Snickers.

"Yeah, well, he crossed the line this time. I'll get at y'all," Polo said, hopping into his '67 Nova and peeling off.

Polo was boiling as he sped through the streets of Long Beach. All he could think about was how he would beat Sid's ass. Once he pulled up on his block, he double-parked his car in front of the house his sister stayed in. As he cut off the engine, he didn't notice the two black Lincoln town cars parked directly across the street. All of a sudden, the window rolled down and Russian henchman, including Mad Max, pointed their fully automatic assault rifles at his car. Polo opened the door, still fuming about what Sid did to his sister. The sight of machine guns woke him up like a fresh cup of Colombian coffee.

"Oh, shit- -"

RAT-TAT-TAT-TAT!!!!!

The rapid fire of slugs pierced holes through the car, tearing Polo's body apart as he struggled to get out the door. Polo squealed in pain and shock until he slumped to the ground. Max hopped out of the car and walked up to Polo's corpse and fired until his clip was empty. "Welcome to the big leagues," he said as Sid strolled out of the house.

Max waved for one of his men to bring the money. A fat Russian handed Sid the bag. "That's $50,000, and there's more whenever you see another one of those sons of bitches," Max said, patting him on the cheek.

"A'ight, guys, let's move out. We'll be in touch."

CHAPTER 41

GET OUT OF JAIL FREE CARD

*S*moke stood outside the bar, running down sales and serving fiends, with no worries. The rest of the old heads on the block were too scared to try and reason with him. They knew how hot-headed Smoke could get if confronted. As he went to make a sale, he spotted a green Taurus speeding up the one-way street. Smoke knew exactly who was inside and went to make a run for it, but was stopped by the undercover task force in the blue Chevy Impala. They found a gun on Smoke, along with a bundle of crack.

"Look like you're not goin' home today, buddy," an officer said as he slapped the cuffs on him.

SMOKE ALREADY HAD two offenses on the books. A third might put him in jail for life. There was no way he could let that happen, especially since he had a kid on the way. There was only one thing left to do

"He is so cute," Breezy's cousin, Jasmine, said as they sat in the playground, watching Mike and his team of hustlers play ball.

"Girl, leave that nigga alone. He's spoken for," Kia proclaimed.

"Spoken for? By who? That Spanish bitch? Please. That bitch don't hold no weight on my cousin," Breezy said with vanity while checking her watch.

Just then, Taliban walked through the playground gate and approached the girls. "Damn, y'all out here like y'all tryna catch or something. Ay, Breezy, some nigga came through the block lookin' for you," he said.

"Oh, that's Kev. I told him to pick me up at the playground," Breezy stated with a smile.

"You and Kev really hitting it off, huh?" Gi-Gi said sounding surprised.

"That's because he can't get enough of this ass I got," Breezy joked, smacking her left cheek, which got a glance from Taliban.

Just then, Montega zoomed down the street on a black and white Yamaha Raptor, with his homie, Lil Man, following on a blue and white Banshee. They pulled onto the basketball court, where he spotted his sister and her girlfriends. On the back of Montega's four-wheeler, was his new squeeze, Juicy. At 16, Juicy was a half-Puerto Rican, half-Mexican, redbone with long, dark, red hair and a body that could have gotten a grown man locked up for getting near it.

The girls watched as Montega got off the huge four-wheeler before assisting his little shorty, who was dressed in a short blue jean skirt, a white shirt that exposed her midriff and a pair of Kitson Chucks.

The girls were always taken by Montega's swag and his good looks. At 5 foot 9, he weighed close to 175 pounds and had a chiseled body that was accentuated in a wife beater, black Polo cargo shorts and a pair of black Stan Smiths. Montega was slowly becoming a regular source of conversation with the neighborhood females.

"Hey, brother," Jasmine greeted him as he approached.

His shorty, Juicy, leaned on the four-wheeler and watched the guys play basketball while Lil Man and Razor kicked it by the wall. "What 'sup, sis?" Montega said, giving Jasmine a hug.

"I see you like 'em with beans, salsa, and rice," Gi-Gi joked, getting a few snickers from the girls.

Ignoring her sarcasm, Montega smiled politely. He wouldn't let the girls embarrass his girl like they did whenever Taliban brought a girl around. "Aren't chu gonna introduce your little girlfriend to your sister?" Kia asked.

"Fuck, no. The less people she know, the better. Besides, the way y'all bitches act, she don't need to pick up none of your traits," Montega replied coolly.

Breezy frowned, and before she could fire back, she heard the sound of screeching tires burning up the street. "Oh, shit, the law," Montega said. He got low and pulled out his gun. He quickly stuffed it into his sister's pocketbook and walked towards Juicy as the detectives got out of their car.

Kia was used to hiding guns and drugs whenever the cops came; the cops rarely searched her or her girlfriends, but they loved to harass the dudes.

"Breezy, ain't that your dad?" Kia asked, pointing to the brown-skinned detective with the small fade and thick mustache.

"Yeah, that's him. Quick, give me your shades," Breezy said as a pack of 14th District detectives walked onto the courts.

Kia handed Breezy her shades as her father and his partner, an Italian, walked up to Mike and flashed their badges. "Michael Harris, we have a warrant for your arrest," Detective Gary Whitehead informed him.

"What's the charge?" Mike snarled.

"Murder," Detective Lucca said tersely as he placed Mike's hands behind his back and cuffed him.

Mike looked at his homie, Reek. "Yo, call my girl and tell her to call the lawyer. This some bullshit."

When Lucca saw the Puerto Rican kid sitting on the four-wheeler staring at him, he approached. "You got a problem with your eyes?"

"It's a fucking free country," Lil Man snapped fearlessly.

"Oh, yeah?" Lucca sneered, pulling out his pocket knife. "Well, if it's a free country, then I guess I gotta right to do this."

Lil Man watched as the detective punctured all four of the four-wheeler's tires, then walked away, laughing. Montega watched as Mike was placed into the back seat of the squad car and hauled off to jail. He only had one question: How did the police know about the murder? And who told them?

CHAPTER 42

KILL THE QUEEN

Stephon's phone rang, which brought him out of a daydream. "Hello?" Stephon answered.

"Yo, where Diamond at?" a husky male voice asked.

"Who the fuck is this?"

"It's Butch. Who the fuck is this?" he growled.

"This is Diamond's boyfriend. That's who the fuck I am," Stephon snapped.

"Boy, give me the phone. That's probably my cousin," Diamond said as she walked into the room with a white, fluffy towel wrapped around her.

She snatched the phone from Stephon's hand. "Hello?"

"Yo, what's up, cuz?" Butch said.

"Oh, hey, cuz. How's everything going?" Diamond asked while looking over at her jealous boyfriend, who was eyeing her like a hawk.

"Not good, Ma. The Ape Gang hit one of our spots in Los Santos. Them niggas ain't let nobody live, baby girl. We need to punish these marks. But, fuck all that. What's up with you? You got that lame answering your phone now? When you start that?

"I was in the tub at the time," she tried to explain.

"Well, still check that mark," Butch advised. "What's wrong with you, baby girl? You ain't been out with us in months. All you do is lay up with the ex-middleweight champion. You need to get your mind right, cuz. Don't let no nigga fuck up your business. Seriously."

Diamond rolled her eyes. She hated when he lectured her when she was wrong. The truth was, she was falling for Stephon and would probably do anything for him, including staying locked down in the house. "A'ight, cuz, I'll call you later," she said before hanging up.

Ever since Diamond and Stephon linked up, he had been pressing her. Stephon was so fascinated with her, he moved from New York to Los Angeles so that he could be close to her. That made him overprotective and very jealous.

He would pummel any guy who tried to make a play on her. Earlier, Diamond had thought it was cute, but when he started keeping her sheltered in the house, her attitude changed. It had gotten so bad that he lost his edge and his title to some second-rate amateur. His career now in limbo, he spent most of his time with Diamond. When she cut off her cell phone, she looked over at him. "Why are you still staring at me?" she asked.

"Who was that?" he demanded, folding his arms.

"That was my cousin. Why do you have to act so jealous all the time? You need to chill. That could've been someone important," she griped.

Seeing her displeasure, Stephon quickly softened up. "I'm sorry. I just don't want anybody around you. You're my heart, baby," he said walking up to her.

"And you're mine, too, but you gotta give me space. Don't you trust me?" she asked innocently, her sparkling, brown eyes gazing into his.

"Of course, I trust you, but I don't trust those niggas out there," he confessed.

Diamond got up to get herself together. "Where are you going?" he asked.

"Home. I haven't been there in far too long, and I need to get myself focused. Now, go have some fun with the guys and give me a call tonight. Maybe we can go out to dinner," she said, kissing him.

"Alright, but at least take Bain with you for your own protection. I don't have any use for a bodyguard anymore," he said sadly.

"Aww, boo, cheer up. You still have me," Diamond assured him.

Although Stephon was no longer the middleweight champ, Diamond still loved him. She knew what love meant, and when she fell for someone, she fell hard. Once the seven-foot giant got in the passenger's side of the silver Lexis GS 400, Diamond drove off and headed for the mansion. On the way uptown, she noticed through her rear view mirror that she was being followed.

The black Suburban had been following her ever since she'd left Stephon's place. Instincts told her not to go home until she found out who the hell was back there. Could it be Stephon? She thought.

Out of nowhere, another SUV smashed into the side of her Lexis. Diamond quickly regained control and floored the gas. "Bain, hold on. And shield your head," she said as the car bolted forward.

She heard the sound of gunfire as a volley of bullets punched through the back window. Diamond swerved in and out of traffic, trying to shake the assassins. As she dropped into the far right lane, a glut of traffic slowed the assassins, giving her just enough time to escape.

Diamond stepped on it, but slammed on the brakes when she spotted a car double-parked up ahead. The Lexis smashed into the back of a Toyota Camry, causing the air bags to deploy. Bain quickly opened the passenger's side door and rolled out as Diamond followed on the same side. She grabbed her bag just as the driver's side door got ambushed with lead. The Suburban stopped and Ape Gang members hopped out with machine guns, spraying bullets. Diamond and Bain stayed low as she pulled out her semiautomatic Glock .40 with the extended magazine. Bain had his trusty Colt.45 automatic, ready to fire. Diamond crawled to the next parked vehicle and looked underneath, glimpsing at the feet of the assassins. She took aim and fired.

BOOM! BOOM! BOOM!

A few bullets caught the feet of one of the assassins, causing his palm to lock on tight to the trigger of his gun from the pain. He mistakenly killed two of his own members before he fell to the ground.

Diamond downed him with a head shot, which he took without warning. While the rest were distracted, Bain swung around the car and fired at the rest of the men who were trying to reload their weapons. Diamond dropped one of them and kept firing until her clip was on E.

Innocent bystanders ran for cover, leaving their cars as they ducked and hid from the loud gunshots. Diamond dropped down as bullets came her way. She reached into her bag, pulled out a fresh clip, and reloaded. Before she could get up to return fire, she heard a different round of gunshots in the distance. With the Ape Gang on top of them, a police helicopter hovered overhead and a SWAT team quickly started blocking off the area.

Diamond grabbed her purse and tossed the gun and clip in the sewer drain. She then nodded at Bain, and they trotted off for an alley, just as the Ape Gang turned their weapons on the SWAT team and fired. The Africans battled it out with the cops until the last man fell.

By this time, Diamond and Bain were three blocks away. The first person she thought of was her boo. "Bain, I have to call Stephon," she said pulling out her cell phone and dialing his number. She got the voice mail. She was confused. He always kept his phone on, in case she called.

She prayed nothing was wrong as she called her cousin, Butch, to let him know what had happened and where she was. Too far away, Butch called Butta on the three-way and gave him her location.

It was a good thing Butta was at a restaurant nearby because cops had swarmed over the whole area. When Butta pulled up in his white Excursion, with his right-hand man, A-Z, by his side, Diamond and Bain got in and headed for Stephon's mansion, hoping that they weren't too late.

CHAPTER 43

WHEN A WOMAN'S FED UP

*D*iamond tried to call Stephon's cell phone once more, but again, all she got was his voice mail. Out of frustration and fear, she threw the phone down. Once they pulled up, all four jumped out when they saw an unusual Dodge Challenger parked out front. A-Z handed Diamond one of his black P-89 twin Rugers and cautiously walked into the mansion, behind Bain. A-Z was a cold white boy with blue eyes and a crew cut fade. He was skinny, but he rode hard when things got dramatic. Big Butta fucked with him tough and kept him on the wing.

Together, they searched the first floor. There was no sign of an intruder. No sign of false entry. All of a sudden, they heard noises upstairs, squeals and grunts. Someone was in the house. They all headed up the spiral staircase, checking every room. When they finally reached the master bedroom, once again Bain took lead. Slowly, he twisted the knob, then pushed the door. It swung open and bounced against the wall, knocking a picture of Stephon and Diamond to the floor.

When Bain rushed inside with his gun drawn, his eyes widened with surprise. Lying on the bed were Stephon and some white woman. They both were completely naked, trying to cover themselves up with the quilt. When Diamond walked into the room, assuming that her boyfriend was dead, what she saw devastated her and broke her heart.

Both Stephon and the white girl lay there with their mouths agape as Diamond stood there, with her hands on her hips and a sneer on her face. "Diamond, baby, I can explain."

"Oh, you can explain?" Diamond snarled as her left eyebrow arched in anger. "What? She accidentally came to the wrong house, found the wrong man, stumbled out of her clothes, and fell onto your dick? Is that what you were gonna tell me? And to think, I was worried about you."

"Diamond, please-"

"Just shut up," she snapped, finally fed up with his lies.

She aimed the gun at him while giving A-Z and Butta the nod to grip him up.

"Wait. What the fuck are y'all doing?" Stephon asked, panic stricken as the two approached. "Bain, do something."

"Bain is no longer your concern. Besides, you don't need a body-guard where you're goin, boo-boo," Diamond promised him as A-Z snatched the chick off the bed and flung her down to the floor.

As Butta went to grab Stephon, the boxer cocked his arm to swing, but Butta's 450-pound body was quicker on the draw. "Go ahead and try that boxing shit with me if you want, dog. I'll bust ya ass, you flea-ass nigga," Butta warned with the gun to Stephon's head. "Now, get ya broke-ass dressed before you're fighting for your life in the emergency room."

Stephon did exactly as they said. He threw on some clothes, wondering where this was going. Diamond studied the girl on the ground and shook her head. Not only was she mad that he had cheated on her, but with a skank?"

As soon as Stephon was fully dressed, A-Z clobbered him on the back of the head, knocking him out cold. Diamond drew her gun and pointed it at the girl's face. "Suck on it," she demanded. "You like to suck black barrels, don't you? Well, suck on this hammer."

The chick hesitated until Diamond shouted, "Suck on it, bitch!"

Trembling with fear, the chick placed the barrel in her wide mouth. Disgusted, Diamond pulled the trigger, blowing her brains out. Butta and A-Z tied Stephon's wrists, arms and ankles with duct tape as Diamond bent down to look at Stephon one last time.

"How could you betray the woman who always put you first?" she asked before kissing him on the forehead. Using the girl's panties, she gagged him.

They carried him downstairs and threw him in the trunk of his brand new AMG Mercedes Benz. Inside the house, Diamond opened several jugs of gasoline and poured it on the flooring before setting the house ablaze. She then came outside with a bag and shovel in her hand. "You sure you good from here?" Butta asked.

"I'll be fine. Thanks for everything. We'll be in touch," Diamond replied.

"You know Scar's gonna ask questions about his brother," Butta added.

"Fuck him. Let's keep this between us, though."

"You ain't got to tell me that. I live by the code, and my man A-Z ain't no rat, either," Butta stated before jumping back in his truck and pulling off just as the house was engulfed in flames.

Diamond and Bain headed the opposite way, blasting Jay-Z's "Say Hello" on the stereo. By the time she arrived on the outskirts of LA, to a place that overlooked the city, it had gotten dark and the city's lights glowed below. Every time she visited the place, it made her think of JR. Diamond took the shovel and got out. As soon as she popped the trunk, she began to beat Stephon with the shovel. She pounded and pounded on him until he was a bloody, pulpy corpse. Bain pulled Stephon out of the trunk and laid him on the ground. Taking the shovel from Diamond, he dug a deep hole. Diamond went into the car and pulled out the bag and dumped it into the ditch: every picture that she and Stephon ever took together, along with shirts, panties and everything else that made her think of him. She poured gasoline into the ditch and set it on fire.

Diamond stood there for a second, thinking about what she was doing. Part of her wanted to stop, because what she was doing would kill her inside. Not to mention she had killed a high-profile Underworld member's brother. The other part of her was saying that she was already gone and fuck who didn't like it. Looking at Bain, she gave him a simple nod. Bain dumped Stephon's mutilated body in the makeshift grave. The fire licked at the corpse for a while, then Diamond told him to shovel dirt in and be done with it. She told herself not to cry, but a lone teardrop found its way down her cheek, fell off her chin and landed on the grave below. At that moment, she realized that love was her worst enemy. She vowed never again to get that close to another man. Love was for the weak. And at that point, she needed all the strength she could to make it to the top.

CHAPTER 44

NEWS REPORT

"Oh, yes, right there. Yes! Yes! Yes!" Clyde pounded her out, doggie style. "Ummm, ssss, ohhh, yes, baby."

Clyde could feel himself reaching his peak, but all of a sudden, he was distracted by a news report on his 43-inch.

"Good evening, I'm Barbara Benson, and you're watching 'Fox News at Ten'. A tragic fire broke out today in the Redondo Beach section of Los Angeles, leaving a woman dead. Police say that the house belonged to ex-middleweight boxing champion Stephon 'Baby-face' Butler."

When Clyde heard that, he pushed the broad off of him, fearing that the dead woman was his sister.

"Police found a Caucasian woman murdered, with a gunshot to the head. There was no sign of Butler anywhere. Police suspect that Butler shot the woman and fled after torching the house. If anyone knows of Stephon Butler's whereabouts please call our hotline..."

Clyde couldn't believe his ears. He knew that Stephon's life started going south right after he lost the title belt, but he had no idea it was that bad. When the reporter spoke of a white woman killed in the house, he was relieved that it wasn't Diamond. His thoughts were now on Deshawn, wondering how he was taking this loss. With his dick still hard and Tammie still horny, he pulled off the condom and lay back to watch the next segment. Knowing that she wouldn't get it any other way, Tammie took his dick and started polishing it off inside her mouth.

"In Sherman Oaks, police say witnesses saw this Lexis crash into the back of a double-parked car as armed men opened fire on the vehicle with automatic weapons. Witnesses say a huge man and a black woman exited this vehicle and returned fire before escaping," the reporter said as the TV flashed scenes where the shootout took place.

"Get the fuck outta here," Clyde said in amazement as he watched.

"It's good, daddy?" Tammie asked, lifting her head up.

"Not you. I'm watching the news," he replied, pushing her head back down to finish the job.

The reporter continued. "Police say the woman and the accomplice managed to kill three armed men and evade a SWAT team. The vehicle that they were driving was registered to Stephon Butler."

Clyde frowned when he heard that. What the hell is going on, he thought. It was obvious that Stephon got around and was probably fucking every bitch in the city. He knew he had to get down to the bottom of all this. "Ahh, shit, yeah!" he gasped.

She popped up with a big smile while wiping her mouth. "Did you like that, baby?"

"Yeah, that shit was bomb...now, get out!"

CHAPTER 45

CURRAN FROMHOLD - CORRECTIONAL FACILITY
PHILADELPHIA, PA STATE ROAD

*M*ike repeatedly dialed Jennifer's number and got no answer. Hissing with frustration, he decided to call Reek. On the first ring, Reek answered. "Yo, big homie."

"Hello, you have a direct call from…"

Reek pressed five and answered. "Mike, what's good, my nigga?" he said, happy to hear from him.

"Ain't shit. How's everything going out there?" Mike asked while massaging his temple.

"Everything good. Your cousin definitely looked out. I just sent you a stack [$1,000] the other day."

"Yeah, I got it, but that's not why I'm calling. Look, I need you to drive past my girl's crib and grab that bread I got stashed in the safe for me. She actin' real weird, not answering the phone and shit," Mike explained.

"Say no more, my nigga, I'm on it," Reek said.

"Good looking out, bol," Mike said feeling, a bit better.

"No doubt. Oh, yeah, before I forget, you know the shorty, Jazz, who be with Taliban and Montega's sister, Kia?"

"Uh-huh, I know the bitch."

"Yeah, well, she wants to holla at chu, so I gave her your address and PP number so she could come see you," Reek stated.

"I ain't worried 'bout no bitch, right now. I'm facing a murder, dog. What I need is hat bread," Mike emphasized.

"A'ight, I'm on it," Reek said before hanging up.

Reek hopped into his green Cadillac Eldorado and headed for the playground. There, he spotted Montega, his brother, Taliban, and Razor, chilling by the gates. Rolling down the passenger's side window, Reek said, "What ch'all doin' right now?"

"Shit," Montega replied.

"Why don't y'all take this ride with me up to Chestnut Hill?," Reek suggested.

Once all three were in, Reek drove to Mike's crib, located in a nice, quiet neighborhood. As soon as they pulled up, Montega recognized the place. He had been there plenty of times to cook up coke for Mike. But, this was the first time that it ever looked so plain.

When the four got out, they headed for the front door. Reek rang the bell. No one answered. As he tried again, Montega stepped up on the storm drain and looked inside the window. "Yo, ain't no furniture in this muthafucka," he observed, squinting through the glass.

"Fuck you mean, ain't no furniture?" Reek asked, bewildered, before taking a look for himself.

Montega stepped down and walked up to the door and gave it a thunderous kick. The door swung in, and Razor looked at him with shock. "I see you been spending a lotta time with J-Rider and Killa lately," Razor joked, referring to their homies who loved to burglarize houses.

Montega smirked devilishly and walked inside. Reek and the rest followed. When they got to the basement, Reek spotted the open safe on the floor and shook his head when he saw nothing inside but some worthless papers. All he could manage to say was, "Ain't that a bitch."

CHAPTER 46

ONE YEAR LATER

*I*n an old-fashioned barber shop, Richard Zelinski sat in the chair while his barber shaved his face. In front of the shop, six Russian mafia soldiers stood around talking, while Zelinski talked to his underboss, Semok Budinov, as his bodyguards, Boe, Fatso and Pete, also sat in on the conversation. Semok needed to discuss Clyde White's army destroying his club the previous night.

"Mr. Zelinski, I'm through being embarrassed by this guy. Something has to be done. You told me that this man wouldn't be a problem after Max murdered Charles. Now his son is running around here like he owns the state," Semok complained.

As the barber angled the chair forward, he grabbed the scissors and began clipping the loose ends of hair. Zelinski replied, "These things that you speak of are little consequence. After tonight, you will understand what I mean. What I want to know about now is our girl. How is she doing?"

"She's really something, Zelinski. I don't think I've ever seen a woman so persistent, so ambitious. It's amazing. Not only is she hot, but she's serious. She now buys over 2,000 kilos a month. Maybe

196

soon, she'll be buying our whole shipment," Budinov exaggerated to make his point.

"I think I'd like to meet her. Set it up for me, will you?" Zelinski said just as his barber finished.

Semok nodded his head and faked a smile, "I'll get right on it."

Diamond lay back in her new boyfriend Hector's estate while enjoying the pleasure of getting her pussy eaten. She raked her fingers through his hair. "Ummm, that feels so good, poppy," she purred.

HECTOR WAS a Mexican drug lord who was head of the Sinaloa cartel. His cartel produced some of the finest heroin in Mexico, smuggled into America. His only competition was the heroin coming from Afghanistan, the stuff Verningo Castor had coming in from Colombia, and the heroin in Cuba.

When Diamond met Hector, she immediately talked with him about starting a new era in her business. Hearing so much about her, then seeing her in the flesh, Hector fell in love. Her beauty was exquisite, and her confidence and poise were well beyond her years. Never had he met a woman with such a touch of class.

From that point on, Hector was infected by her poisonous attraction and didn't stop until he had her in his bed.

As Diamond climaxed, her cell phone rang. Her pussy still pulsating, she lifted Hector's head from between her legs and answered it. Business first, she always said.

"Yes?" she said.

"Hello, pretty. How are you?"

"Mr. Budinov? I didn't expect to get a call from you, being as though it's not the end of the month. How can I help you?" she asked, brushing her hair behind her ear and crossing her legs on the edge of the bed.

"Please, Diamond, I told you to call me Semok. You make me feel like such an old man," he said.

Diamond giggled as Hector watched, feeling a little jealous that another man had amused his woman. "I need you to come and see me at my estate. I've got someone who's been dying to meet you."

"Oh, yeah, who?" she asked, moving to the edge of the bed, re-crossing her smooth, succulent legs.

"I prefer not to speak his name at this moment. But, you'll see when you get here."

"Okay, Semok, I'll be there tomorrow at, let's say, seven o'clock?"

"Seven o'clock is perfect. I'll see you then," he said and hung up.

Diamond closed her phone, then looked over at Hector, who was trying to hide his jealousy with a smile. However, Diamond saw right through him. With a devilish smile, she unfolded her legs and said seductively, "Come on, poppy. Come to mommy and finish what you started."

Like a trained dog, Hector got up and went right back to work. Diamond lay back, looking up at the ceiling with her legs spread as Hector's head dove between her open thighs. She didn't realize the evil smile that she had planted on her face proved that she knew how much power she had over a man. She was a man's favorite drug. And, at the moment, Hector was on cloud nine. Right then, it was about pleasure. Tomorrow, it would be business. Big business.

CHAPTER 47

LAST OF A DYING BREED

On an early Sunday morning, Diamond awoke from her bed to find Hector gone. It was no surprise. She knew that he was a very busy man. She got out of bed, and walked into her bathroom, squirted some toothpaste on her toothbrush, and brushed her teeth on the way back to her room. She turned on the TV news to see what was going on in the city, and saw a story about a firebombing and the death of a sports agent. She frowned and then grunted with a mouthful of suds.

Hoping for a better way to start the day, she turned off the TV and went to get showered and dressed. She knew Bain was probably downstairs, waiting for her in the living room. She wondered at times if he ever got any sleep. Now, dressed in a black J. Mendel dress and Westwood Vivienne shoes, she grabbed her Michael Kors handbag and headed down the steps. Just as she expected, Bain was standing by the marble fireplace, sipping on a cup of straight black coffee. His Desert Eagle was resting on the counter, waiting to take its place in the holster.

Diamond took one last look at herself in the full-length mirror. "You ready to go?"

Bain picked up the Desert Eagle and stuffed it inside his jacket as Diamond tossed him the keys to her bulletproof, white Audi A8. She had a lot to do today. She wanted to get a head start, so she and Hector could have some playtime later on tonight.

As Bain pulled out past the mansion gates and headed down the street, two black vehicles began to trail them. As the sedan cruised past all the large palm trees on the strip, the vehicles following them began to speed up. Diamond noticed this when she pulled out her make-up kit to check her eye liner. Snapping it shut, she spotted two more vehicles barreling towards them.

Both vehicles skidded to a halt and blocked them from the front. Bain skidded to a stop, then put the car in reverse, but the two vehicles from behind hemmed them in. Diamond pulled out a chrome Beretta and cocked it back, while Bain whipped out his Eagle, waiting for a war with the Ape Gang. But nothing happened.

As the two waited, tense and confused, men with M-16s got out of their SUVs. Even though their skin was dark, they were not Africans. In fact, they looked Spanish. They weren't pointing their guns, either. They just stood at attention, like royal guards, as someone in a cream-colored suit got out and approached them. Bain clutched his gun, but Diamond urged him to relax.

She cracked her window. "What's with the circus act?"

"I apologize for the rude intrusion, but I thought this would be the only way to get your attention, Diamond," the man in the suit said, bringing a frown to her face. "I am Jose Ramos, and I'm here on behalf of a man named Diego Elcano. He requested that I find you and bring you to his home. He has scheduled a flight for me to take you to--"

"Hold up for a second," Diamond interrupted him, "Who does this Diego Elcano think he is? First of all, I don't know you or him from the man on the moon. Second, I'm very busy, as you can see. So, you can tell this ... this man, or whoever he is- -"

"He's your grandfather," Jose interjected, stopping Diamond in her tracks.

For a few moments, she didn't quite know what to say. "My...my
... grandfather?"

"Yes, and he is a very powerful man in Cuba. Most importantly, he
wants to see his granddaughter immediately."

Diamond looked away and took a deep breath, trying to think.
This was all too unexpected. When she finally made up her mind, she
looked back at Jose and opened the door to get out. "Take me to him,"
she demanded.

After rescheduling the meeting with Russians, eight hours later,
the leer jet landed on a private landing strip, not far from the jungle.
Diamond was picked up by a black Hummer, escorted by other
armored jeeps. On the way to the estate, she looked out the window,
taking in the scenery. It was the most beautiful island she'd seen.
Besides the gentle slopes and broad grasslands, Cuba was landscaped
with towering mountains, deep bays, sandy beaches, and colorful
coral reefs.

The driver traveled through the sultry climate of the Sierra
Maestra range on the southeast coast.

As Diamond passed a huge field of steep terrain, she noticed
people scattered about with buckets and farming equipment. Jose
noticed her interest and leaned over. "Those are your grandfather's
farmers. These are his fields."

"What sort of fields are they -- cocaine?" Diamond asked.

"No, your grandfather doesn't deal with coca plant. He thinks they
are a waste of time and money. These are opium poppies used for
heroin."

The entourage stopped at a warehouse hidden in the jungle and
got out. When they walked inside, they found people hard at work.
Jose continued, "These people also work for your grandfather. This is
one of five warehouses he owns. What you seeing is one stage of the
development of heroin. Inside the petals of the opium poppies are
egg- shaped seed pods that are dripping with a milky substance. It's
called crude opium. Once it gets to a gum-like stage and turns darker,
it is packaged into kilos.

"For years, your grandfather has been selling nothing but pure white powder and making a huge profit," he said before pivoting to get into the car.

"I thought heroin was a brownish color," Diamond said.

"It can be, depending on where it comes from. But, the purest heroin is white, with a bitter taste, almost like Chinese heroin. Out here, kilos get sold on the black market for less than $20,000 apiece. In America, they're sold for $80,000. Your grandfather didn't want to deal with smuggling, so he dealt with the black marketing," Jose explained as they pulled up to a mansion surrounded by opium poppy fields and paramilitaries armed with AK-47s.

"So, what is it that he wants with me?" she asked as they stopped in the front of the mansion's entrance.

Jose turned and stared at Diamond. "Diamond, your grandfather is sick, very sick. He's on his deathbed, and the last request of a dying man is that he see his only grandchild."

Diamond looked at the big mansion before finding the courage to get out. She had so many questions that she wanted to ask her grandfather, starting with his abandonment of her mother. There were so many things she wanted to tell him, but when she entered the room where the nurses were checking his blood pressure, all that changed.

What she saw was a frail, wrinkled, old man with a respirator strapped to his face. As the women parted for her, Diego waved her over to him. Slowly, Diamond made her way to his bedside and saw his old face transformed into a big smile. Pulling the respirator off his face, he said, "So, you are the last of a dying breed. You're twice as beautiful as your mother, my child."

Diamond smiled and nodded in respect for the old man. He spat out words in the midst of a spasm of coughs. "I'm glad that...cough... cough...the last thing...cough...cough...I got to see...cough...was your pretty face...Come kiss my forehead, child."

Diamond bent over the bed and kissed him on the forehead. He stared at Diamond the whole time. As she rose up, the respirator flat-lined with a monotone buzz. Diamond stepped back as the nurses tried to revive him, but there was nothing they could do. When it's your time to go, it's your time. As Diamond looked on, Jose stood beside her. "What is to happen to my grandfather's legacy?" she asked.

"It's all yours, under one condition," Jose replied.

"What's that?" Diamond said, turning to face him.

"Your grandfather wants you to stay in Cuba and run the family business."

"And if I don't want to stay?" Diamond asked before turning back to look at her grandfather.

"Then, I will handle all of his affairs until you are ready to take the oath," Jose answered.

Diamond watched as the doctor wrote down the time of death. "I'm a be honest with you. I'm not ready to take on such a huge responsibility. But, I will tell you this: Cut the line for the black market. From now on, anything that comes out of my grandfather's fields comes directly to me. You understand?"

"But how will we get it there?" Jose asked in confusion.

Diamond grinned slyly. "Don't worry. I'll find a way. I always do. Trust me."

The following month, Diamond sat on the empty pier with Butch and all the others. The sun was dipping below the horizon, and everyone was clueless about what they were about to see.

"What are we waiting for?" Butch said over Diamond's shoulder.

Diamond checked her watch. "Any minute now."

Suddenly, bubbles in the water shot to the surface. Right before their eyes, miniature submarines began to emerge. The guys counted ten.

Diamond smirked devilishly. "Get the workers and tell them to bring the trucks up to the docks. We have a shitload of heroin to move. And, we only got a week before the next load comes," she instructed.

Butch couldn't believe his eyes. Diamond had really done it this time. Whoever her connect was, he was definitely about his work. Little did he know, the real connect was his little cousin, in the flesh, the Black Kiss of Death, who was the last of a dying breed.

CHAPTER 48

A RUSSIAN MAFIA HIT

The meeting with Clyde and his whole commission was on a yacht docked by the harbor. The yacht was equipped with 15 armed men with HK MP-5s on guard. Seated at a table on the deck, Clyde parlayed with his 15-man organization. Reese Chubs, Cheeko Raw, and Shug were there, along with a few other big boys, like heavy-set self-made millionaire, Miami George, and the playboy gangsta, Tony Wright.

"I'm glad to see everyone here. It's been awhile since we last saw each other like this. I must say, I'm proud to be a part of this new era for Great White. Before we get into other business, Shug, I need to ask you about our problem in Philly," Clyde said.

"It's all handled. I had my little cousin, Mike, take care of our problem," Shug replied confidently.

"Did he?" Clyde inquired.

"Damn right, he got 'em. But, some clown who was there got booked on some bullshit charges and ratted him out. Now, he's sitting in the county. I gotta get my little man back on the streets."

"Don't sweat it. I'll have Scar's shorty, Tanya, go down there and represent him. Tanya is the best. Don't worry, she'll handle it, trust me," Clyde replied before turning his attention to Tommy. "What about the people responsible for my father's murder?"

"Word through the underground is that the Russian mob boss, a guy named Zelinski, and the Colombian drug lord, Castor, were the ones who put the hit out. They said your father and Castor had been beefing since you were in diapers. There's still no word on how the Russians came in the picture, but with two big empires joining up, they can do a lot of damage. We could either join them or try to take both of 'em down."

"Wait, what does a Colombian drug lord have to do with some Russians?" Clyde asked in confusion.

"Verningo's got the whole U.S. southeast on smash. This guy is supplying a lot of people. Could be supplying the Russians, too," Cheeko Raw added.

"How do we find this guy?" Clyde inquired.

"This nigga has spots all over Miami. Not only that, he has a Colombian army of die-hards. The motherfucker's a dangerous dude. I suggest we stay in our lane and worry about these Russians, because if you're not willing to start a war in Colombia, I think you should leave them alone, ya feel me?" Tommy advised.

Clyde nodded. There was no way he would get his hands that dirty. "And, what about this bitch running around the city, tearing shit up with some crazy war with the Ape Gang?" he asked, looking around for answers. There were none.

"If anyone knows who she is, it's that fucking nigga, Steel. Word on the street is Steel was part of the plot that got her boyfriend killed. I think Iceman and a few other dudes were a part of that, too. That's how they got smoked," Chavo mentioned.

"Damn, she was the one that killed Iceman? He was a street sweeper himself," Reese Chubs said, amazed.

"Man, the bitch puttin' work in on whoever gets in the way of her drug operation. And, let me tell you, I don't know where she's gettin' it from, but her heroin is 100% pure white powder."

Clyde rubbed his chin as he did some thinking. "I think we just might have to pay Steel a visit so we can find out who this bitch is and who she deals with. Now, if there--"

Boom! Boom! Boom!

The gunshots had come from the harbor, causing everyone to dive to the deck. "What the fuck?" Shug shouted with his head crouched low as he crawled to the window to see what was going on.

When he stood, he saw an army of gunmen dressed in black suits with HK assault rifles, firing at his security. "Oh, shit, it's the fucking Russians. "They're here!" He reached for his .40 that was tucked on his hip.

Clyde popped up like bread out of a toaster, firing out the window at the assassins. While he battled, Justin ran for the door, out to the edge of the deck, to bust off at the Russians. Shug and the rest of the men took a position on the yacht and joined the gun battle. With the bullets flying, Clyde dove for cover.

While the Russians were spread out along the parking lot, beyond the harbor, taking cover behind some vehicles, Mad Max held his fully auto AK-47 with the scope, picking off men like they were ducks in a pond. He got Reese Chubs in his sight and fired.

On deck, Clyde watched as Reese caught bullets in the chest and neck. He slumped down into the dark water. Clyde stayed low, with his arms shielding his head helplessly, while Shug crawled to the cabin door and went inside. Cheeko Raw then got hit in the stomach and leg. Clyde almost shitted on himself when he saw that. Shug came back out with massive firepower. Holding a 47 mm grenade launcher with a 10-round drum, he took aim. Mad Max had Clyde in his scope, but then he saw something fearsome hurtling right at him.

"Oh, fuck!" he gasped as he took off running, just as a grenade hit the side of the car he was hiding behind.

BA-BOOM!

The explosion knocked Mad Max to the ground. But, he popped right back up and sprinted for safety. Clyde quickly picked up a gun after seeing Shug cock back another grenade into the chamber and fire.

BA-BOOM!

Another car got torched and several Russian goons went down. Shug's arsenal was too much for them. The Russians beat a hasty retreat, just as Clyde got up and joined Shug. The Russian piled up into their cars and peeled out of the area.

When Clyde turned and saw Cheeko Raw dead on the ground, the anger inside him started to boil. Someone would pay for this. He wanted to scream in anguish but that showed weakness, and Clyde refused to show his hand in front of his men. He knew then that the Russians weren't playing games. They wanted him dead.

CHAPTER 49

THE MEET

*D*iamond rode in the three-car entourage full of armed men, including Bain, Butch, 4-5, and Butta. On the way to Zelinski's mansion, Diamond marveled at the humongous ranch that featured cattle, tall trees and armed guards. The mansion was also huge, occupying almost 26,000 square feet.

Once the car pulled up to the front, Bain stepped out and opened the door for Diamond. The rest of her men followed and were greeted by the hostess, who ushered them inside. They walked down a hallway into the living room, where Semok and Zelinski were seated on a white, wrap-around sectional. Both men stood when Diamond stepped into the room. She wore a white, two-piece, trimmed business suit with cream pumps, and wiggled to the couch across from them.

After shaking hands, she took a seat, keeping her back arched and her legs crossed. She nodded her head modestly as Semok spoke highly of her to his boss. "So, Diamond. You are the one who's making us so rich off of the cocaine we supply you with. Semok told me that you were beautiful, but he didn't tell me how radiant you were in person," Zelinski complimented and Diamond smiled.

"I hear that you're having some trouble with a notorious South African gang. I would like to offer you my assistance," Zelinski said.

"That won't be necessary. I have the situation under control. But thank you, anyway," Diamond replied, forcing a smile.

Zelinski looked over at Semok in shock. "A woman with balls. I love it. It's not every day one comes across someone as dazzling and as dangerous as you, my dear. I may have to ask you out to dinner one day when I'm not so busy," Zelinski said elegantly.

"I'd be honored," Diamond replied modestly.

Zelinski looked over at Semok, who seemed a bit put off. "Semok, why don't you show our guests around while Diamond and I talk about an important matter. Show them where the bar is. I'm sure they're thirsty."

Diamond could see that Semok had no choice in the matter. As the men walked out, Zelinski looked back at Diamond and moved closer. "There's something I need to ask of you when you do catch Tanetche Agugbo. He has a very rare diamond that I will pay top dollar for. If you can retrieve it, you will be handsomely rewarded."

"What kind of diamond are we talking about?" Diamond inquired.

"It's called the Inar diamond, and it was found in Petra, Jordan. It is believed to be the rarest diamond in the world. Somehow, the Agugbo brothers have gotten their hands on it," Zelinski explained.

"I'll do everything in my power to get you that stone," Diamond assured.

After the brief meeting, Diamond and her people headed back to her new mansion in Ladera Heights. "So, what happened back there?" Butch asked as the driver pulled up to the entrance of her mansion.

"A whole bunch of things that have nothing to do with me," Diamond said, getting out. "I'll talk to you later."

After Bain shut the door, the entourage pulled off. Diamond checked her watch; she was supposed to see Hector later on. Bain stepped in the door and proceeded down the foyer. Diamond followed, searching in her Gucci bag for something. Out of nowhere,

Bain was clobbered with a 2x4. For the first time, Diamond heard his voice. He grunted before getting knocked to the ground.

Another swing knocked him out cold. Not one to run away, Diamond kicked off her shoes and rushed at the intruder, whose face was hidden behind a ski mask. Seeing her drop her bag and charge, the man swung the 2x4 again, but Diamond dipped under the blow, causing the wood to slam into the marble floor.

With perfect calculations, Diamond kicked the wood out of his hand. The intruder swung an open hand, but Diamond blocked the hit and struck him in his chest with the palm of her hand, stunning him.

From there, another masked assailant came from behind and wrapped his arms around hers as another came to rush her from the front. Diamond football punted the rushing man in the face, crumbling him to the floor like a Dorito chip. She then head butted the one behind her in the nose, twisted his wrist, and flipped him onto his back.

When she kicked him in the jaw, the first intruder with the 2x4 recovered and came back for more. This time, he tried to take her head-on with martial arts.

Diamond threw a flurry of punches, but the intruder was skilled at the art of self-defense; from hooks to jabs, he blocked them and returned punches of his own. Diamond slipped under his arm and came back with a backhand chop to the neck. As the man got more aggressive, she kicked him in the nuts, bending him over before she kneed him in the face.

Five men were down, and it seemed like more were emerging from inside her home. Diamond had no choice but to get out of there. As she turned to flee, her jaw ran into a fist that stopped everything. Her vision went blurry before her body could hit the floor.

CHAPTER 50

CUTTING OUT THE SMALL FISH

"Wake up, sleeping beauty," a voice said just before Diamond felt cold water splash against her face and body.

As she painfully gasped for breath, her eyes opened to see that her arms were over her head and her wrists were duct-taped to the pipes hanging from the basement ceiling. She was also without her shoes and shirt. The only thing she had on were her white Michael Kors pants and a black Agent Provocateur bra.

As she looked over her shoulders, she saw Bain dangling upside down, quiet, but alive. Before she could speak to him, the muscular African dressed in all-black smacked her to reality.

"That was for this," he said, pointing to his broken nose and swollen black eyes.

Diamond looked at the rest of the men standing behind him and smirked with sarcasm. Some had bruised faces. Others had bruised egos. Before she could say something that would surely get her killed, the door upstairs opened and a darker man who looked like he ran with the Ape Gang appeared.

Defiantly, she stared at the man with the beady eyes in the face as he frowned and said with a raspy voice, "What's your name?"

Diamond never flinched, nor did she respond. The man looked at his enforcer and gave the signal, while stepping back.

"With pleasure," the man with the broken nose said, stepping up.

He struck her in the stomach with an uppercut, then in the side with a hook, taking her wind away.

"Now, I will ask you again. What is your name?" the beady eyed man said, louder than before.

When Diamond was able to inhale, she curled up her lip with disgust and spit dead in his eye. This time the beady-eyed man needed no help from his men. He returned Diamond's remark with a hard slap to her face. Before she could recuperate, he punched her in the stomach. Embarrassed, he wiped what he could of the spit from his face and grabbed her by her long hair, pulling her head back.

"You think you're big shit, bitch, huh? You think you can use those pretty lips of yours to get your way out of this? I'm here to let you know that your reign is over."

"If I ever get out of here, I'm gonna kill you so quick your heart will still be trying to function with your brain," Diamond threatened.

The man laughed as he looked at his soldiers, who were amused, as well. "When the boss gets here, the only one doing the killing will be me. I hear you like to kiss. Well, you can kiss your pretty ass goodbye in a few minutes."

As he released her hair, he struck her in the jaw again with his closed fist. His cell phone rung in his pocket. The man pulled it out and answered it. After speaking briefly, he closed the cell phone and looked at one of his men. "Go let the boss in," he ordered.

He then looked back at Diamond arrogantly. "You should know before you die that I am the best tracker in the U.S. There's nobody I can't hunt down. Not even the notorious Black Kiss of Death."

Diamond could no longer hear the man talking. Her mind was somewhere else. Yeah, she was dazed by the punch, but she still held her ground. She knew she was going to die, but there was no way that she would give anyone the satisfaction of seeing her beg for her life.

Then came the sound of steps coming down the basement. At that moment, Diamond knew that her reign as queen had come to an end. As soon as she looked in the eyes of the man the tracker called "Boss," she froze, and so did he.

Mr. White, I give you the Black Kiss of Death. I took your advice about her dealing with the Russians, so I staked out their ranch. Guess who was there, visiting?" the tracker announced proudly.

Clyde looked in shock at his homies, Shug and Tommy, then back at his sister. Diamond stared at her brother with no emotion.

"What makes you so sure this is her?" Clyde asked with some doubt.

"I just told you. I staked out a- -"

"Man, let her down, Dawg," Tommy said, cutting him off. "That ain't her."

The tracker frowned. "But, sir, she's --"

"You heard what he said. Let her down. She's not the Black Kiss of Death. She's my sister," Clyde proclaimed.

The tracker looked at Diamond: no expression. Shaking his head, he had his men cut her loose. Once they brought her down, she massaged her sore wrists, then looked into the man's beady eyes. "You're a good tracker," she complimented.

"One of the best. Look, no hard feelings"

"Don't sweat it," Diamond said as she put a hand on his shoulder. "I know you were only doing your job. But, I never lie when I swear."

As the tracker turned to leave, Diamond picked up a loose pipe she spotted on the floor and cracked it over his skull. Blood spilled out of his head. Everyone backed up as the tracker's body collapsed to the floor. "Shit, did you just see that?" Shug asked Tommy, who stood there in awe.

"Let him down," Diamond ordered, pointing to Bain.

Her brother turned to glare at Diamond. "You got a lot of explaining to do."

"I don't have to explain shit to no one," Diamond shouted before walking by him.

"You may not want to talk now, but one day, you're gonna need me again," Clyde said seriously with a sinister smile. "Mark my words."

Later that week, Diamond and Hector went out for lunch. Hector had to meet with his client, who had come all the way from Northern California. Every month, the two met at a restaurant to discuss their business and where the next load would be dropped off. Hector didn't really want Diamond to know his moves, so he spoke in Spanish the whole time. Little did he know, Diamond knew three different foreign languages. Spanish was one of them. When Hector's client, Jesus "El Chango" Vargas, arrived, the two embraced and shook hands. Hector introduced him to Diamond, letting him know from the rip that she was his girl. Vargas couldn't seem to take his eyes off of her. She was like a bewitching spell.

Diamond glanced at him and smiled every now and then. Vargas was a handsome man, just like Hector, but she had no interest in hooking up with the boss of the Mexican Mafia, also known as "El Eme." If anything, she was more interested in cutting the small fish out and taking Hector's biggest client for herself. El Eme was a very large organization that dealt heavily in drugs. Diamond listened attentively, faking like she didn't understand a word they said. While the two talked business, Diamond found out about Hector's client. She also found out that Hector was charging an arm and a leg for his supply. Mexican heroin was only worth, $50,000 to $80,000 a key, yet Hector charged his clients $100,000.

She could see the man's frustration, knowing in the back of his mind that Hector was ripping him off. Before the three departed, Hector went to use the bathroom while Diamond waited with Vargas. As she sat patiently, she asked in Spanish, "So you say Hector charges you $100,000 a key, does he?"

Vargas was immediately flustered. "Yeah, but that doesn't concern little girls like you."

"Hah!" Diamond richly laughed. "You are very funny. So, tell me, how does a person get in contact with you if they want to do business?"

Vargas smirked at the thought of potentially doing business with her. *What does she have, that Hector doesn't,* he thought. However, he enjoyed the little game he thought she was playing. "I'm sorry, Miss, but there's nothing that you can give me that Hector hasn't already given me."

Diamond pulled out a piece of paper and wrote down her number. Sliding it across the table, she said, "What if I say I can get you pure white heroin? The type that can kill you with one sniff if you don't step on it two or three times. What if I tell you that the going rate for something like this will only cost you $60,000?"

"I would say you're crazy," Vargas said, taking the number and storing it in his pocket.

"You have no idea," Diamond responded as Hector returned. The conversation got sidelined.

"You ready?" he asked, catching them deep in conversation.

Diamond looked up at him. "Yes, I'm ready. It was very nice meeting you, Mr. Vargas." She slowly got up and walked off. Vargas watched her exquisite ass wiggle down the aisle. Hector gave the Mexican Mafia boss a fake smile and shook his hand before exiting the restaurant.

As soon as he got in the car, he snapped. "What the fuck was that about?" he shouted.

"What?" Diamond asked, confused.

"You know what I'm talking about. That intimate little talk you two were having. What the fuck is going on?" Hector demanded.

"Hector, please, it was nothing. Just small talk. Don't be so jealous. Really, you twist everything I- -"

BAM!

Hector slammed his fist on the steering wheel. She stared at him in silence. "You know what? You can take me the fuck home. I don't have to--"

"Shut the fuck up!" Hector shouted while grabbing her arm.

"Let go of my arm, Hector," she said calmly.

He released her and put the car in gear. The two remained silent all the way to the mansion. When they arrived, Diamond opened the door, got out, and slammed the door.

When they were inside, Bain came out of the living room and gave her a welcoming nod, but he could tell she wasn't in the mood for niceties. Hector was saddled with guilt; he had never acted like that before. Something about her brought out this ugly side of him. He walked up the steps and into the bedroom. Diamond emerged from the bathroom wearing a black robe.

"I wish to apologize," he began. She just brushed by him without saying a word. "Diamond, I'm sorry. I wasn't myself."

Diamond sat in front of the mirror, blow drying her hair. Seeing that she still wasn't trying to hear it, he decided he had to take some type of chance. As Diamond combed her hair, he came up behind her and kissed her on the neck. Diamond quickly nudged him away, but he continued. "Get the fuck off of me," she said, pushing him again.

Hector scooped her out of the chair and flung her on the bed. Her robe flew open, exposing her goodies. Hector dove head-first between her legs.

Diamond sandwiched his head in a leg lock. "No, boy, stop," she said, tightening the squeeze. Hector wouldn't relent. He stretched his tongue out as far as he could and licked her outer vaginal lips. Diamond felt faint pulsations of pleasure and started to weaken. Given more leeway, Hector's probing tongue cracked the door open and went after her juicy pearl. "Ummm, boy, didn't I tell you to stop?" Diamond moaned as her resistance gave up on her.

Hector's dick was as hard as a lifer with two shanks in an upstate prison yard. From her pussy, his mouth traveled up to her juicy titties and nursed on her hard, brown nipples like a baby. He then stuck his six-inch shaft inside her and fucked her like a jack rabbit. Although he wasn't the consummate lover, it was make-up sex, after all, which is always a turn-on. "Uhhh, shit, Diamond!" he gasped as she pulsated her vaginal wall like a porn star.

Diamond knew that he couldn't hold out much longer. He never had much stamina, so she had to get hers before it was too late. Diamond pulled his face to her breasts so he could stimulate her nipples. It was like a shock wave shooting directly to her pussy. "Oh, yes, suck my titties. I'm having an orgasm," she sighed, gripping the back of his head.

Anticipating his eruption, Diamond pushed him out of her just as he started to nut.

She knew how bad he wanted to have a kid with her, but that was out of the question. She was in the prime of her life; the last thing she wanted was a baby.

That night, as she and Hector lay in the bed, she said innocently, "Baby?"

"Yes, my dear?" Hector replied, with his arms around her.

"You know you my boo, right?" she asked.

"Yeah, Mommy, I know," he replied.

"And you know I'd ride for you, every time, right?"

"Yes, I know, Mommy. Why do you say this?" he asked cautiously.

"Because if you ever put your hands on me again like you did in the car, I'll leave you right where you stand."

Hector kissed her forehead, thinking that she was just talking. Little did he know how serious she was and how dangerous she could be.

CHAPTER 51

THE PRESENT

*C*lyde sat on his couch with the phone to his ear. As much as he didn't want to believe that his little sister was the Black Kiss of Death, Tommy told him otherwise.

"Yeah, Dawg. You should have believed it when you saw her hanging from the ceiling that day. We got the nigga Buck right here to confirm it. Remember the nigga JR she was dealing with? Well, he was the boyfriend who got killed, and she damn sure put that work in on Iceman, believe it or not. Check this out, she took all JR's affairs from drugs to the studio he had put together for unsigned hype. Oh, and that white heroin that everyone's going crazy about. Well, turns out it didn't come from China. It came from Cuba. Now, I know how much you don't give a shit about her, but me personally, I think you need to holla at your sister. It's obvious the Russians don't know who she is, and I don't think she knows what's going on, either.

"A'ight, good looking out. I'll get back with you after I figure something out." Clyde said before hanging up.

Staring out in space for a few minutes, Clyde shook his head.

Diamond had really made a way for herself. His only problem was, how was he going to convince her to bring her talents home?

~

DIAMOND CRUISED through LA in her red Ferrari with a black Suburban full of shooters behind her for back up, just in case she ran into the Ape Gang again. She was headed to a meeting. At 21 years old, she was the smartest, prettiest, and most feared woman moving bricks out on the streets. Since her boyfriend, Hector, had taken a flight to meet some clients, this was a perfect time for Diamond to handle her own business without him nosing around.

For two and half years, she had been with the Mexican drug dealer. His jealousy and insecurity had caused him to lose focus on what really mattered: money and his cartel. His obsession with Diamond had weakened his will and affected his business. He couldn't control himself when it came to her. His temper and jealousy had gotten uglier over time. Diamond couldn't understand why men got that way with her, but it was something that gnawed at her. She fondly reminisced about her first love, JR.

She used to visit his gravesite every Sunday, but she found herself too busy to do that now. She had a reputation in the streets to preserve, and as a woman, the game was always that much more diffi-cult. As she traveled down memory lane, she vibed off of the song, *Best of Me* by Mya, featuring Jadakiss. She wondered if she could ever replicate the love that she had for JR. The relationship she had now was taking its toll on her. Diamond sang all the way to the restaurant. She gave the valet her ticket, then followed Bain inside. The hostess looked through the reservation book, then said, "Ah, Ms. Reynolds, your table is this way, but I was under the impression you would be alone."

"Oh, this is my...friend," she lied. "He'll be joining me, if that's okay with you."

The hostess looked up at the huge, bald-headed black man with the imposing stare. "No, it's not a problem," she replied meekly.

"Thank you," Diamond said before following the waitress to where her guest was seated.

Immediately, he stood and shook her hand. "Diamond, it's good to see you again."

"You, too, Mr. Vargas," she said graciously as he pulled out a chair for her to sit.

For a year and a half, Diamond had been secretly doing business with the Mexican Mafia behind Hector's back. Some would see that as snaking her own boyfriend. To Diamond, it was all about power. She not only flooded the Triads with heroin, but now she had the Mexican Mafia on her line. Slowly but surely, she was starting up a buzz in cities such as, Boston, Dallas, Detroit, Baltimore, Camden, and Trenton.

Because of Hector's outrageous prices, a lot of his clients abandoned him and dealt with Diamond. Others dealt with Castor, or the Agugbo brothers. Even though Diamond's and Vargas' relationship was strictly business, Vargas really wanted Diamond for himself and hoped that one day he would capture her fancy.

While Diamond and Vargas conversed like two old friends, outside, Diamond's men were collecting the duffle bags of money from the trunk of Vargas' car. This was how he would re-up. The bricks would be sent to a location, then Vargas' men would take care of the rest.

After the meeting, Diamond shook hands with Vargas, then headed out of the restaurant, looking like a movie star in white Max Mara fitted slacks, a gold Marc Jacobs blouse, and white Hermes calfskin Gladiator sandals that matched her handbag. She had her long hair tinted brownish gold and kept it in a loose ponytail. Vargas stared as she left, fascinated by her curvaceous hips and apple-shaped ass.

CHAPTER 52

GREED

*D*eep inside the ghetto of South Central LA, Steel and his homie, Sid, rode with two others in a Chevy Impala. Steel had to make a stop at the supermarket to pick up some baking soda and a couple of bags of ice. The four men hopped out and passed through the electric doors. Steel pulled out his cell phone and called Buck's number, but didn't get an answer. "Fuck, where is this nigga?" he griped.

"He still ain't answerin'?" Sid asked.

"Nope, and that dumb muthafucka has to load."

"Well, let's check the strip club. You know how that mark is with them hoes," Sid suggested.

After buying what they needed, they drove to the strip club. When they got to the place where Buck liked to hang out, they searched the nude scenery, but there was no sign of him. As they turned to leave, Butta and four shooters came rushing down the steps, with Macs poised.

Steel took cover and dropped the first dude with a shot to the neck. Sid fired his Caltech as he tried to make it to the back, but before he reached the dressing room, he got wet up by the hail of bullets. He staggered forward and tumbled over a waitress who was crouching down, covering her ears from the loud noise. Before Sid fell on his back, one last bullet from Butta's gun thudded between his eyes. Steel watched as his cohorts fell, one by one. Thinking fast, he quickly put a naked stripper in a choke hold and used her as a shield as he backed his way towards the emergency exit. He fired a volley, killing one of Butta's men.

By the time he got to the back, the woman was full of holes. He dropped her lifeless body to the ground. As soon as he got out the door, he was slugged with the butt of 4-5's 4x4 bulldog and slumped to the ground. Dazed, Steel looked up and saw the barrel of a gun stuck in his face. 4-5 smiled before pulling the trigger. "Long kiss, nigga."

BOOM!

IN SAN LEANDRO, outside of Oakland, Butch counted, packaged and distributed all of the bricks that they had just received from another submarine shipment. A-Z helped with the count. Seeing that there was an extra brick, he recounted. When he got the same amount, he secretly stuffed it under his shirt and took it to his car. After all the trucks were packed and ready to move out, A-Z headed for the city to holla at one of Butta's workers. Once he arrived, he beeped his horn at the young bol in charge of the lookout. "Ay, Cuz, where Meechy at?" he asked.

"I don't know, A-Z. He was just out here," the lookout explained.

Up the block, officers in a tinted black Crown Victoria surveyed the whole block. When they saw the lookout go to a red Cadillac Escalade and saw the white guy inside, they thought he was making a sale. "Alright, guy, we got a buyer," Sergeant Kasem Moss said through his walkie-talkie before putting his car in gear.

As A-Z spoke with the lookout, his eyes ballooned at the sight of police cars closing in from all angles. The lookout hauled ass through one of the alleys, but was hit by a cop car on the other end. A-Z also tried to make a run for it, but Sergeant Moss was right there with his gun drawn. "Put your fucking hands up!" he commanded.

A-Z did as instructed. Once he was placed in the back of the Crown Victoria, he watched as the officers searched his vehicle. When he saw them emerge with a big plastic bag, he knew they had found the handgun and the brick of heroin. "Well, well, well, look what we got here, Sarge. I think we hit the jackpot," one undercover officer rejoiced.

Moss walked towards the squad car A-Z was in and peeked in. "And to think, we thought you were just some buyer. Looks like we gotcha, buddy."

A-Z put his head down, anticipating all the hard time he would have to do, especially if the feds got involved.

CHAPTER 53

THE FIRST LADY

*A*fter an intense training exercise with her martial arts instructor, Diamond stepped to the side to take a seat. Drained and tired, dressed in an all-black cat suit and tube socks, she toweled herself off, crossed her legs, and cracked open a bottle of Fiji spring water as she watched her trainer circle another one of his students.

Before she could watch them battle it out, her phone rang. It was A-Z. "Hey, white boy, what's up?"

"Yo, what's crackin', girl? What you doin'?" A-Z asked.

"Nothing. You know, it's Thursday. I gotta stay in shape," she replied.

"Oh, so you're at your martial arts class, right?" he asked lamely.

"Yeah, why?" she asked suspiciously.

"Nothing, I was…uh, just seeing what you were up to," he said hesitantly.

Diamond took her cell phone from her ear and looked at it, slightly vexed. A-Z never called her regular line unless it was an emergency. But, to call and have nothing to say was questionable. She quickly snapped her phone shut, grabbed her gym bag, and headed out the door. As soon as she got outside, LAPD officers swarmed around her. Diamond looked over at Bain, who was handcuffed and being escorted to a paddy wagon. She shook her head in disbelief as a small squadron of officers pointed guns at her face.

She dropped her gym bag and put her hands up before Sergeant Moss walked up to her and slapped the cuffs on her. "Diamond White, you are under arrest for drug trafficking and the possession of a controlled substance. You have the right to speak to an attorney. If you give up that right, anything you say can and will be used against you in a court of law..."

CLYDE'S PHONE rang in the cigar room as he and Justin played pool. Seeing it was Tommy, he answered. "Yo, TG what's up?"

"Yo, Dawg, are you watching the news?"

"Naw, why?" Clyde asked, raising his eyebrows.

"Man, I think you need to turn that shit on, cuz," Tommy suggested.

Clyde hit the remote for the big screen and watched as a reporter delivered the story.

"Just a few hours ago, police arrested 21-year-old Diamond White." Clyde's and Justin's mouths simultaneously almost hit the floor. "White was charged today with drug trafficking and possession of nearly 100 kilograms of heroin. An informant led the police to a ranch out in Los Santos where he claims that White may have distributed nearly 1,000 kilos of heroin not long before her arrest. White's fingerprints also matched prints lifted from the steering wheel of ex-middleweight boxing champion, Stephon Butler's white Lexis that was connected to a violent shooting in LA over two years ago. White's bail is set at a quarter of a million dollars."

Justin looked over at Clyde in shock. "Can you believe that shit?"

Clyde replied, "What's not to believe?"

~

Later on that day, as Diamond sat in a cold jail cell, she couldn't stop thinking about the betrayal of A-Z. She was relieved that he hadn't mentioned all of the murders, especially Stephon Butler's. And, after being questioned for hours about her fingerprints being in the Lexus, the detectives seemed satisfied with her answers. She was his girl-friend. End of story. As she sat on the cold, steel bench, the turnkey guard came down the walkway. "Diamond White? You made bail," a fat, nasty, white guard said, opening the bullpen.

DIAMOND WALKED by with a grateful smile. When she got outside the district, she looked around for Butch's Tahoe, but didn't see it anywhere. Instead, there was stretch limousine sitting out in the parking lot. Diamond knew who was inside and rolled her eyes.

Clyde once told her that she would need him one day, and now that day had come. It was time for her to explain everything. When she got into the back seat, Bain was already seated with Clyde and Justin.

"So, are you ready to tell me what you've been up to? Or, do you want to spend a shitload of time behind bars in a women's federal prison? They got that snitch hidden so good, even the Black Kiss of Death can't get him without help."

"You'd be surprised," Diamond corrected him.

Clyde stared at his sister in wonder. Diamond knew there was no other way. She swallowed her pride. "Okay, damn."

She then explained everything that happened from the moment JR was killed to the underlying cause of her arrest, leaving both Clyde and Justin breathless, especially when she spoke of her visit to Cuba.

"So what happened with the car crash?" Clyde asked.

"Bain and I made a run for it. We got a ride from Butta and A-Z to Stephon's house, but we found the girl dead and Stephon was gone," she lied, glancing over at Bain to make sure he was still riding with her. "I think he may have been abducted."

"You sure you didn't kill the broad after finding her in the house?" Justin asked, wandering close to the truth.

Diamond rolled her eyes. "Why would I kill his sports agent? Like I said, he was gone when we got there. And the house was already flaming."

Clyde stated the obvious. "You do realize that the people you are dealing with on the cocaine tip killed our pop, don't you?"

"Business is never personal, Clyde. You should know that."

"You say that like you're serious," Justin observed.

Diamond ignored Justin and looked at her brother. "So what now?" she asked.

"Now we go to New York. There's a lot of people that are looking for answers, and there's one who might need to help you with your situation."

A few hours later, Clyde's private Leer jet landed at the JFK International Airport, in New York. From there, they were taken to a large skyscraper in downtown, Manhattan, on 57th Street, where they took the elevator to the 12th floor. There, the boss of all bosses, Carlton Butler, sat behind a long table with the members of the Underworld, along with his son, to greet them.

Once everyone was seated, Carlton began. "Diamond, this is really a surprise for me to see you here today. Your father wanted something much different for you, but what's done is done, right? Before we get started, I understand you dated my son, Stephon. I also found out that you had his Lexis the day he disappeared. You care to enlighten me about this?" Carlton asked.

Deshawn studied the woman in the black Ferragamo skirt suit and pumps as she removed her Louie shades. She explained her story the same way she explained it to her brother. It was a brilliant acting job; they believed her. Diamond even faked a few tears, leading them to believe that Stephon was still alive. Carlton felt her pain, then introduced her to some people who could help her with her problems.

"Diamond, the Underworld doesn't just dabble in illegal activities. We also deal with some very powerful people in government. Anything is possible if you have these people in your corner. They can locate a government witness testifying against you; they can get all the charges dropped. All these things are possible if you cut all the ties with the Russians and join the Underworld as our First Lady," Mr. Butler promised.

Diamond looked around at all the big faces, then sat back and crossed her legs. "I'll join under one condition."

"Name it," Mr. Butler replied.

"I get to bring who I want into this organization with me. And, I want Verningo Castor dead."

Everyone looked around at each other with worried faces. This was risky, but not wanting to lose a potential member, Mr. Butler said, "You got yourself a deal, Ms. White."

"Alright, then. I'm in."

Each man nodded in agreement, except for Deshawn. He was still unsure about the woman, especially after hearing all the rumors about the disappearance of his brother.

That day, Deshawn saw the whole White Family in a different light. He vowed that if he ever found out that Diamond had a hand in Stephon's murder, the whole Great White Organization would burn to the ground. "So what about the Russians?" Clyde asked Diamond. "How do you plan to cut your business with them?"

Diamond gave her brother a wink and a smirk, then got up from the table to leave.

CHAPTER 54

DOUBT AND DECEPTION

*T*he large receiving room inside the CFCF county jail on the State Road was packed with visitors to see loved ones. Like always, Mike sat across from his new girlfriend, Jasmine, as they discussed what was going on out on the streets. For two years, Jasmine had been coming up to visit Mike every week. It didn't take long for love to blossom.

Jasmine didn't care how much time Mike got; she was loyal and would ride it out with him as long as he stayed true to her. Jasmine was a 5 foot 3, 126-pound, petite redbone with straight black hair that dropped past her shoulders. She was blessed with a nice ass and a nice set of breasts that Mike always fantasized about sucking on.

"I talked to your cousin, Shug, the other day," Jasmine told him. "He said that he fired your lawyer and hired one of the top lawyers in the country. Her name is Latanya Gibson. She's supposed to be coming up to see you soon."

"Man, none of that shit matters if this nigga Smoke still runnin' around the streets like he ain't no rat," Mike replied disappointedly.

"I heard KK cousins, Flex and Mick, tried to get Smoke, but Mick ended up getting killed. Flex got away, but then Razor iced him a week later," Jasmine said, spilling the beans.

"Razor? My young bol, Razor?" Mike asked, stunned.

"Yup. Something about Razor telling Flex he couldn't roll out with them during a hit. Razor told them that three was a crowd. Flex took it personal. They got into an argument and they drew their guns. They said Flex had his safety on and Razor shot him. Now KK's trying to get involved."

"KK better fall back, if he know what I know. Kia's little brother ain't goin' for that," Mike warned.

"Who, Kenny?" Jasmine said. "The one they call Montega?"

"Yeah, young bol a gun on the low. I ain't even gonna hold you."

"Oh, yeah? But, he seems so quiet and to himself. All he wanna do is sell drugs and ride dirt bikes and four-wheelers all day," Jasmine said naively.

Mike recalled the night Montega killed Gangwar for him at Shrimpie's bar. It was then he realized that Montega had heart and was way more dangerous than any other hustler on the block. It was also the reason Mike gave Reek strict orders not to sell Montega anything over two ounces. Deep down, Mike knew that Montega's rep could destroy what he had built. That scared Mike; with some money, there was no telling what Montega was capable of.

ON A COOL and sunny afternoon in the Big Apple, Deshawn Butler dined in front of a Manhattan restaurant on Chelsey Pier. It was a spot where people enjoyed brunch or an early dinner outdoors. Deshawn and his brother, Stephon, loved to meet there and try to hit on actresses or a singer. Stephon's disappearance had disturbed him. Deshawn knew that he'd moved out to LA to be with Diamond, so her claim that she was ignorant about what happened to him sounded bogus. Deshawn was shocked at how much control Diamond had over his brother. Stephon's life had deteriorated once he moved out west. He had neglected his career and his friends to be with her. He always resented that.

Now Stephon was missing, and a hundred questions were floating in his head. The main one was: Did Stephon kill his sports agent and flee? If so, why? Deshawn snapped out of his mental investigation as a red C-class Benz slowly rode by and parked up the street. Deshawn dug into his pocket and pulled out a fresh pack of Newports. Giving the box a few taps before he removed the plastic, he pulled out a cigarette just as the women in tan business attire sashayed his way.

"I figured you'd be here," she said, setting her briefcase down and taking a seat across from him.

"Tanya! What are you doing here?" he wondered.

"Checking up on my man. I see you're still smoking those cancer sticks. I thought you told me you stopped. They'll be the death of you one day," she said before pulling the pin from her bun and letting her hair fall down.

"Well, I guess old habits die hard," Deshawn replied while watching her shake her long hair out.

Tanya was a pretty brown-skinned beauty who happened to be Deshawn's accountant, lawyer, and lover. The two grew up together in the same neighborhood in Brooklyn. Both had an ambition to leave the 'hood and become somebody important. Ironically, they got rich helping each other out.

Tanya watched as Deshawn lit his Newport and puffed away.

"Still haven't got any word on your brother?" she asked as she sat down and crossed her legs.

"Nope, and, truthfully, I don't think I ever will. Stephon never disappeared before. Right now, I'm just trying to handle the fact that I may never see my brother again. Shit hurts bad, Tanya."

Tanya felt his pain. She had never seen him so down. He was always so strong-minded, fearless and confident. Leaning forward, she placed her hand over his in the middle of the table. "Don't worry, baby, everything's gonna be alright. I'm here for you if you need anything."

Deshawn looked at his girlfriend's hand and smiled. But, before he could say anything in return, someone walked up to the table. This time, the undercover shooters that were hidden in the midst of all the customers, got up and approached. Seeing it was Hillary Agugbo, the African crime boss, Deshawn signaled for them to remain seated.

"Mr. Butler, it's nice to see you up and about," Hillary said pleasantly.

Tanya released Deshawn's hand and eased back in her chair. "Hillary, by all means, have a seat," Deshawn insisted.

Once the South African was seated, the waitress stopped by the table to take their order. "Just a glass of Pellegrino for me," Tanya said.

"I'll have a glass of freshly-squeezed orange juice," Hilary said, folding his hands.

The waitress then looked at Deshawn. "And you, sir?"

"Hennessy straight, and fill it to the brim," Deshawn said.

Hillary paused to look at Deshawn. "I take it you're still distraught about your brother. I have some information about him that might be of value."

"What is it?" Deshawn asked, putting out his cigarette.

"A few months back, we believe that your brother was associated with the Black Kiss of Death. My brother saw her in LA and had one of his men follow her all the way across town, to a nice, tidy mansion. But, before he could strike, he was called off. When he went back to the mansion, it had burned down to the ground. Simon traced the house to Stephon Butler, your brother."

Deshawn thought long and hard about what he had just heard. Clyde had told him stories about a mysterious woman running around LA trying to control whatever she got her hands on. Come to find out, it was Clyde's very own sister. Raking his fingers across his bald head in frustration, he asked, "Why didn't you tell me this sooner? Why wait damn near two years later?"

"Because we thought you were in on it. At that point, we didn't know who to trust. Throughout the years, we've lost almost a hundred men, including Tanetche's wife."

"Well, why trust us now?" Tanya asked.

Hillary calmly replied, "After seeing what happened on the news, I realize that you couldn't have known about this bitch. That is why I am here now."

Deshawn tried to think back to his meeting with Diamond. It was already too late to retaliate. Diamond had been welcomed into the Underworld. And, in the Underworld, a boss couldn't kill another boss unless the council okayed it.

CHAPTER 55

A NIGHT BEFORE THE NEW YEAR

*I*n Pennsgrove, New Jersey, on Route 60, in a motel called the Westly Inn, A-Z sat in a room with a bottle of Grey Goose vodka, a pack of cigarettes, and a jar of Dro. He had been hiding out as part of the federal witness protection program. He was set to go to court the 10th of January to testify against Diamond on major drug charges.

After sparking up a joint, he turned on the TV to watch a movie. It was 11:49 PM, and A-Z was getting a little woozy off the weed. He got up to check on the officers who were supposed to be out front. They were gone. As A-Z started to panic, Butta's wide body squeezed through the door.

A-Z cursed, "What kind of fucking witness protection is this?" he mumbled before turning to see Butta come into the bedroom.

"Ain't no protection for you, muthafucka," Butta stated.

Butta smacked A-Z on the side of his head with the gun. A-Z stumbled over the television and spilled to the floor.

"Yo, man, wait, I can explain!" A-Z pleaded while pulling himself to his feet.

"I trusted ya ass. Put you under my wing and you gonna play us like this. Like we wasn't gonna find you. You a bitch-ass nigga, A-Z. And, the worst kind of bitch-ass nigga is the one who act like they thorough when, really, they weak. You shoulda rode it out. You know Diamond woulda got you out of a jam. No, but you was too fuckin' weak. Fuck it, though," Butta said, aiming his .357 and turning up the volume on the TV. It was the final count down to the New Year. "5…4…3…"

"Butta, wait. Don't do this!" A-Z begged.

"Long kiss, you snitch-ass nigga," Butta said.

"2…1…Happy New Year!"

BOOM!

CHAPTER 56

THE SNOW WHITE QUEEN

*D*iamond sat behind the defendant's table, next to her lawyer, Latanya Gibson, waiting as the DA tried to stall for another court date. It was obvious that they weren't ready. "Ms. Anderson, I won't grant your motion for a continuance because you do not have your witness here to testify today. I'm sorry, but I will have to deny your motion and proceed, without the witness," the judge proclaimed to the district attorney.

The DA was speechless. A silent courtroom waited for the DA. She stood and said, "Council has no further evidence, your honor."

After a brief recess, the jury came back with the verdict. "In the case of the United States versus Diamond White, the jury finds the defendant, Diamond White, not guilty."

The DA turned to look at Diamond and Tanya, shocked. Both women rose and hugged each other before heading through the throng of spectators. Although Clyde wasn't there, there were still spies hovering about to report back to him.

As she exited the courthouse, the news reporters crowded Diamond to get an interview. But, Diamond's bodyguard, Bain, quickly escorted her straight to her limousine. When she was inside, the phone rang. "Hello?" she answered.

"Hello, Diamond. Congratulations," Zelinski said.

"Thanks. You know what? Why don't we celebrate at dinner tomorrow night? My treat," Diamond suggested.

"Sure," Zelinski eagerly replied. "That was exactly what I had in mind. How about Mr. Chow's. I love it there."

"You got it. Eight o'clock. I'll see you then," Diamond said before hanging up.

Staring into space, Diamond thought for a moment. Taking a deep breath, she dialed Semok's number. After the third ring, he answered. "Hello?"

"Semok, it's Diamond. I need to talk to you today about something. It's very important."

"Okay, but you didn't give me a chance to congratulate you on embarrassing the district attorney," he said.

"Congratulate me later," Diamond replied before giving him the time and the place.

After hanging up the phone, she ordered the driver to take her home. Diamond couldn't wait to get there and celebrate with Hector. Although they had been arguing lately, they still settled their differences with fabulous make-up sex.

When Diamond arrived at Hector's estate, she got out and had Bain keep the engine running as she rushed through the door and up the steps to see him and tell him about everything that happened in court. When she got to his room, he was sitting on the bed, talking on the phone. "Okay, Jack, thanks again," he said before hanging up.

Diamond walked over to hug him, but he stood and pulled back from her. With an arched eyebrow, she folded her arms over her breasts. "What the fuck is wrong with you?"

"You want to know what's wrong with me? How about your secret dinners with Jose, huh? What the fuck is that about?" Hector shouted.

Diamond's face softened. She didn't know Hector had a private investigator watching her. She definitely didn't want to hurt him or have him thinking that something was going on. Unfolding her arms,

she said, "Baby, believe me. It's not what you think it is. Me and Jose -
-"

He gave her a wicked backhand across her face, sending her spit spewing out of her mouth.

"You lying bitch!" he shouted before balling his fist to strike again.

As he cocked his fist back, Diamond did the same with her blue steel .357 revolver, stopping Hector in his tracks. Seeing the gun pointed at him, he took a big swallow and challenged her. "What chu gonna do? Shoot me? You ain't got the guts."

"You're right," Diamond replied with tears rolling down her cheeks, "I don't have the guts to shoot you. But, I damn sure got the heart to kill you."

BOOM!

The bullet slammed in the center of his neck exiting though his spinal cord and out his back, paralyzing him as he fell to the ground. Hector choked on his own blood. Diamond squatted down to look at him in the eyes sadly. "I'm sorry, Hector. I'm so sorry. But, I made a promise to myself never to let you put your hands on me again," she whispered to him before kissing him on the lips.

Hector's eyes widened because he had a feeling about what would happen next. Diamond aimed at his forehead just as Bain came running into the room to see what was going on. Diamond ended Hector's life with a head shot.

BOOM!

Afterwards, she called Butch to dispose of the body. Sadly, she looked at Hector once more. As much as she wanted to break down, she wouldn't let it happen. She then headed out the door for the meeting with the underboss of the Russian Mafia. On her way, her conscience continuously ate at her. She felt bad for what she had done. She knew she was out of line for not telling him about what was really going on, which gave him every right to be angry. This is what her conscience was telling her. However, her pride was saying that it didn't give him the right to put his hands on her. She wasn't that type of female. Once she pulled up to the restaurant, she had to get herself together before she became an emotional wreck.

Inside, Semok Budinov was already seated and ordering his favorite dish. As he sat and waited, he watched his two undercover henchmen to see if their position wasn't compromised. Looking over to his right, he saw a large African-American who he thought he had seen before someplace. The guy sat at the table, reading the sports section while enjoying an apple danish and a cup of coffee.

Semok wondered how a guy that young drank so much coffee. Then, he studied his belly and said to himself, "Go figure!"

As Semok tried to recall where he'd seen the guy, Diamond walked in the busy restaurant and sat across from him.

"You order already?" she asked.

"Yeah, I was hungry. If you want, I'll get you a waiter."

"No, no, that won't be necessary. I'll be brief with you. I'm not buying anything else from you guys. My reason is that I've been offered a better deal with my brother."

Semok frowned. "Your bother?"

"Yes, Clyde White," she replied with a poker face.

Semok also played a good game of poker. "Oh, I see."

"The reason I came here today is to offer you a deal," Diamond said.

"Offer me a deal?" Semok asked, confused.

"Yes, I'm giving you a chance to make your money in the Underworld with the Great White Organization," she said, her elbows pressed to the table and her chin resting on her hands.

Semok had to smile it off because he was completely confused. "Listen, Diamond --"

"Let me tell you something, Semok," Diamond said, cutting him off. "I know that your people killed my father. So, don't think otherwise. I also know that you're tired of being under Zelinski's thumb and want to take control of the Russian Mafia. I am here to give you that chance," Diamond explained.

"And, what about Richard?"

"Aren't you the underboss?" she asked.

"Yeah, so?"

"And, you and the rest of the Russian Mafia are tight, right?"

"Why, yes, of course," he replied, wondering what she was getting at.

"Well, let me handle the Russian don. You just buy him a nice suit and a pretty casket. Deal?" she asked while extending her hand halfway across the table.

Semok liked what he heard. He knew that if Zelinski stepped down, he would give the job to his son. However, if the boss died, everyone would vote for Semok because the men loved him. Smiling broadly, Semok shook Diamond's soft, manicured hand.

"You got yourself a deal," he stated.

"Good, just make sure he's not heavily guarded when we meet tomorrow at Mr. Chow's. I'll take care of the rest. Oh, and give me Mad Max's number. I have a job for him, as well," she replied before she gave an odd hand signal.

Out of the mist of the customers, several shooters who were seated in different areas of the restaurant stood and began to make their way to the exit, including the guy that Semok thought he'd seen before. It all came back to him. He had seen him with Diamond. His name was Butta.

CHAPTER 57

THE LIP GLOSS DON

*O*n a new location in Long Island, New York, Tanetche, watched the news on CNN as Diamond walked out of the federal courtroom and into the safety of her limousine. "That bitch got away," he said, throwing the remote at the TV. Tanetche's anger blazed every time he saw her face. He thought about how his wife had died in a car bombing that was meant for him.

"That anger will eat you up, Tanetche." Hillary said, looking into the fiery eyes of his brother.

"She killed Shelly," Tanetche said with clenched teeth. "The only reason that bitch is alive is because of that manipulating mother-fucker, Carlton Butler. Fuck him. He doesn't run shit."

"Brother, calm down. Why don't you take a trip with me to South Africa? You could use the vacation," Hillary suggested, putting a hand on his shoulder.

Tanetche swatted it away. "I don't want no vacation. I want revenge, and I won't rest until I kill that bitch!"

"Ever since you got into this war with her, you've gone over the edge," Simon said, taking a seat on the couch.

"That's because he hasn't been able to kill this one," Hillary joked as the two shared a laugh.

Tanetche glared at his brother. Although it was just a joke, he knew his brother was telling the truth. Throughout the Agugbo brothers' rise to power, they never had a problem getting rid of troublemakers. But, this bitch Diamond just wouldn't go away.

Tanetche stormed out of the living room and walked upstairs to pack his bags. "Where are you going?" Hillary asked.

"I'm going back to LA, and I won't leave until that bitch is in the ground."

Hillary then turned to his brother, Simon. "No matter what she's done, she's still Clyde's sister. Follow him, and make sure you keep an eye on him. He's hot-headed and stubborn. I don't want him to fall into any trap because his pride got in the way."

Simon nodded and went to prepare for his trip out west. He would leave a tracking device in his brother's luggage.

AT MR. CHOW'S, Mr. Zelinski sat at an isolated table so he and Diamond could be alone. The only person nearby would be his hit man, Mad Max, who took up a spot in another booth a few feet away. A few minutes later, Diamond arrived in a brand-new, black and white, Maybach 57's.

Diamond hopped out of the vehicle dressed in a silver Armani silk V-neck dress that came up to her mid-thigh. She wore Jimmy Choo sandals and had her hair in a tight bun. In her hand was a silver suitcase.

She was also accessorized with an iced-out diamond necklace and studded three-karat earrings. She was dressed to kill. When she got to Zelinski's table, he was mesmerized by her beauty. "Good evening," she said pleasantly as the hostess pulled out a chair for her across from Zelinski.

Diamond sat the briefcase beside her on the floor. "Hello, Diamond. Might I say that you are one fine work of art," he complimented her. "I took the liberty of ordering your food for you, if you don't mind."

"No, that's fine, thank you," Diamond responded gratefully as she looked down at the steaming plate of peppered lobster with a touch of garlic sauce and lemonade Pellegrino, string beans and spring rolls with fried seaweed.

After they ate, they drank wine and chatted as if they've known each other for years. Diamond checked her diamond-faced women's Chopard. Seeing that it was getting late and most of the customers had already left, she decided to wrap it up. "Well, Mr. Zelinski..."

"Please, Diamond, call me Richard," he said gobbling some more string beans.

"Richard, I want to let you know that it's been real good doing business with you. Unfortunately, I have something I must confess," she said, bringing a curious expression to the Russian don's face.

He asked, "And what might that be?"

Diamond circled the brim of her wine glass with her fingers. "I no longer need to buy your product. I've joined my brother's organization. So, I just wanted to say goodbye," she said with a pretty smile, showing a perfect set of white teeth.

Zelinski frowned. "And who might your brother be?" he said, already knowing the truth.

"Clyde White. Have you heard of him?" Diamond asked, looking dead into his eyes and seeing fear.

"No, I haven't heard of him," he lied. He glanced over at Mad Max, who was enjoying his bottle of champagne.

Wiping his mouth with a napkin, he said, "Okay, will you excuse me? I have to use the restroom," he said, giving Mad Max the eye. His assassin would take it from here.

Zelinski couldn't believe that she would have the audacity to tell him that she was his enemy's sister, let alone walk out on his business. Inside the bathroom, Zelinski washed his hands as Mad Max walked inside, holding a gun with a silencer. "What are you doing in here? Kill that bitch. She's Clyde's- -"

CHEWK!

A subsonic 9 mm bullet struck Lewinski in the stomach.

The Russian don was stunned to see blood pouring from his gut. He then looked up at Mad Max, who pulled the trigger again.

Chewk! Chewk! Chewk!

Zelinski staggered back and fell against the sink, then onto the floor. Mad Max stood over his dying victim and finished him off with a fatal shot to the dome.

Chewk!

As Diamond sat at the table, finishing her meal, Mad Max came out of the bathroom and walked by the table. "The job is done."

He then grabbed the briefcase Diamond had just placed on the table. She then got up and headed straight for the valet. Max couldn't resist opening the briefcase to look at his reward. He paused for a moment before he opened it. There was the million dollars he was promised for killing Zelinski, all in neat bundles.

Little did he know, it was all counterfeit. Closing the case, he headed for the exit just as Diamond pulled out of the parking lot.

It had begun to rain, with lightning and thunder. Diamond stopped at the corner of the block and reached under her seat for the black electronic box. When she reached it, she pulled out the extended antenna, flicked the switch, and said, "This is for you, daddy."

The bomb inside Mad Max's briefcase exploded with a big bang. Diamond watched the bright explosion through her rear view mirror. She pulled out her lip gloss and applied some to her luscious lips, then puckered up and blew a kiss at herself before pulling off at the light.

CHAPTER 58

SOMEBODY'S GOTTA DIE

"*I* would like to introduce one of the newest members of our organization," Clyde announced, easing back in his chair in front of the Underworld council. "Carlos Morin. Carlos is from Miami and can be a big asset to us as far as --"

"How can he be a big asset to us when Verningo Castor has control of the whole southeast? What good is he?" Diamond interrupted. All eyes at the long table were now on her. "No one is an asset until we kill the man that is responsible for the death of my father. Nobody, not even you, George," she said, looking at Miami George.

Clyde shook his head in frustration. For over a year and a half now, Diamond had been a part of the Great White Organization, and no one, especially Deshawn Butler, could stand her. Sure, she was beautiful and had good business sense, but Diamond had become an arrogant little bitch. No man in the circle could tell her a thing without getting cursed out. Her outbursts during meetings had become a major obstacle.

Like always, Chavo spoke up. "Diamond, you do understand that

Verningo Castor is a very important man in Colombia and in the American southeast. We're not ready to start a major war with --"

"Clyde, what the fuck is this?" Diamond interjected again, pointing to Chavo as if he was a domestic servant. "I mean, really."

Diamond didn't care too much for Chavo or what he had to say. Over the years, he had become an arrogant son of a bitch himself. Plus, he was a coward. And, he wasn't the only one in the circle who was afraid of his own shadow. As far as Diamond was concerned, the only ones who had any balls were Semok Budinov, Tomas Gonzales, and Shug.

Diamond continued. "What was the reason for putting together a bunch of pussies?" Now the men turned to snarl at her.

"Diamond, I think you need to shut up and let us discuss business," Justin replied, tired of her mouth.

"What business do you have? You're not even a boss. You don't even know how to run a business, so why the fuck are you even here?" she fired back.

"Got-dammit, that's enough. Now, Justin, you chill out. And, Diamond, if you got a problem with this meeting today, you can roll out. Now." Clyde announced angrily.

"My pleasure," she said, getting up to leave.

Once she left the room, Semok joked, "Well, at least she lasted a little longer than last time."

His joke eased the tension and had the men chuckling, except for Clyde and Deshawn. They feared that appointing Diamond as a boss was a big mistake, one that might have to be corrected before it was too late.

When Diamond got in her car, she sat in silence for a while, thinking about how it would have been if JR was still alive. She then wondered if she would ever find another man with just half his swagger. Her thoughts were interrupted by her cell phone. Seeing that it was Clyde, she frowned. 'What do you want, Clyde?"

"I want you to know that this war that you started with the Agugbo brothers must end. You may not know this, but throughout the years they have been good allies to- -"

CLICK!

"Yeah, yeah, yeah, whatever. The day I listen to that bullshit will be the day I meet Casanova," Diamond muttered after hanging up on her brother. Just then, her phone vibrated again. Diamond started to ignore it until she saw a different name on the caller ID screen. Seeing that it was Butta, she answered. "I'm gonna pick up my dress now. Bye."

Diamond put the car in drive and pulled off. Watching her vehicle exit out of the parking lot, Tanetche put the Expedition in drive and followed. Diamond got on the phone again.

"Yo, cuz," Butch said.

"Butch, where's Butta's wedding being held?" Diamond asked.

"Behind his fiancée's parent's mansion in Merina Del Ray," Butch replied.

"How big are we talking?" she asked, referring to the crib.

"It's only a couple of acres," Butch answered.

After getting the address, she got ready and headed for the wedding, with Tanetche hot on her trail. As she looked at her watch, she saw that she was running late and hoped that they hadn't kissed yet or she wouldn't forgive herself. The ceremony only consisted of close to 200 people inside. As Diamond walked in, she was fortunate to catch the two exchanging vows.

Afterwards, Butta raised his wife's veil from over her face and kissed her, sealing the deal that was sure to last a lifetime. Diamond clapped her hands as her womanly instincts got the best of her. She then wiped her eyes with a tissue. She pictured JR and her in that exact spot. It tore her up because she knew that special day would never come.

After the wedding, everyone gave their congrats, along with envelopes full of cash, to the bride. When the two lovebirds were out in front of the mansion, Diamond approached them, causing Butta to stop in his tracks and tell his wife to wait for him in the car. Diamond gave him a big hug. "Congratulations, fat boy," she said.

"I'm glad you could make it, ma," Butta said with a big smile.

"Oh, please. You know I wouldn't miss this for the world," she said, pinching his cheek.

Looking at his half-black, half-Italian wife, Diamond said, "She's beautiful."

"She a'ight," Butta replied, blushing.

"Let me tell you something. Don't be like these other guys out here who don't have no respect for a woman. They say only a real man knows what his woman is worth, and from the looks of her, you got a winning hand, so treat her right. Most important, stay faithful because these bitches out here don't want nothin' but your money," Diamond advised.

Across the street, Tanetche watched Diamond stand at the top of the mansion's steps, talking to the fat black guy in the white tuxedo. The more he looked at her, the more he thought of his wife, who didn't deserve to die. No longer able to control his temper, he grabbed his gold plated mini AK-74 and got out.

A few cars away, Hillary's lieutenant, Raymond, sat behind the wheel of a black Grand Prix. His orders were to keep an eye on Tanetche, just in case he did something stupid. Seeing Tanetche jump out with an AK machine gun gave him no choice but to follow him. However, Tanetche was already in motion. As Diamond talked with Butta, she didn't peep Tanetche walking up the steps until it was too late.

The only one to spot him fast enough was Butta. "Diamond, look out!" he shouted as he pushed her behind him, then reached for the Glock inside his coat.

As his hand gripped the handle, bullets from the AK peppered his fat belly. Butta stumbled back, knocking Diamond to the ground. That accident saved her: bullets whizzed over her, hitting innocent bystanders.

By the time Tanetche's clip was empty, Butta's heavy body had fallen on top of Diamond. His white tuxedo was soaked in blood. Seeing this, Tanetche took off running, but Butch and the rest of Diamond's protectors caught up with him. Out of nowhere, 4-5 tackled Tanetche to the ground and an angry mob began stomping and punching him. When Bain was able to get Butta off of Diamond, she got up and found him bleeding profusely. When his screaming wife came out of the car, Diamond focused on the crowd of men beating Tanetche on the ground. "Stop!" she said. "Tie the bastard up and put him in the trunk."

The men removed there neckties and did as told. Butch and 4-5 got into Tanetche's Expedition, along with Bain and Diamond. Tanetche's unconscious body had been stuffed in the trunk. Raymond watched the whole thing, cursing Tanetche for making such a foolish move. He then got on the phone and called Simon. "Hello?" Simon answered.

"Yeah, Simon. They have your brother," Raymond said.

"What? Who?"

"The Black Kiss of Death. I'm following her as we speak. He tried to take her out at some wedding, but ended up killing the groom and a few other people. They have him now," Raymond explained while making the same turn as the Expedition made.

When the vehicle stopped at a nearby stash house, Raymond gave Simon the address, then waited for him to get there. In the basement, Tanetche awoke to find himself handcuffed to a metal chair and bound at his ankles. When he looked up, he saw Butch, 4-5 and Bain staring at him.

A pair of clicking high heels clopped down the steps. Diamond walked towards him. In her hand were a pair of jumper cables, connected to a powerful battery. Tanetche stared at her drowsily as she clamped the cables on both sides of the steel chair.

"You need me to do anything else?" Butch asked, wanting to get back to the mansion.

"No, go 'head. I'll be right behind you," she replied.

Once the man left, Diamond and Bain were left in the basement with Tanetche. "You know what? You are pathetic," Diamond told him as she circled him with clenched teeth. "You didn't have the guts to walk up on me and pull the trigger, did you? You just had to do it from a distance and risk killing innocent people."

Tanetche gave a hurtful smile of sarcasm. "You know, they say that death smiles back at you. Well, Hah-hah-hah, bitch!"

Diamond walked over to the electric lever, ignoring his sarcasms. "You know what they say about the bitch who laughs now," she said, flicking on the box.

Tanetche's laughter quickly turned into shouts of pain as electric volts shot through his body.

"They cry later," she said before flicking the switch back off. Tanetche slumped over in pain.

"Now, I'm only going to ask you this once. The Inar diamond. Where is it?" Diamond asked.

"Fuck that diamond, and fuck you!" Tanetche bellowed, as spit flew from his mouth.

Out front Simon had finally appeared with four men in black, all armed with assault rifles. Raymond got out of his car and guided the men to the house he saw Diamond enter with Tanetche.

"Ahhh!" Tanetche screamed as Diamond juiced him again.

"Okay, fuck the diamond. I want you to look at this pretty face because it will be the last face you'll ever see again. You killed my boyfriend, I killed your wife. You tried to kill me. You failed. Now, payback's a bitch, ain't it?" she said, lifting the switch again as she blew him a kiss. "Come, Bain, if he wants to die with the fucking diamond, then let's not get in the way. Long kiss."

Diamond headed back up the steps just as she heard the sound of gunfire out front. Simon, Raymond and the rest of the team took out the three guards who were waiting for Diamond. Simon rushed inside the house and searched every room. When he got down to the basement, Diamond was nowhere to be found, but his brother was slowly cooking. Simon rushed to the box and turned it off. Tanetche's tensed body bowed over as his brother removed the clamps and then shot off the links on the cuffs. Feeling for a pulse, he found a faint heartbeat. He and his men then carried Tanetche to the vehicle, grateful they got there when they did. He then looked at Raymond, who was beside him. With clenched teeth, he said, "Show me the house where he was captured."

CHAPTER 59

DEAD OR IN JAIL

*L*ater that night, as Butch sat in the hospital's emergency waiting room with 4-5 and Butta's bride, praying for the doctor to give them an update on Butta's condition, the nurse came out of the operating room. Everyone stood up.

The woman shook her head. "I'm sorry, but we did all that we could. He didn't make it."

On hearing that, everyone broke out in tears, including Butch. He and 4-5 were so upset, they had to leave the hospital. Once they got to the parking lot, Butch wiped his eyes and reached for his keys. As soon as he pressed the alarm button, out of nowhere, Ape Gang members surrounded them. Walking through the cordon of armed men was Simon.

4-5 quickly reached for his gun, but he caught a slug from one of Simon's henchmen. His lifeless body fell to the ground. "Hold up," Simon told his men.

Butch looked at all the guns that were pointed at him and knew that they wanted him alive. But, before anything else could escalate,

SWAT members swarmed the hospital's parking lot. They arrested everyone, including Butch, who was strapped up with a Mac-10.

Both he and Simon looked in each other's eyes as the officers cuffed them from behind. Although Butch knew he was going to sit for a while, he had a funny feeling he would never see the South African again. One day, Diamond would make sure of it.

EPILOGUE

On a beautiful Friday evening in Philadelphia, the sun had fallen from the sky as the wind blew calmly amongst the tombstones in the graveyard. Montega sat in front of his mother's stone, holding 12 single roses, which he placed on her grave, one by one. It was his mother's birthday and every September 5th he visited her and brought her up-to-date about all that he had done during another year without her.

"Well, mom, I still haven't found your killer, and I'm sure as hell not rich yet, but I'm not gonna give up. Don't worry. You're not a grandma, yet. I always strap up at least most of the time. Me and Tasha are cool, but she wants me to be something I'm not. You ain't raise me to be no weak nigga. Juicy's fine. She says hi. That's my heart, right there. She's my rider, but she's not who I see myself being with forever. She's not that girl I always dream about. I still haven't found that perfect somebody that you used to say I would find, but I'm a keep lookin'. Right now, I'm just taking it one day at a time. I love you, mom, and I miss you a lot." He placed the last rose on her grave and stood.

Just then, someone walked up on him. Montega turned to see

Stacy standing behind him, smiling. "I figured you would be out here," she said.

"Stacy! What are you doing here?" Montega asked.

"Kenny, there's something I think you should know, something that I should have told you a long time ago," she said, taking his hand and looking him in his eyes.

Montega frowned. "What is it?"

Stacy looked over at his mother's grave, then back at him. "Kenny, I don't know who it is, and I don't know where that person is, but before you were born, your mother had another child."

"What?" Montega gasped, all the more confused. "Stacy, what are you trying to say?"

Stacy could see the confusion in his face and said, "What I'm trying to say is that you have a brother."

CARLOS MORIN PULLED up to a parking lot on Collins Avenue, not far from the sandy beaches of Miami. Three vehicles away, a white limousine awaited him. Carlos parked his Corvette and got out, throwing on some shades to block the intense sunlight. He wore a pair of tan Hugo Boss khaki shorts, a white Polo shirt by Ralph Lauren and white Ferragamo sneakers. Carlos' dark, shoulder-length hair was slicked back, and his copper complexion glistened. As he approached the limousine, a man in a suit got out and held the door open for him. Carlos gave him a nod and entered. The man closed the door and stood guard. Inside, Carlos was face-to-face with his boss, the one and only, Verningo Castor.

Carlos smiled at the Colombian. "You were right. They did not suspect anything."

"I told you this from the beginning," Castor replied. "Now that you are in, I want you to get as much information about the Great White Family as you can. Because when the time comes, I'm going to wipe them off the face of the earth. And, that includes that bitch, Diamond White."